Here's what people are saying about

Hiring Managers

"Too many writers try to educate others without proven success for themselves. Bermont gives readers real business-world experience, not theory!"
—Bryan West, Director of Consumer Business, APC Corp.

"Unbelievable...this book gives away so many secrets it should be illegal! This book is worth its weight in gold!"
—Nat Hanan, Director of Enterprise Sales

"Bermont's advice is real-life and right on the money!"
—Steven Weintraub, President, Pre-Paid Communications

"Great book...not only is it full of terrific advice...this book is actually fun to read!"
—Paula Maslov, Controller, Friendship Village

Career Experts and Job Recruiters

"Many job-seekers think today's point-and-click Internet technology has made job-hunting easier. Not so! It has made it more competitive and many of the old rules still apply. A recruiter needs to select the best candidates. Bermont gives you a clear, step-by-step approach that will separate you from the competition and increase your opportunities for successful job placement."
—Anita Grant, Technical Recruiter

"One of the best books I have ever read....Insightful, practical, and full of expert tips...This book is ideal for someone starting a career, or an old pro looking for a career change."
—Jason McClure, America's Success Coach
(*www.AmericasSuccessCoach.com*)

"Mr. Bermont has written an incredibly comprehensive, informative and effective tool that every job-seeker should have. The tips and 'insider' advice he gives show tremendous insight into job hunting, and should give anyone who reads his book a huge advantage in this ultra-competitive job market."
—Frazer Donaldson, President, LionSearch, Inc.
(*www.lionsearch.net*)

Celebrity Experts and Media

"Excellent...outstanding...the best job-hunting book I have ever read!"

—Les Brown, Author, Speaker, Radio and Television Celebrity

"Whether you are job hunting for the first time or have years of work experience, this book gives you the most up-to-date and essential tips and techniques you need to get the job you want...even in tough times!"

—Brian Tracy, Author, Speaker, and Consultant

"Great strategies to crush the fears associated with finding a job and practical ways to release the power to get the job you really want."

—Karen S. Hinds, Author of *Get Along, Get Ahead*

"Comprehensive. Extraordinarily timely and shrewdly perceptive."

—*The Book Reader*

Job-Hunters

"My only regret was that I didn't read this book sooner. Bermont's secrets gave me the confidence and direction I needed. After reading this book, I landed a fantastic job!"

—Kenneth Weine, Evanston, IL

"I always wanted to work overseas. The information in this book helped me land the job of my dreams in Kyoto, Japan!"

—Lucas Zastrow, Formerly of Iowa City, Iowa

"This is the best job-hunting book I have ever read!"

—Esther Taylor, Winnipeg, Manitoba

"Read book = Get job"

—Lance Bush, Fuquay Varina, NC

"After reading "*10 Insider Secrets...*" I was motivated to get the job of my dreams! I am now making more money...while doing something I enjoy. I highly recommend that anyone...who aspires to do better in life...read this book."

—Pete Cialkowski, Schererville, IN

10 **Insider**
Secrets
to a
Winning
Job Search

**Everything You Need to
Get the Job You Want
in 24 Hours—Or Less**

Todd Bermont

CAREER
PRESS

Franklin Lakes, NJ

10 INSIDER SECRETS TO A WINNING JOB SEARCH
EDITED AND TYPESET BY KATE HENCHES
Cover design by DesignConcept
Printed in the U.S.A. by Book-mart Press

To order this title, please call toll-free 1-800-CAREER-1 (NJ and Canada: 201-848-0310) to order using VISA or MasterCard, or for further information on books from Career Press.

The Career Press, Inc., 3 Tice Road, PO Box 687,
Franklin Lakes, NJ 07417
www.careerpress.com

Library of Congress Cataloging-in-Publication Data

Bermont, Todd, 1964-
    10 insider secrets to a winning job search : everything you need to get the job you want in 24 hours—or less / Todd Bermont.— [Rev. ed.]
       p. cm.
    Revision of the 1st ed., c2002.
    ISBN 1-56414-740-1 (paper)
    1. Job hunting—Handbooks, manuals, etc. 2. Employment interviewing. I. Title: Ten insider secrets to job hunting success!. II. Title: Everything you need to get the job you want in 24 hours—or less!. III. Title: Insider secrets to job hunting success!. IV. Title: Secrets to job hunting success!. V. Title.

HF5382.7.B465 2004
650.14--dc22

                                                        2003069602

Dedication

To my mother, Margot Bermont, my wife, Paula, and to my wonderful family and friends. Their tremendous love and support has given me the courage to follow a dream. I will always remember the advice my mother gave me in her final days...

"I would rather regret what I did do than what I didn't do!"

Living by those words has changed my life!

Acknowledgments

I am deeply grateful to everyone who has helped me in the preparation of this manuscript. Thank you to Caryn Cialkowski, Harold Bermont, Sharon Maslov, Cheryl Southern, Debra Golden, Jennifer Fischer, Jeff Meyer, and a special thank you to my wife, Paula.

Also, thank you to the following individuals for your tremendous support and encouragement: Andrew Pultman, Nathaniel Bermont, Eric Bermont, and Debbie Bermont. In addition, I would like to thank The 3rd Coast Café of Chicago for their endless cups of delicious coffee that helped keep me at the top of my game while writing this book.

I would also like to thank my previous employers for providing me with an outstanding foundation for my success: Royal Dutch Shell Corporation, NCR Corporation, IBM Corporation, and American Power Conversion Corporation.

Most importantly, I would like to thank each of you, the readers, for your confidence in me, in this book, and in your own ability to succeed. In purchasing this book, you have invested your valuable time and money in what I have to say. I hope to exceed your expectations and help you land the job you want as quickly as possible.

Author's Note

Welcome to *10 Insider Secrets to a Winning Job Search!* Since coming out with my first book, *10 Insider Secrets To Job Hunting Success*, I have had the privilege of coaching clients, speaking in front of numerous groups, and appearing live on both radio and television (including CNN and FOX), and have been featured in countless newspapers throughout the country, including the national edition of *CareerBuilder*.

As a result, I had the opportunity to talk to and gain feedback from thousands of people just like you. Even though my first book was often ranked the #1 "Most Popular" job-hunting book on sites such as *Amazon.com* and *BN.com* (Barnes & Noble), being a perfectionist, I wanted to add new and exciting topics and perspectives to make this book the best job-hunting resource ever created!

All of the information contained in this book is based on my *real-life* job hiring, job hunting, job interviewing, speaking, and training experiences. My goal in writing this book is to provide you with the best possible foundation you need to get the job you want fast—even in difficult times!

This book is written to give *you* a complete step-by-step guide on how to get a job in *any* economy. It is my intention to offer you an entirely new perspective on job hunting that comes from both sides of the interview desk.

10 Insider Secrets to a Winning Job Search is designed to provide you with an *unfair* advantage when searching for a job, and to help you have *fun* with the process. It is my sincerest hope that the secrets, strategies, tips, and techniques you find here are beneficial not only in your job hunt, but also in your personal life.

With that being said, I would like to thank you for investing your valuable time and money in this book I hope that you will be thrilled with your investment. Please enjoy!

Sincerely,

Todd L. Bermont

Contents

Introduction

Congratulations! You have taken an important step towards having a successful job search and getting the job you have always wanted! This book is written to give you an *unfair* advantage. You'll feel confident and enthusiastic about yourself and the job hunt. More importantly, you'll interview to win…so you can get the job you want, at a salary you desire!

The Secrets in This Book Work!

Using these secrets, I have found jobs in both good times and bad, landed *three* job offers in one week (during a recession), earned numerous job promotions, and received *six* job offers my senior year of college. You, too, can achieve this kind of success if you follow the tips and techniques in this book.

Whether you want a position in a large corporation or a small entrepreneurial firm, after reading this book, you will jump into the job hunt like a champion and interview to win!

It Takes 24 Hours to Get the Ball Rolling!

This book teaches you everything you need to know to get the job you want—and how to *sell* yourself throughout the process. It is a complete job-hunting roadmap. The directions are logical, easy to follow, and designed to show you exactly how to get your ideal job fast!

If you spend 24 solid hours following the advice in this book, you will have the foundation you need to succeed, even in today's job market!

With this book, you will:

- Maintain a winning attitude throughout your job search.
- Discover the job you really want.
- Convince firms to hire you even when no positions are open.
- Write attention-grabbing resumes and cover letters.
- Network and market yourself to maximize your job opportunities.
- Be prepared for even the most rigorous job interviews.
- Answer the most difficult interview questions.
- Interview to win even on the toughest job interviews.
- Learn how to negotiate your job offers to receive top dollar.

I'll Share *Real-Life* Experience... From Both Sides of the Interviewing Desk!

The secrets in this book are based on my own personal experience both as a job-hunter as well as a job-interviewer. I have been in your shoes. I understand the frustrations and challenges that can often accompany a job search and how to overcome them. As a hiring manager, I have also been in the interviewer's shoes. I will share with their perspectives and how to use that information to your advantage.

While today I may be a "job-hunting expert," it certainly wasn't always that way. In fact, there have been many times when I have flat out failed in my pursuit of the ideal job. Even now, when I forget to embrace one or more of the secrets in this book, I can still be humbled.

However, having learned the secrets in this book, I no longer fear interviews, doubt myself, or get frustrated at circumstances. Instead, I approach every opportunity with confidence and excitement. Now, I have the career of my dreams and I am happier than ever.

If I Can Do It, You Can Too!

As an author and professional speaker, even to this day, I still have to job hunt on a daily basis. The only difference is now I interview for jobs that last anywhere from five minutes to several days, instead of finding an opportunity that will last for years. To appear on radio or TV, I have to go through the same kinds of grueling interviews that you do.

Whenever a corporation or university considers hiring me to speak, they put me through the wringer. On average, to make a media appearance or to win a speaking engagement, I have to go through at least three to four job interviews. In this book, I'll share with you the same tips and techniques I use in my own job searches.

Certainly, the job-hunting process is a lot easier for me now then it was years ago. After all, I have gone through hundreds of interviews, been hired many times, and I have had the good fortune of sitting on the other side of the interviewing desk as a hiring manager.

However, I am far from perfect. What I can tell you is that when I follow the secrets in this book, typically I succeed. It's when I get too cocky, and forget one or two of them, that I get slapped back into reality.

I Once Lost the Opportunity of a Lifetime!

The opportunity was with Procter & Gamble. For years I had wanted to work for them. Finally, I was granted an interview. To me, this job opportunity was the chance of a lifetime. I was both eager and nervous at the same time. Unfortunately, while I was extremely excited about the opportunity, I wasn't nearly as prepared for what I was about to encounter.

All of a sudden, as I was walking to the interview, my knees started to buckle and my legs began to quiver. Then, my hands started to sweat more than the outside of an air conditioner on a hot day. No matter how many times I wiped my hands on my suit pants, they still were dripping wet. I kept telling myself to relax. But the more I told myself that, the more nervous I got.

When I got to the interview, there was not just one person interviewing me, but two. When I shook their hands, they must have thought they were shaking a cold fish. They told me to take a seat. I almost missed the chair as I went to sit down. That's when things went from bad to worse.

First, I was asked to tell them about myself. I didn't know where to start. I rambled and rambled and finally stopped when I could see one of the interviewers staring out the window in complete boredom. Then, they asked me what my biggest challenge was and how I overcame it. I had no clue.

Have you ever just had your mind go completely blank? Well, that's what happened to me.

The interview went so badly, that to save face at the end, I actually told the interviewers, "*I greatly appreciate your time today. However, after learning more about the position, I have to say that I don't think this is the right job for me.*"

Afterwards, I was devastated. Here, I was interviewing with a company for which I had always wanted to work and I totally blew it! It didn't matter that I got the last word, I just lost a dream job opportunity.

I Was Determined to Succeed

After failing, I decided never again would I bomb another interview so badly. Never again would I go into an interview so unprepared. Never again would I be so nervous that my legs would tremble or my hands would drip with sweat. No! From that point on, I have been determined to succeed and, fortunately, have been able to enjoy many great achievements.

How I Did It!

10 Insider Secrets to a Winning Job Search is the culmination of what I have learned over the years to be the foundation for success. You could read nine separate books on *careers, cover letters, job interviewing, job hunting, motivation, negotiating, networking, resumes,* and *selling* and still not get the information you'll discover in this book!

Throughout this book, you'll see many references to the art of selling. The reason is plain and simple. In order for you to get a job, you have to sell yourself throughout the entire job-hunting process. The interesting thing about job hunting is, while you are the salesperson, you are also the product. This book will help you balance both roles to get the sale—a great job offer!

Gain Confidence and Achieve Success

You'll feel so confident in yourself, and have such a good game plan for your search, that you'll actually look forward to job hunting. You'll even realize that you can really enjoy the interviewing process. In the end, you will succeed!

You'll Get the Job You Have Always Wanted!

My ultimate goal for this book is for you to get the job you want, at a salary you desire, as quickly as possible. With that being said, I would like to once again thank you for investing your valuable time and money in this book. I hope you are delighted with your investment. Please enjoy!

Secret #1

Believe in Yourself

- 10 ways to develop and maintain a positive attitude throughout your job search.

The most basic, yet perhaps the most essential secret to any successful job search is to believe in yourself and your ability to succeed! After all, if you don't believe in yourself...who will? Optimism fosters clear thought, energy, enthusiasm and productivity. When you believe that you are a *great* person...you can achieve *great* things!

Whether dating, investing, playing sports, or job hunting, it's much easier to succeed when you are confident and happy, versus being down and depressed. When you feel positive about yourself and your situation, it is easier to enjoy all that life has to offer—including job hunting!

Developing and maintaining a positive attitude is an essential ingredient to any successful job search. Following, I will take you through 10 ways that, in as little as 30 seconds or less, can help you develop and maintain a positive mental attitude throughout your job hunt.

10 Ways to Develop and Maintain a Positive Attitude

1. Believe that "you are great."
2. Understand that everything happens for a reason.
3. Get some R, R, and R (Rest, relaxation, and reflection).
4. Tell yourself, "I can do it!"
5. Think of interviewing as a numbers game.
6. Surround yourself with positive people.
7. Don't take rejection personally.
8. Treat interviewing like a job.
9. Focus on what you can control.
10. Visualize success.

1. Believe That "You Are Great"

Wait! You're wondering whether or not you're a great person? Stop right there. Every person, in his or her own way, is *great*! You don't believe me? Well, start believing! If you don't believe in yourself and your abilities how can you expect others to believe in you? If you lack confidence because you feel others are more qualified...forget it!

The Word "Qualified" Is Subjective

You don't need the Department of Agriculture to place a big, blue "Interview Approved" stamp on your forehead. Being qualified is totally subjective. The key is to position yourself so you become qualified. Don't worry. By the time you finish this book, you will be able to present your qualities and characteristics so no one can defeat you.

Remember Tony the Tiger from the Kellogg's Frosted Flakes commercials and how he used to say, "They're grrreeeeaaaaat!" If you want to feel good...go to a mirror, look at yourself, and smile. Then, like Tony the Tiger, yell out...as loud as you can... "I am grrreeeeaaaaat!" Say it loud and with conviction. I know it sounds silly...but try it. I guarantee you will have a smile on your face. Say it often enough and you will believe it. You are great! Don't let anyone tell you otherwise!

Still Bummed? Try Creating a List of Your Accomplishments

If you are still having difficulty believing in yourself, take out a sheet of paper and write down as many of your accomplishments as you possibly can. Write down anything that comes to mind. And don't worry about staying focused on just work-related accomplishments.

Your accomplishments can be something as simple as scoring a goal in a soccer game, getting a good grade in a difficult class, successfully leading a group project, winning a major sale, or solving a difficult customer situation. Be it in our relationships, our family life, in school, or in our careers, we have all had numerous accomplishments throughout our lives. By taking the time to write down some of your many accomplishments you begin to realize that you truly are a *great* person.

2. Understand That Everything Happens for a Reason

Right now, many of you might be experiencing difficult times. Maybe that's why you purchased this book. But don't feel sorry for yourself or make excuses for your situation. These feelings will only sabotage your efforts.

One of my friends recently lost his job...even though he was working upwards to 14 hours a day. He was devastated when the company decided to let him go. He had worked as hard as humanly possible and had to travel almost all of the time. On top of that, he was a top producer. Yet, in the end, what was his reward? A pink slip! In fact, he even had to take legal action against the company just to recoup what he was owed in bonus money.

I had a long conversation with him. I said, "You know what? This is the best thing that could have happened to you." At first, he thought I was crazy. How could losing a job possibly be good?

I said to him, "You have had no life. Your entire life was the company. Look at you. You don't have a relationship. Your health is not good. You're constantly going to the doctor. And let's face it, when was the last time you took a vacation where you relaxed and didn't check voice mail and e-mail every day?"

He started to smile. "You are right," he said. Even though he had been making more money than ever, he wasn't happy because he had no balance in his life. With his new perspective, he suddenly realized losing his job was an opportunity to regain his life, health, and balance, not a failure like he had originally thought. He was now free to find a new job that would allow him everything he truly wanted in life.

As Anthony Robbins states in many of his programs, sometimes it takes a tremendous amount of pain to force us to make changes for the better. Think about it, when you are complacent with something in your life, do you go through the effort to change it? Sometimes it takes losing a job to provide the incentive to find a much better position.

If You Were Laid Off or Fired...

This is an opportunity, not a hurdle. Be proud of who you are and what you have accomplished in your life. Just like with my friend, everything happens for a reason. You may not know what that reason is today. However, in five years, you will look back on this time and be glad you went through this discovery process. This is the universe's way of saying it is time to take a time-out and improve your situation. After all, you deserve better!

Tell yourself that you lost your job so you can finally be free to find the job of your dreams or to regain balance in your life. Every person I know who has lost his or her job ultimately ended up in a much better situation. You will too! You deserve a better situation and you will find it!

If You Are Graduating or Are Currently Employed...

It is okay. You just haven't found the right opportunity yet. Be full of pride. Celebrate your successes and accomplishments. Believe that you are an extraordinary person and you will get the job you want. If you got rejected on some interviews, it is only because there is something better for you elsewhere.

Not All Opportunities Will Be Right For You

I can tell you firsthand that even I get rejected on interviews from time to time. You might think, *Wait a minute...you're the author of a job-hunting book, why do you even go on interviews, let alone experience rejection. I thought you knew it all.*

Well, as an author and a speaker, I am constantly being interviewed for speaking engagements and radio and television appearances. Just like you, I have to sell myself to win each and every opportunity. I can totally relate to what you are going through. Although I am an "expert" on the topic, sometimes even I don't succeed.

Whenever I get rejected, I try to take a step back and recap the situation. I try to see what I can learn from an interview so I don't repeat the same mistakes again. Then, I think to myself, *There was a reason why I didn't succeed on this interview.* I try to figure out what that reason was and then I tell myself, *It just wasn't the right opportunity for me.*

By realizing that everything happens for a reason, you can take solace in knowing that no matter what challenges are thrown your way, ultimately you will be in a much better situation to succeed. Every step you take is getting you that much closer to happiness and success!

3. Get some R, R, and R (Rest, Relaxation, and Reflection)

Before starting any job hunt, it is critical to have as much energy and enthusiasm as possible. Whether you have lost your job, or you just want to find something better, I always recommend taking some time off to rest, relax, and reflect.

One of the best ways I have found to reenergize myself is to do something outdoors. Be it a walk on the beach, a hike, a bicycle ride, or going to the pond to watch the ducks, I have found that doing something outdoors does a world of good for my mental state of being. It helps me temporarily escape my daily problems and best of all...it is free!

Personally, I love taking long walks to reflect on my current situation. It is amazing the ideas I can get as a result of just taking a walk. Like you, there are times when I can get disgusted over a situation or an outcome.

To overcome this frustration, I try to dissect the situation by asking myself questions such as *Why did this happen? What can I learn? How could I have done it differently? Where did I do well and how can I improve? How will going through this make me a better person?* By answering these questions, I always end up feeling better.

Don't Be Afraid to Be Honest With Yourself

If you lost your job or if you are unhappy in your current career, try to understand why. Be objective with yourself. Sometimes the truth does hurt. However, it's better you learn now, so you can avoid similar situations and outcomes in the future.

There once was a time when I was a manager for American Power Conversion (APC) where I almost got fired. This was my first job as a manager. I was so focused on wanting to impress upper management that I was totally failing in my management duties.

Luckily, my boss at the time suggested I have my employees conduct a review of me. When I did this, I was shocked at the comments my employees made about me. They wrote statements such as "Didn't go to bat for us" and "Doesn't listen to our needs."

Until I went through this process, I had no idea that I had become the type of boss for whom I myself had always hated to work. Fortunately, I had the opportunity to learn from my mistakes and correct them before I got fired. From then on out, I have always had my employees review me. Thankfully, my reviews have always been better ever since.

However, not everyone is fortunate enough to be given a second opportunity to learn before losing a job. If you fail in this category, or if you just are flat miserable on your current job, ask yourself some tough questions that will help you move on to success.

Ask yourself questions such as, *Where can I make improvements? What do I really want in an ideal job? Where do I want to focus my energies? What can I do differently in the future to have a better outcome?*

Look Past the Negatives

See all of the positives you have experienced throughout your career. Summarize your learning experiences. Ask yourself what you liked most and what you liked least about your last position. This will help you focus your job hunt.

Ideally you want to find a job that maximizes the things you like most and minimizes those you like least. While this is such a simple concept, people often fail to take into account their true likes and dislikes. Then they wonder why they end up switching jobs or getting fired every two to three years.

By taking the time to rest, relax, and reflect you get a better perspective on your current situation and gain the energy you need to succeed. You can then jump into your job hunt with the excitement of a lion being fed a nice juicy steak.

4. Tell Yourself, "I Can Do It!"

Keep your spirits up! A great way to feel confident at any time is to yell out with joy and confidence, "*I can do it!*"

Remember when John Belushi shouted out, "Let's do it!" in the movie *Animal House?* Try going to a mirror and scream like John Belushi, "I can do it!" Then yell out, "I will get the job I want!" When you shout with conviction, "I can do it! I will get the job I want!" you will believe it.

Ever notice how it's the positive people who always seem to be the happiest and most successful? Upbeat people are fun to be around. They are also the ones who tend to get the most out of life. A positive attitude is contagious. Those who catch it are forever cured.

You can do it! You will get the job of your dreams!

5. Think of Interviewing as a Numbers Game

At times, your job hunt may become frustrating, especially if you experience rejection. However, don't let it get you down or strip away your confidence. Depending on the job you are trying to get, it may take as many as 10 interviews just to get one offer. But by reading this book, you are increasing your chances for success. Look at each rejection as bringing you one interview closer to getting the job you really want.

If you get rejected after an interview, say to yourself, *This job wasn't a good fit. I deserve better. I am too good for them. Besides, I am one interview closer to getting the job I really want!*

Don't get emotionally attached to any single opportunity. Focus on the process and what you can learn from each situation. If you get rejected, try to understand why. In fact, there is absolutely nothing wrong with calling an interviewer and asking why you didn't get the offer. After all, you invested valuable time and energy preparing for and going on the interview. You have a right to know.

Not every position will be the right job for you. Interviewing is a numbers game. Each rejection serves as an opportunity to improve, as well as a stepping-stone that gets you that much closer to your ideal job.

6. Surround Yourself With Positive People

When going through an arduous job hunt, it is easy to be sidetracked by negative thoughts and pessimistic people. But to succeed you must avoid these damaging elements as much as possible. Dwelling on the negative will only hurt your efforts. Instead, focus on the positives. Surround yourself with people who will encourage you and motivate you. When you are around positive people you'll think and perform like a winner!

Job Hunting Is Like Real Estate

They say it is always better to buy the cheapest house in a good neighborhood than to buy the most expensive house in a questionable area. The value of the lowest priced house in a good neighborhood is almost always boosted by the presence of the more expensive houses.

When you surround yourself with positive and motivating people, like a good neighborhood, their enriching attitudes will rub off on you and boost your morale, success, and overall value. These positive influences can only help you succeed.

If you have negative friends, stay away from them while you're job hunting. If members of your family are negative, tell them to keep their thoughts to themselves unless they have something constructive to say. I know this can be difficult, especially when dealing with family, but attitude is *so* important!

Attitude Can Often Determine Success or Failure

Like it or not, each one of us emits energy, be it positive energy or negative. Subconsciously, we tune into the frequencies of others. Don't make the mistake of spending most of your time commiserating with people that are frustrated and out of work. You'll soak up their negative energy like a dry sponge.

Instead, surround yourself with positive people who are succeeding in what they do. Employed and happy people are much more likely to help you succeed than those who are negative and unemployed. So, be positive, confident, and surround yourself with motivating people who will help you succeed!

7. Don't Take Rejection Personally

One of the most difficult tasks of any job hunt is to not take rejection personally. However, in job hunting, there are many things that are beyond your control. Just understand that this process is the universe's gift to help you find a much more fulfilling opportunity. Rarely in life does something worthwhile ever come easy.

Each bump in the road is a step on your stairway to success. If an interviewer wants to hire a Yale graduate and you went to Ohio State, there is nothing you can do to change it. Not every situation will be the right one for you. If the only thing the interviewer was interested in was where you went to school, then most likely you wouldn't want to work for him anyway. Don't take it personally. Rejection is just a part of the job-hunting process.

8. Treat Interviewing Like a Job

Typically, the people that have the greatest success at job hunting are those who treat the job hunt like a job in itself. This attitude fosters motivation and productivity.

After all, getting a new job is a job in itself. Anyone who tells you otherwise is mistaken. There are many steps you can take to treat your job hunt like a job...and put yourself in a position to succeed.

Dress the Part Every Day

If you are trying to get a job that requires formal business attire, then wear something professional every day. When you dress the part, you live it and feel it. You never know during the course of any given day when you might run into someone who can hire you. I have known of people who found jobs just by talking to complete strangers while in airports, bus stations, local coffee shops, or even on a commuter train. If an opportunity presents itself, you want to be at your very best.

When you dress for success, you achieve it. Even if you have a phone interview, dress as if you were interviewing in person. When you dress the part, you will communicate much more effectively and you put yourself in a much better frame of mind to succeed.

Believe it or not, the person you are talking to can subconsciously sense how you are dressed...even over the phone.

If the job you are striving for requires business casual attire, rather than formal, then wear that every day. The key is to dress how you would if you were on the job. Doing so energetically puts you in the proper frame of mind.

Establish a Virtual Office

Another way to treat the job hunt like a job is to go to a "virtual" office every day. The secret is to go somewhere. Some of my clients have gone to places such as the library, while others have gone to a coffee shop or a bookstore café. Some have even gone to the extent of renting an executive office suite. Others have found friends that could lend them a spare desk where they work.

Look for a place that is within your budget. Yet find a location where you can be productive. When you get out of the house, you feel better about yourself. You also avoid distractions such as the television, the Internet, children, and housework. Ultimately, you become much more productive, confident, and proud.

Get a New E-mail Address

In today's day and age, almost everyone is connected to the Internet. Most companies prefer to communicate electronically. Having a professional e-mail address allows you to level the playing field.

I suggest you create a new address just for your job search. That way your job-hunting related e-mails won't get confused with "junk mail" and other mail that is less important. Plus, new accounts are much less likely to receive annoying spam.

When you are creating your account, make it as professional as possible. Don't use something silly such as a nickname, a number, or a cutesy phrase. Instead, try to use your first initial and your last name. That way, interviewers will recognize your incoming e-mails. If the ideal e-mail ID isn't available, then try your full name. Everything you do conveys an image. Something as minute as your e-mail address can make or break someone's impression of you.

If You Don't Have Your Own Computer...

With today's technology, there are many ways you can establish an e-mail account without having you own computer. Sites such as *Hotmail.com* and *Yahoo.com* provide this service either for free or for a nominal fee. These sites store your e-mail online so you can access it from any computer. You can go to a local Internet café to get on a computer, or just ask a friend if you can use theirs.

Have a Personal Business Card

When you have a personal business card you convey a more positive and professional image. Plus, most people feel more important and confident when they have a business card. Perhaps best of all, business cards are especially convenient to use when networking.

Creating a Business Card Is Easy

There are numerous software solutions you can use to design a business card. In fact, many word processors even provide templates. Business cards are very inexpensive to produce. Typically, you can print out 500 for the cost of eating a meal in a restaurant. Either you can buy business card stock paper for your computer printer or you can take your file to a local printer or copy shop.

If you don't have a computer, most printing companies and copy shops can assist you in creating a professional card. Either route you choose, the cost of producing a professional business card is relatively inexpensive and well worth the investment.

Make Your Business Card Simple, Yet Professional

If you are not sure what it should look like, go into your drawer or file cabinet and take out a handful of old business cards you have collected throughout the years. If you don't have any, then call up a friend and ask to see some of theirs.

Include a Logo or Picture

For your logo, you can use your initials in a bigger and different font or you can put your picture there. I know, I know, people have always said that you don't want to put a picture on anything when job hunting. However, my feeling is that if you want to, then go right ahead.

Let's face it, if someone is going to reject you on the basis of your appearance, isn't it better not to waste the time and energy on the interview? Having a picture on your card can help interviewers put a face to your name. However, do what is most comfortable for you.

Give Yourself a Title

For a title, put whatever the position is that you are trying to get. If you want to get an accounting position, then put *"accountant."* If you want a sales position, then put something like *"sales representative"* or *"account manager."* Or just put your name on the card without a title.

Provide Important Contact Information

Include your address, phone number, and e-mail address. Provide information that makes you most accessible. If you have a cell phone, you may want to use that in lieu of your home phone.

The following is an illustration of a business card using myself as an example. This will give you a good idea of a generic layout you could use for your own card. However, if you don't like mine, most software packages have a variety of templates and fonts you can use.

TLB   Todd L. Bermont

555 N. State Parkway   Direct: 555-555-5400
#555   Fax: 555-555-5777
Chicago, IL 60610   tbermont@hotmail.com

Use Voice mail

One of my biggest "pet peeves," when I have interviewed people in the past, was when I called someone who either didn't have voice mail or didn't have a professional greeting. The worst messages are those that have loud music and you can't even hear what the message is saying.

Forget Answering Machines

Only voice mail can provide you with the professionalism that you need to succeed in today's competitive times. No, I don't work for your phone company. The bottom line is that if you don't have voice mail and you are on the phone, your interviewer will get a busy signal. This will happen regardless of whether or not you have a recording machine. And if you are not home, even with an answering machine, your phone could ring endlessly. In either case, an interviewer may never call you again. Often, you only get one chance. Don't blow it with a cheap recording device.

Voice mail is available from most phone companies including cellular phone providers. Typically, it is very inexpensive. If you don't have it, get it! Recording machines are just not professional or reliable.

Have a Professional Greeting

Interviewers don't want to hear rock music, a computer-generated voice, or your kids on your recorded message. They want to hear a professional greeting from you. Your greeting is just one more way you can demonstrate the high caliber individual that you are.

Here is an example of a greeting I often use:
Thank you for calling the voice mail box of Todd Bermont. You have reached my voice mail mailbox because I have briefly stepped away from my desk. Please leave your message after the tone and I will try to return your call within three business hours. Thank you and have a great day!

Notice, I don't say I am either on the phone or away from my desk. I just say I am away from my desk. There is a reason for this. How is your interviewer supposed to know which one it is?

If you aren't home, but the interviewer thinks you are on the phone, they may have an unrealistic expectation that you will get back to them quickly. It's better just to say you "stepped away from the desk." That way you can exceed the expectation, rather than risk falling short.

Dedicate the Proper Time and Effort to Your Job Hunt

If you were working at a full-time or part-time job, most likely you would go to work every day and consistently show up on time. Searching for a job requires the same effort. To be successful, you must dedicate a certain amount of time solely to the purpose of the job hunt.

If you are unemployed: Dedicate a minimum of eight hours a day to your job-hunting activities. This can be spent in a variety of ways from doing research, to networking, to improving your resume. Practice counts as well. Think about it, a football team will practice an entire week to play just one, three-hour game. You need to put that kind of effort into your job search.

If you are employed or a student: Devote at least two to three hours a day. If you cannot afford to do that, then schedule two or three days out of the week, when you can spend that amount of time. Treat job hunting, in this case, like a part-time job.

I understand you might think this is difficult. But if you don't take job hunting seriously, you will not get the job you want, in the timeframe you desire. After all, your competition is taking it very seriously!

When you treat your job search like a job, you will have a higher self-esteem, be more productive and will convey a more positive image. Ultimately, treating your job hunt like a job will directly contribute to the success you achieve and the level of your morale throughout the process.

9. Focus on What You Can Control

In life, as well as in job hunting, there are many things we can't control. We can't control things such as the economy, politics, taxes, and whether or not the country is at war. However, there are many things we can control. We can control aspects such as:

- Diet.
- Exercise.
- Attitude.
- Organization.
- Focus.

When you focus on those things that you can control somehow the things you can't control become less cumbersome. I know when I eat right, exercise regularly, properly focus my energies, and organize, I have a much more positive attitude about myself. Plus, I am much more productive.

Focusing on those areas you can control will help you immensely. It will give you a sense of accomplishment every day. If you would like some further resources on personal enrichment, there are many programs as well as books that can help. Les Brown, Brian Tracy, and Anthony Robbins are three individuals whose advice over the years has had a very positive influence on my life. Each one of them has a variety of products and services that can motivate you in the areas you can control.

10. Visualize Success

Perhaps the best exercise of all is visualization. When my mother was alive she used to always try to convince us kids, that when we were down or scared about a situation, to visualize a good outcome. Being a typical child, her words usually went in one ear, and out the other. However, over the years, I have learned the value of her advice. I wish I had listened years ago. Visualization really works.

Every morning when you wake up, take a few moments to close your eyes and visualize success. Visualize an interviewer reaching across the desk and shaking your hand, saying, "*Congratulations, welcome to our team.*" Or, "*Congratulations...You're hired!*"

Before every interview, visualize the outcome you want. If it is a phone interview, visualize the interviewer asking you to come in for a second interview. If you are interviewing in person, visualize the interviewer offering you a job.

When You Visualize Success, You Achieve It

Hopefully by now you are feeling better about yourself and your situation. When you believe in yourself, you can succeed at almost anything. Thomas Edison failed thousands of times before he finally found the solution to inventing the lightbulb. Colonel Harlan Sanders went to thousands of restaurants before he finally found someone willing to take a chance on his recipe for chicken.

Both Thomas Edison and Colonel Sanders had one thing in common. They believed in themselves. If you believe...you will achieve! So before moving on to the next chapter, close your eyes and visualize success. You are great! You can do it! You will get the job you want at a salary you desire!

Secret #1: Believe in Yourself
—Checklist Summary—

√ Say out loud..."*I am great!*"
√ Everything happens for a reason.
√ Get some rest, relaxation, and reflection.
√ Interviewing is just a numbers game.
√ Surround yourself with positive people.
√ Smile and shout..."*I can do it!*"
√ Don't take rejection personally.
√ Treat the job search like a job.
√ Focus on what you can control.
√ When you visualize success...you achieve it.

A positive attitude is contagious. Those who catch it are forever cured!

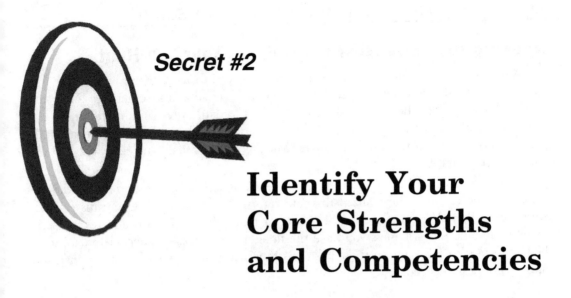

Secret #2

Identify Your Core Strengths and Competencies

- The four cornerstones of strengths and competencies.
- Convert strengths and competencies into benefits.

Losing a job or searching for a new position can be frustrating. It can be especially difficult if you have the pressures of unpaid bills, supporting loved ones, or dealing with an unbearable boss. It can certainly be tempting to just jump into the job hunt and put the misery behind you or to just dive into the help-wanted ads and mail off resumes.

However, before you do so, it is important to take a step back to assess your strengths, capabilities, and talents. Then, determine what it is you really want to accomplish and do for a living.

Create a Solid Foundation

The best way to jumpstart your job search is to first identify your core strengths and competencies—what you are good at. You will be amazed at how proud of yourself and more confident in your abilities and opportunities you become when you take the time to acknowledge your positives. These core strengths and competencies are the foundation on which your job hunt is built.

Insider Tip

During your interviews, more than 80 percent of the time you will be asked, "What are some of your greatest strengths?" By articulating your strengths and competencies now, you will be much more prepared when asked this question in your next interview.

Knowing Your Strengths Helps Focus Your Job Hunt

When you know what you are good at, it helps you focus your job hunt on those jobs you are most likely able to get. Unfortunately, even the best sometimes forget to do this. Ever heard of the basketball player Michael Jordan? After winning three championships in the early 1990s, he decided to retire from basketball to try baseball and golf. Because he was a tremendous athlete, Michael was confident he could succeed at these other sports, too.

As it turned out, Michael didn't perform nearly as well in those sports as he did in basketball. Fortunately, he realized this and returned to basketball, where his talents were most aligned. He went on to win several more championships and to conquer many more milestones. Unless you have the financial resources of Michael Jordan, it is best to focus your job hunt on those positions in which you have a talent and expertise, and would best succeed.

Insider Tip

During your interviews, most likely you will be asked, "Why did you choose this occupation?" By articulating your strengths and competencies, you have a strong foundation on which to answer this question.

Separate Yourself From the Competition

As of yet, I am not aware of any human clones. One of the beauties of life is that we are all unique. Each of us has positives and negatives. I have yet to meet a perfect person, but, I have yet to meet someone who didn't have numerous redeeming factors.

The key is to use your positives to your advantage. In job interviewing, it is your core strengths and competencies, along with your personality and appearance that ultimately differentiate you from your competition.

Identifying your core strengths is like reading a fuel gauge in a car. When driving, the more gas you have, the further you can travel. Similarly, the more skills and experience you have accumulated throughout your career, the further you can go in your work-related endeavors.

When you review your strengths, be honest with yourself. It will help you identify those positions you realistically can consider. For example, if you have just graduated from college, it would be pretty difficult to get a position as vice president. However, if you have been in the workforce for many years and have significant management experience, perhaps the position is more realistic.

In your career, just as in driving, you can always put more gas in your tank and travel further. The key is to determine your destination and draw a road map (plan) of how to get there. Each job you hold and degree you attain along the way, in conjunction with the knowledge and experience you gain, serves as more fuel for your career.

To see how far you can realistically travel at this point in your career, assess your core strengths and competencies. You will be able to identify the jobs that you want, as well as those that you have the best opportunity to get. Everyone has unique strengths. Identify yours so you can focus your efforts where you are most likely to get hired.

Job Interviewing is Like Dating

In dating, your appearance may be important to some people, while others might look for someone with a great personality. Some may want to date a person who comes from a good family background, while others may fancy a person with a good sense of humor and cute laugh.

Whether it's our personality, our looks, our smile, or our sense of humor, we all have different strengths and attributes that make each of us attractive to someone else. The same is true in interviewing. Some interviewers look for candidates with a great personality or extensive work experience. While others may want someone with corporate expertise or who is a team player.

The key is to identify your greatest selling points so you can make yourself as appealing to your potential employers as possible. I know you have a tremendous ability to succeed. Be it in school, on the job, or in your personal life, I am confident you have developed many marketable strengths and competencies. Now is the time to articulate them.

I have never been in an interview situation without being asked the question, "What are your strengths?" Because it is so common, you need to be prepared. There are four cornerstones you can use to articulate your strengths and competencies.

The Four Cornerstones of Strengths and Competencies

1. Personality and subconscious energy.
2. Personal and job-related accomplishments.
3. Work-related skills.
4. Job-related knowledge and credentials.

1. Personality and Subconscious Energy

Have you ever met someone on the street and immediately felt comfortable with that person? Conversely, has anyone ever rubbed you the wrong way before you even had the chance to meet them? What causes this? Often it is their personality and the subconscious energy they emit.

Subconscious energy can be described as waves of power that can't be seen, but can certainly be felt. Each of us, whether we choose to acknowledge it, is a transmitter of energy. How we feel about ourselves and our lives determines the frequency of energy that we release. People who are happy in life and proud of who they are have an unmistakable glow about them that can be understood, even without them talking. Conversely, those who are depressed and ashamed walk around with a "cloud" over their head.

In job hunting, and in life in general, how you feel about yourself and your situation will absolutely determine the frequency of energy that you produce. That energy will significantly impact the type of people you attract in your life and the quality of life that you live.

What Level of Energy Are You Broadcasting?

If you have gone from one bad job to another or one bad relationship to another, perhaps you should question the feelings you have about your life and about you. Your energy is like a radio. When you tune into AM 1000, you are tuning into a station that is transmitting at that frequency. Everyone else in town who tunes into that same frequency will hear the same station.

In subconscious energy, when you are broadcasting depressed, frustrated, and insecure waves, you will only attract others into your life who are tuned into those same negative frequencies. On the other hand, if you make a conscious decision to be proud of yourself, and to cherish all the positive things you have in life, you'll attract people who are winners and who will want to help you in your pursuit of the ideal job. The energy you transmit will impact your entire job search from networking to job interviewing.

Gratitude: The Easiest Way to Establish Positive Energy

Gratitude is powerful. One of the best ways to change negative energy into positive is to focus on those things in life for which you are most thankful. Often, in life, we can take things for granted. Just being able to walk is something to be grateful for. How many people out there are disabled and unable to simply walk up a flight of stairs?

If I fall into the trap of feeling sorry for myself, I place my emphasis on gratitude instead of frustration and disappointment, and it doesn't take long to snap out of it. In job hunting it's easy to fall into a trap of doom and gloom. After all, there are many others who are more than happy to join you in that trap. Instead, focus on all of the good things in your life.

Rather than focusing on your lack of a job, or a rejection you just encountered, think about positives such as having a family and good friends, having your health, having love in your life, or having experienced wonderful things.

Try Starting Each Day by Focusing on Gratitude

Get into the habit of every morning articulating at least five things in your life for which you are grateful. You can pick any five. Just be genuine in what you choose. When you start each day with gratitude, you'll tune into a positive frequency that'll attract success and happiness in your life and your job hunt. It sure beats waking up "on the wrong side of the bed." When I start my days thinking about the good in life, I almost always have a great day. When I forget to do this, it is amazing how many distractions, roadblocks, and frustrations pop up.

Personality:
The Conscious Visualization of Subconscious Energy

As previously mentioned, each of us, at all times, is broadcasting waves of energy that can't be seen, but is indeed felt by the subconscious mind. However, there is a conscious representation of this subconscious energy you transmit—your personality. While each job interviewer will have an immediate subconscious feeling about you, they will consciously relate to your personality.

Understanding and being able to articulate your personality will help you focus your job hunt and sell yourself during interviews. There are both general and work-related aspects to our personalities:

1. **General** personality traits provide insight into your overall personality, both inside and outside the workplace. Are you easygoing? Do you have an outgoing personality? Descriptions such as positive, creative, people-oriented, competitive, driven, empathetic, assertive, flexible, and motivated are examples of your general personality strengths.

2. **Work-related** personality traits describe aspects of your personality that are more relevant to the workplace and on-the-job performance. Descriptions such as team-oriented, goal-oriented, strategic-thinker, natural-leader, conscientious, detail-oriented, and problem-solver are examples of job-related personality strengths.

If I asked you what your greatest personality traits were, what would you say?

Insider Tip

When interviewers say, "Tell me about yourself," what they are really looking for are the aspects of your personality, both general and work-related, and if they make you the most viable candidate for the position.

---

2. Personal and Job-Related Accomplishments

Accomplishments are quantifiable results that you have achieved throughout your life and career. This second cornerstone provides an objective insight into your abilities and achievements. Interviewers often use accomplishments both as a way to differentiate one candidate from another, as well as a means to justify their decisions based on emotion. As we discussed on page 31, energy can't be seen, it is only felt. That energy often stimulates emotions, either in a positive or a negative way, within the interviewer. An interviewer may feel very enthusiastic about you without exactly knowing why, and to justify this excitement, he or she will often use your accomplishments as a means to logically explain his or her feelings.

Accomplishments Generate
Interest Throughout the Job Hunt

Because energy has no bounds, it flows into your resumes, into your cover letters, and into your networking and interviews. This energy will always stimulate emotions within anyone encountered. As early as possible in your job-hunting process, you'll want to articulate your many accomplishments. You'll find that the more accomplishments you identify, building your confidence, the more positive your energy frequency will be.

Once you have created a list of accomplishments, you can draw from it in everything from your resumes to your interviews. As with personality, there are two categories of accomplishments: personal and job-related.

1. **Personal** accomplishments summarize achievements of your life outside of work. Examples may include charitable activities, community service, offices held, and sports championships.

2. **Work-related** accomplishments demonstrate successes you've had on the job. Achievements such as getting a great review, making the "100-Percent Club," winning a company award, being featured in a corporate magazine, reducing expenses by 25 percent, and receiving job promotions are all examples of job-related accomplishments.

What accomplishments have you achieved? Focus on those accomplishments that are most applicable for the positions you are seeking and those that are most quantifiable. Saying you reduced costs is a great accomplishment. But, what makes that accomplishment even stronger is if you can say you reduced costs by 15 percent resulting in saving over $100,000. Now that's an accomplishment that will make an interviewer drool with excitement.

3. Work-Related Skills

While accomplishments focus on quantifiable results you have already achieved, work-related skills demonstrate what you can do in the future. This is an important category for potential employers because it is your skill set that shows whether or not you have the tools and aptitude to succeed once on the job. Interviewers may love your personality, and be impressed by your accomplishments, but if they don't think you have the right tools to succeed, they won't hire you.

With this in mind, it is absolutely critical that you take the time to summarize the work-related skills you possess. When articulating your skills, there are two areas you should consider: your cognitive (thinking) skills and your functional skills (what you can do).

1. **Cognitive** skills describe the capabilities of your mind and personality and provide insight into your thought process. Examples of cognitive skills include problem-solving skills, interpersonal skills, and creative skills.

2. **Functional** skills describe what you are physically capable of doing on the job. Examples of functional skills include, managing people, reducing

expenses, implementing computer rollouts, developing budgets, quality control, report generation, large account sales, graphic design, and customer service.

Those of you who don't have work experience should focus more on your cognitive skills than functional. If you have experience, then employers will most likely focus more heavily on your functional abilities.

Regardless of what position you will interview for, interviewers will expect to see some sort of evidence that you have the skills and aptitude necessary to perform effectively on the job.

Demonstrate Quantifiable Evidence of Your Skills

If you think you possess a particular skill, prepare some examples of results from your previous experience to prove your case. Interviewers are going to expect you to provide proof of your claims. So it's best to be prepared.

Let's say you believe that you have phenomenal selling skills. Evidence such as, "Grew sales by double-digits during the last fiscal year" or "Achieved quota three years in a row" would be appropriate.

If you have a unique ability to reduce expenses, include the amount by which you reduced expenses in your previous job, such as, "Went out for bid and saved the corporation $10,000" or "Implemented a new phone system allowing the company to reduce staff by 10 percent and save more than $75,000 per year."

If you have fantastic management skills, then give examples such as, "Reduced employee turnover by 25 percent" and "Increased productivity by 14 percent."

Insider Tip

When managers create a position, they compile a list of criteria that they would like to see in an ideal candidate. Work-related skills typically are the foundation for this list.

4. Job-Related Knowledge and Credentials

Job-related knowledge is learned in school and on the job, and will help you succeed in the position you are trying to get. Unlike the other categories of strengths and competencies, career knowledge focuses more on what you know rather than on what you have done or can do. Those of you without strong work experience should put more emphasis on career knowledge in your interviews.

If you are trying to get a job in the computer industry, knowledge, such as knowing a specific programming language, or a credential, such as a certification in a certain operating system, may be beneficial. If you were applying for an inventory management position, knowledge such as "Just-In-Time (JIT)" and "Vertical Process Management" would be more appropriate. If you want to go into marketing, you had better know the Four P's of the Marketing Mix.

Simply look back throughout your career and summarize your key elements of knowledge that will be most applicable for the job you are trying to get. Perhaps you know how to use spreadsheets and word processing software. If you are interviewing for an accounting position this knowledge could be very beneficial. However, if you were interviewing for a fireman or security position, this would not be as applicable.

What Makes You Great?

Don't wait until an interview to list what makes you great. Start now by brainstorming about all of your strengths and competencies using the four cornerstones we have discussed. Remember: the more you focus on the good in you and your life, the better the outcomes will be.

Write down as many core strengths and competencies as possible. Following, I have created a few simple worksheets for you to use. Try to keep your descriptions to four words or less. In doing this, you will gain focus, build your confidence, and be more realistic in identifying the kinds of jobs you can get. After this exercise, you will realize that you truly are a spectacular person, and you'll be more motivated throughout your job hunt.

Insider Tip

Throughout your job hunt, interviewers will ask, "Why should I hire you?" By using the four cornerstones of defining your personal strengths and competencies, you'll be able to tell them why.

Strengths and Competencies
Worksheet 1

General Personality Traits:
(outgoing, social, empathetic, creative, motivated, etc.)

1. _____
2. _____
3. _____

Work-related Personality Traits:
(team-oriented, conscientious, detail-oriented, multi-tasking, etc.)

1. _____
2. _____
3. _____

Personal Accomplishments:
(charity, fraternity, community service, etc.)

1. _____
2. _____
3. _____

Job-Related Accomplishments:
(100-percent club, manager's award, featured in a company newsletter, etc.)

1. _____
2. _____
3. _____

Strengths and Competencies
Worksheet 2

Cognitive Skills:
(interpersonal, problem-solving, creativity, etc.)
1. _____
2. _____
3. _____

Functional Skills:
(managing people, reducing expenses, processing payroll, large-account sales, etc.)
1. _____
2. _____
3. _____

Job-Related Knowledge:
(collections, year-end reporting, procurement, marketing, accounting, advertising, etc.)
1. _____
2. _____
3. _____

Job-Related Credentials:
(certifications, degrees, CPA, MBA, etc.)
1. _____
2. _____
3. _____

Other marketable skills and competencies:
1. _____
2. _____
3. _____
4. _____
5. _____
6. _____
7. _____
8. _____
9. _____
10. _____

Convert Your Strengths and Competencies Into Benefits

Congratulations! By identifying your strengths and competencies, you have taken a major step towards a successful job search, and, hopefully, you are feeling better about yourself and your abilities. However, identifying your positive attributes is only half the battle. Where the true salesmanship comes into play is in your ability to translate how your strengths and competencies will benefit your potential employers.

Think about some of the jobs for which you might want to interview. Put yourself in the shoes of an interviewer. If you were the interviewer, what kind of strengths and competencies would you want your ideal candidates to possess? Why? Then, think about how these skills and aptitudes would benefit the company in relation to the other candidates having those skills and aptitudes. What would you come up with?

On your interviews, not only are you going to have to relate your strengths and competencies, you are going to have to convert them into selling points that will make companies want to hire you!

> ### *Insider Tip*
> Your key selling points and their related benefits are what interviewers are looking for when they ask, "Why should I hire you over other candidates I am considering?"

If You Are About To Graduate From School...

A success might be how you led a group to recieving high score on a class project. Your selling points might be your leadership skills and your ability to work as a team player. The benefit may be that you'll be easily integrated into the company and will work well with others.

Perhaps you are certified in Java. How does that make you different from other programmers? Why is that certification beneficial to the company interviewing you? Maybe you developed a Website for a class or organization. Selling points here could be your knowledge of Web design and your ability to manage projects; a benefit may be your ability to make an immediate contribution.

Were you in charge of a fraternity/sorority fund-raiser? If so, you exhibited *leadership* when coordinating people for a common effort. You exhibited *creativity* when forming the idea that raised funds. It took *teamwork* to achieve a goal. You were *successful* in that you raised more money than ever before. You were *marketing savvy* when drawing so many people; and demonstrated your *sales skills* to get those people to participate and donate. A benefit may be your ability to generate new sales and marketing programs. Get the idea?

Work Experience

If you have work experience, recall accomplishments from your current and previous jobs. How about the time you turned that irate customer into a happy customer, saving a huge order? Maybe you were given an excellent appraisal. How about the note you received from a coworker who was grateful for your help on a project? What about the fact that you made quota three years in a row? Maybe it was your creative efforts that helped reduce accounts receivables by 20 percent. Or maybe you excelled and won a corporate award.

Whatever your strengths and competencies, quantify how this experience will help benefit the company looking to hire you.

Come up with a minimum of four strengths and competencies and generate at least one key selling point for each one. From that selling point, quantify what the benefit will be to the company. Ask yourself, *Why does that strength or competency make me the most qualified candidate?*

For example, let's say you are a plant supervisor. Perhaps one of your strengths is that you are a great cost cutter. First come up with a quantifiable example: "I cut the cost of manufacturing by 25 percent on XYZ product for ABC Company."

Now, summarize the selling point in terms that would be applicable to the job for which you are interviewing. In this case, your selling point would be your ability to reduce manufacturing costs.

Finally, articulate the benefits that the company will receive (the "so what"). Why should the company care about this selling point? Here is an example: "If I saved you just 10 percent of your cost of manufacturing, the savings alone would more than pay my salary."

Everyone Has Strengths and Competencies That Can Land a Job!

The key for you is to identify your positive attributes that are most relevant for your targeted jobs. Good interviewers will ask you about your strengths and why they are applicable to the opportunity at hand.

Now, think about the job you really want. Then, go back to your personal strength worksheet and decide what are your three most relevant strengths and competencies to that position. Write them down and quantify them. Come up with some tangible examples that illustrate your selling points. And finally, summarize how those selling points will benefit your potential employers.

Key Selling Points
Worksheet

Strength #1: _____
   Key selling point: _____
   Benefits to company: _____

Strength #2: _____
   Key selling point: _____
   Benefits to company: _____

Strength #3: _____
   Key selling point: _____
   Benefits to company: _____

Secret #2:
Identify Your Core Strengths and Competencies
—Checklist Summary—

√ Focus on building a solid foundation.
√ Be aware of your feelings and the energy created.
√ Identify your strengths and competencies
    using the four cornerstones.
√ Complete the strengths and competencies worksheet.
√ Quantify your most relevant attributes.
√ Convert those attributes into benefits.
√ Complete the Key Selling Points Worksheet.

When you start each day with gratitude, you tune into a positive frequency that'll attract success and happiness into your life and your job hunt.

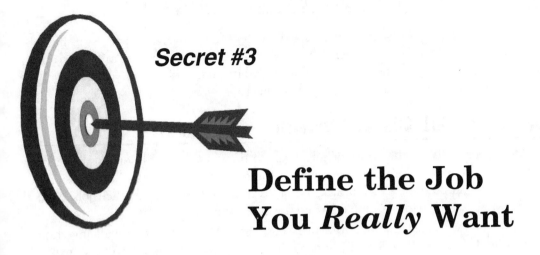

Secret #3

Define the Job You *Really* Want

- ◉   Identify your likes and dislikes.
- ◉   Explore your four P's of career alignment.
- ◉   Define your ideal job using the 10 elements of job satisfaction.

Now that you know your strengths and competencies, you should have a good idea of the jobs you *can* get. But what type of career do you *really* want? Defining the job you want is one of the most important secrets to a successful job search. After all, if you don't know what you want, how are you going to get it?

Recently, I volunteered to critique resumes at a job fair. Out of the almost 100 people, I would say at least 40 had absolutely no idea what they wanted to do for a living and couldn't articulate why someone should hire them. In looking at their resumes, I had to ask questions such as, "What kind of job do you want?" and "What message are you trying to convey?"

In just 15 seconds, I could ascertain that many of these people had no focus or direction. My response was, "If you don't know what you want or what you are good at, how is an interviewer supposed to know?"

You can't expect other people to be able to figure this out for you. You have to come to your own conclusions. It is up to you to tell them.

Your Ideal Job

Sadly, most people believe there is no such thing as an ideal job. These folks never take the time to define their ultimate position, and then they wonder why they can't ever find a job they can enjoy.

In fact, the reason so many people have difficulty finding overall happiness in life is that they never take the time to define what they need and want in life in order to be happy. If you don't make the time to define the traits and attributes of your ideal job, boss, and life, you are destined to a life of mediocrity.

Causes of Job Dissatisfaction

Most people dislike their current jobs because they accepted positions just to earn a buck, rather than those in alignment with their personal interests, skills, passions, values. They can do these jobs but lack the motivation and desire to do their jobs well, and as a result, they wind up unhappy and are often fired.

Have you ever taken the time to define your ideal job? If not, you should! Investing the time to define your ideal job will be one of the wisest investments you will ever make.

Live to Work or Work to *Live*

Including commuting time (on average, upwards to one hour each way) and actual work (usually eight hours a day), most people spend approximately 50 hours a week working. Because the average person sleeps around 56 hours a week, they consume 106 hours a week working and sleeping. There are only 168 hours in a week. That leaves only 62 hours a week of "free" time. Hmmm...50 hours on work...62 hours for pleasure. You spend almost *half* of your waking hours working and commuting!

If you don't enjoy your occupation, the stress, frustration, and lack of fulfillment is going to negatively impact the other facets of your life outside the job. It is critical to have a job that you can enjoy versus a job that just pays the bills.

The most important aspects of my life are health, love, family, friends, and spirituality—and then my job. But if my job is not enjoyable, that negatively impacts everything else. Feelings such as jealousy, embarrassment, lethargy, and frustration take over my thoughts when I am not doing something I enjoy.

Consequently, throughout my career I've always tried to choose professions where I could look forward to work as much as I do leisure. It's very important to me that I have a job I can be proud of. Right or wrong, we often derive our well-being and self-worth from our occupations. These evaluations do not have to be related to money. The ultimate satisfaction is doing work that you enjoy and is in alignment with your goals, beliefs, and desired lifestyle.

Work Can Be Fun!

You can actually enjoy work! As simple as it sounds, the key to enjoying your occupation is to be in the right job for you. When you are in the right job doing something you are passionate about, it no longer feels like work. One of the reasons I have always loved selling-related professions is that for me it is like playing a game every day.

Before I founded my own company, I had several jobs that I was truly passionate about and loved. I remember times, in those jobs, when I couldn't wait for Monday. Have you ever been able to say that?

The best job I had, prior to my business, was when I was a director of a $100 million division for American Power Conversion (APC). In this role I managed their OEM (Original Equipment Manufacturer) effort, focusing on accounts such as IBM, Dell, Hewlett-Packard, and Gateway.

We were in an extremely competitive marketplace and I was fortunate to have a team of sales "all-stars" working for me. It was as if we were playing in a championship game every day.

The position was challenging and rewarding. It allowed me to travel the globe at the company's expense. And due to the quality of my team and the strategies we employed, we consistently had the highest revenue growth and market-share increases in the company.

For years, the job was a dream. Not only was I doing something I loved, I had an excellent income. Then it all changed. The company went through a major reorganization of its management. Unfortunately, the new managers took a lot of the fun and independence out of the position. They started to dictate how I should manage my people and run my business based on political reasons, rather than sound business rationale.

I had always said to myself that once I left APC, I would have to start my own business. I just couldn't envision another situation where I could have been as passionate. But not everyone wants the pressure or hassles that come as a result of being their own boss. I'd be lying to you if I said there weren't times when I questioned my own decision to quit and start my own business.

Most people want to find a job they can enjoy while working for a successful company. It is very possible to find an ideal job working for someone else, as long as you know what it is that you want. You, too, can find the same passion I had working for APC.

Visualize having a job you can enjoy. What would that job be? What kind of qualities and characteristics would that job have? What kind of a boss would you be working for? Would you be working for a small or big company? Would you be working out of the office or in the home? The following is a list of some job characteristics I value. After reviewing my list, try creating one of your own.

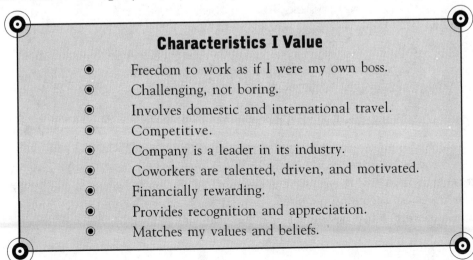

Characteristics I Value

- Freedom to work as if I were my own boss.
- Challenging, not boring.
- Involves domestic and international travel.
- Competitive.
- Company is a leader in its industry.
- Coworkers are talented, driven, and motivated.
- Financially rewarding.
- Provides recognition and appreciation.
- Matches my values and beliefs.

What Characteristics Are Important to You?

Once you find a position that closely matches your desires and beliefs, you will actually look forward to going to work each day. This enjoyment will positively impact everything else in your life.

Throughout my career, I have found three exercises to be extremely beneficial in identifying the ideal job:

1. Identify likes and dislikes.
2. Explore the four P's of career alignment.
3. Define the ideal job using the 10 elements of job satisfaction.

Exercise #1: Identify Your Likes and Dislikes

One of the best ways to figure out what you really want to do for a living is to take a step back, reflect on your previous positions and bosses, and identify what you liked and what you didn't like. Once you capture those thoughts, you can try to find new opportunities that will maximize your likes while minimizing your dislikes.

What positions and bosses did you like? Which ones didn't you like? If you are just graduating from school and you haven't had any jobs in the past, then reflect on your previous courses and instructors. I first tried this exercise when I decided to leave IBM.

Even though I had loved working for IBM, and I was a top performer, I became disenchanted because of compensation. Every year IBM kept doubling my sales quota, without wanting to pay me more money. I had no problem with an increased quota. But I had a big problem with getting the less money to sell more.

When I decided that I wanted to leave, I put together a spreadsheet to try to define my ideal job. I listed all of the things I enjoyed about the job that I currently had...and all of the things I wanted in a future job. Then I ranked each in order of importance.

Some of My Desires for a New Job

- A top-drawer boss like I had at IBM.
- A job that involves travel.
- A job with a market-leader and high quality firm like IBM.
- A job where if successful, I could earn a good income.
- A position that was truly pay-for-performance.

I also wanted to have stock options in the company for which I would work. When I put together this list, it was at the beginning of the bull market of the 1990s and options were just becoming popular. I desired a job where I could utilize the experience and contacts I had developed over the years at IBM.

As a result of doing the exercise, I was extremely focused. I knew exactly the type of position I wanted. In fact, within two weeks of deciding to leave IBM, I had received three job offers, all in the same week. I ended up choosing American Power Conversion (APC) where I enjoyed seven fantastic and rewarding years.

Your Most Favorite Jobs or Courses

What were the traits of your favorite jobs or classes? Who were your favorite bosses or teachers and why? Capture these thoughts. Write them down or create a spreadsheet. Later in this chapter, I will provide you with a worksheet (see page 48) to summarize these reflections.

Your Least Favorite Jobs or Courses

What did you dislike about your least favorite jobs or classes? Why was it so de-motivating? You will find that once you put some of these things down on paper, you can get a better understanding of what you enjoy, and what you don't.

Sometimes it's harder to figure out what we really want than it is to decide what we don't want. Ideally, you want to find a job that maximizes the things you desire and minimizes the aspects you'd like to avoid. It sounds simple, but you'd be surprised at how many people end up in the same dead-end positions because they don't take the time to articulate their likes and dislikes.

I worked at APC more than twice as long as any other company because the job had all the traits I loved, and very few of those that I hated. In fact, when I first took the job at APC, it had every one of the traits I outlined as "wants" on my spreadsheet.

It wasn't until almost seven years later that the negatives began to outweigh the positives. But hey...in this day and age, lasting seven years at one company isn't bad.

Summarize Your Thoughts

The following is a worksheet you can use to capture your reflections. The purpose of this exercise is very simple: Identify what you like and what you don't.

I know this isn't "rocket science," but when you look for a new job, ideally you really want to find one that has more of the things you like and less of the things you don't like.

Identify Your Likes and Dislikes
Worksheet 1

What were your *most* favorite jobs or classes?

_____

_____

_____

_____

_____

_____

What traits made these the *most* favorite?
(freedom, rewarding, travel, pay, challenge, team, etc.)

_____

_____

_____

_____

_____

_____

Who were your *most* favorite bosses or teachers?

_____

_____

_____

_____

_____

_____

What attributes did you like *most* about these bosses or teachers?
(appreciative, mentoring, open-minded, friendly, etc.)

_____

_____

_____

_____

_____

_____

Identify Your Likes and Dislikes
Worksheet 2

What were your *least* favorite jobs or classes?

_____

_____

_____

_____

_____

What traits made these your *least* favorite? (politics, bureaucracy, compensation, effort required, time required, etc.)

_____

_____

_____

_____

_____

Who were your *least* favorite bosses or teachers?

_____

_____

_____

_____

_____

What attributes did you like *least* about these bosses or teachers? (Closed-minded, political, over-aggressive, lack of compassion, etc.)

_____

_____

_____

_____

_____

Your Four P's

Right now, the universe has given you a gift. You have the opportunity to find the job of your dreams, one that you can be truly passionate about and one that allows you to be all that you can be.

Exercise #2: The Four P's of Career Alignment

The second exercise I have found to be helpful in defining an ideal job is to explore what I call the four P's of career alignment: purpose, passions, principles, and possibilities. Purpose is why you are here. Passions are what really motivates you. Principles are the values that are important to you. Possibilities are all the jobs in life that you are capable of doing with the talent you possess.

- ◉ Purpose.
- ◉ Passions.
- ◉ Principles.
- ◉ Possibilities.

Have you lost your job? Are you unhappy in your current position? If so, most likely (if you are honest with yourself) it is because the job is/was not in alignment with one of your four P's.

After all, if you aren't passionate about what you are doing, it's hard to get excited about going to work. It's equally difficult if you are employed on a job that goes against your morals or values. Plus, if you are doing something that doesn't properly utilize the talent you have, odds are you won't be happy either.

Purpose

I am a firm believer that we all were put on this earth for a reason. It would be nice if we were told exactly why we are here on our birth certificate. Unfortunately life doesn't work that way. If you have never asked yourself what your life's purpose is, now is a great opportunity to do so.

Not working in alignment with your purpose can cause great discomfort and dissatisfaction. When I first went into my own business, I went into day trading. I had always been intrigued by the stock market and I thought, *What an easy way to make a ton of money.* Wow, was I wrong. Interestingly enough, I kept sabotaging myself. Every time I was making money too easily, I would make a trade I knew I shouldn't make. For some reason, I would do it anyway and I would wind up giving back most of my profits and then some.

I couldn't figure it out. I was a good trader and I could read a stock chart with the best of them. But for some reason, I kept sabotaging my efforts. Finally, I decided to take a break from trading and go on a trip, by myself, to do some serious soul-searching. I wanted to get to the bottom of why day trading wasn't working out even though I had the talent to succeed.

During that trip, I took out a blank notebook and started reflecting on my four P's. I really wanted to get to the bottom of my self-sabotaging efforts.

What is my life's purpose? The answer I kept coming up with was that I was put on this earth to help people who want to be successful. This was interesting because in my mind, day trading wasn't helping anyone but *me*. Yes, I would try to justify to myself that I was helping others by providing liquidity to the market, but the bottom line was I didn't believe it.

Principles

What are my core principles or values? I came up with values such as giving, loving, competitive, trustworthy, honest, passionate, and sharing. This was a major revelation. The only way to be giving, loving, and sharing in day trading is to lose money. Wow, no wonder I kept sabotaging my efforts.

Every time I was trying to deceive the market on a trade or I was making money, I was going against my core values. When I made money, I wasn't giving. I was taking. When I tried to fake out a market maker, I wasn't being honest. I was being dishonest. Day trading was clearly out of alignment with my life's purpose as well as my core principles.

Knowing that I could no longer trade for a living, I was in a bit of a state of shock. *Okay, now what am I going to do?* At first, I was stumped. Then I thought, *Why don't I write down all the things I enjoy doing and see if I can come up with some conclusions?*

Passions

I wrote a list of things I enjoyed doing in my previous jobs. I then composed a list of aspects I enjoyed doing that weren't necessarily just job related, such as travel and being around friends. In other words, I compiled a list of my passions.

My list included things such as teaching, mentoring, traveling, selling, working with others, competing, being creative, and making my own decisions. This was very revealing as day trading allowed me few of these passions. Yes, it was competitive and allowed me to make my own decisions, but there was no teaching, mentoring, working with others, or traveling. It was Todd against the world and I didn't like that.

So I came up with a great list of wants...Now what?

Possibilities

What are my possibilities? What jobs could I do, with the talent I have, that would be in alignment with my other three P's of Purpose, Principles, and Passions?

I came up with a list of options such as becoming a teacher, going back into sales, becoming a professional speaker, going into real estate, and even considered going back to work for my old company. I had many opportunities from which to choose. Ultimately, I chose what I am doing today.

The Four P's
Worksheet

What is your life's purpose?
(help others, teach, raise a family, motivate others, solve a world problem, etc.)

_____

_____

_____

_____

_____

What are your core principles (values)?
(family-oriented, success-oriented, honest, trustworthy, etc.)

_____

_____

_____

_____

_____

What are your passions?
(freedom, creativity, competition, travel, entertaining, etc.)

_____

_____

_____

_____

_____

What are your possibilities?
(doctor, teacher, salesperson, accountant, firefighter, graphic designer, etc.)

_____

_____

_____

_____

_____

Limit Your Focus

I am sure there are scores of jobs you are capable of doing, but what do you *really* want to do. I took you through a reflection exercise, looking into your likes and dislikes of previous positions and had you explore at your Four P's of career alignment. Now is the time to narrow your focus down to one or two jobs that you really want to do for a living.

Focus on One or Two Types of Jobs

I suggest only trying to focus on one or two types of occupations (not one or two companies) that you want to work at, such as customer service and sales, or technical support and network management. It is difficult enough to be passionate about just one position at a time, let alone multiple ones. Expanding your scope beyond two is nearly impossible.

You will be competing against candidates who know exactly what they want to do for a living. They are going to be very good at articulating why they should be hired. If your concentration is too diluted, you won't have a chance when in competition with those who are more focused.

Interviewers aren't stupid; they can tell right away who is passionate about an opportunity versus who is interviewing just to find a job that'll pay the bills. Interviewers want someone with passion that will put everything they have into the job and hopefully stay with a company for years. Most managers hate turnover and lethargy.

Exercise #3: Define Your Ideal Job

One of the best ways to limit the focus of your job hunt is to use a methodology that considers the 10 elements of job satisfaction. I have used this process throughout my career to determine what I really wanted to do for a living. Once you go through this process and consider these key elements, you will be much more focused throughout your job search.

The 10 Elements of Job Satisfaction

1. Occupation.
2. Industry.
3. Company.
4. Career path.
5. Structure.
6. Hours.
7. Travel.
8. Environment.
9. Location.
10. Compensation and benefits.

1. Occupation

The first element is to define the exact *type* of job that really interests you. The best way to do this is to look at your list of possibilities. From this list determine which occupations allow you to best utilize your strengths. Which of these jobs can you see yourself going to each day? What jobs really interest you? Job satisfaction is in the eye of the beholder.

For example, if your passion in life is cleaning and organizing, being a housekeeper may appeal to you. Driving a truck could be tempting to someone who likes to travel, see the country, and meet new people. Software development can be ideal for someone who loves the challenge of taking a new concept and turning it into a successful product.

Only you know where your passion resides. Don't listen to what others say and think you should be. Had I listened to others, I would have gone to medical school to become a doctor. But, I get woozy at the sight of blood and medical instruments. I don't think I would have lasted too long in medical school. Medicine is not my passion.

Decide what interests you. There are millions of ways to earn a buck. People who like their jobs tend to live longer and happier lives than those who detest going to work each day. Job stress causes people to lose sleep and lead unhealthy lifestyles. When I am under pressure or frustrated, often that unhappiness manifests itself into illness. My worst maladies have always coincided with times I was most stressed about my job.

Typically, people who constantly complain about their jobs don't feel in control of their own destiny. Often, they will stay in jobs they dislike their entire lives because they feel that every job will lead to dissatisfaction. Don't let that become your reality. It is possible to enjoy going to work each day when you choose an occupation that is in alignment with your passions and pleasures.

I enjoy work time almost more than my leisure time because I love helping and interacting with other people, and I thrive on competition and the thrill of the ride. I have worked in situations I hated and that's why I quit those jobs.

Life is too short to do something you don't enjoy. So, clear your mind and think about the following questions:

- What jobs allow you to best capitalize on your core strengths and unique selling points?
- If you could do any occupation in the world, what would you choose?

2. Industry

Once you have decided on the type of job that interests you, your next goal is to determine your *ideal* industry. When I graduated from college, I received six job offers. I knew I wanted to be a salesperson, but what did I want to sell?

The two offers that interested me most were from NCR (a computer manufacturer) and U.S. Steel (a leader in the steel industry). U.S. Steel offered me a starting salary of 25 percent more than NCR. Basically, the choice boiled down to if I wanted to be in the steel industry or the computer industry.

I chose the computer industry and accepted the offer from NCR, even though it was for less money. I have never regretted that decision. Both were tremendous companies. I just opted for the industry that interested me the most at the time. Prior to starting my business, I spent 14 years in the computer industry—and loved it! I thrived on the constant change, abundant opportunities, and rapid innovations.

Just one decision can impact your entire life. Choosing an industry is not a decision to be made lightly. Had I chosen the steel industry, my whole life would have been different—not just my career, but also my experiences, my friends, and even where I would have lived.

Perhaps more importantly, once you choose an industry, depending on the industry and career, you will most likely remain in that industry for a minimum of three job-cycles. Because of the experience and knowledge that is gained through each job, rarely do people switch industries. Once expertise is acquired, it is very difficult to discard that investment, switch industries, and risk being unable to apply that knowledge to a new area.

Sound scary? It's true. So take some time and know what really interests you. Ask yourself, *With my strengths, experiences, and key selling points, which industries should I consider?*

There are thousands of different industries you can choose from. Let's say you wanted to go into customer service. Well, banks have customer service departments, so do manufacturers, doctors, insurers, hotels, and scores of other industries.

Some Major Industry Classifications

- Retail.
- Finance.
- Hospitality.
- Healthcare.
- Manufacturing.
- Information Technology.
- Accounting.
- Law.

As you might guess, often there is quite a bit of overlap between one industry and another. For instance, computer specialists are needed in any industry. Lawyers are needed regardless of the type of business. The main point is to identify what industries interest you.

If you want to be a lawyer, do you want corporate law or real estate law? If you want to go into marketing, do you want to work for an agency or a manufacturer? Do you want to focus on consumer goods or industrial? There are typically scores of industries you can choose from in almost any occupation.

3. Company

Next, ask yourself what type of company you want to join. Do you seek a company that promotes from within or one that hires from the outside? What kind of management philosophies do you value? Do you want the prestige of a big established company or do you want the challenge and opportunity that a smaller start-up offers?

Prestige and opportunity for training and growth comes with working for a company with a *household* name. However, big companies also have a lot of politics, bureaucracies, and rules. What is more important to you? These are important issues to consider when deciding the type of company that is right for you. There are always tradeoffs.

The key is to define a type of company that has more of what you want and less of what you don't want. It sounds so simple. But, I can't tell you how many people hop from job to job and always end up working for the same type of companies.

If you hate politics and bureaucracies, yet you keep getting jobs in large companies, what is the likelihood you will ever be happy? Size and type of company both play major roles in job satisfaction. What kind of company do you want to work for?

4. Career Path

Now that you have decided your ideal job, industry, and type of company, your next decision is to determine which career path to take. This will be your road map (plan).

Choose a career path leading to a good future. No one wants a dead-end job. While nothing that relates to careers is ever written in stone, it is important to decide early on in your job-hunting process what kind of path you want to take.

What is your ultimate destination? Some people want to be an engineer their entire career. Others want to become a manager. Some want to shoot for the top and become the leader of a company. What do you want? Be honest with yourself.

Society puts pressure on us to go into management, but these positions can come with a lot of headaches. There is something to be said for leaving the job at the office at the end of the day.

If you think you want to go into management, do you have the strengths and expertise to do so *now*? If not, are you capable of learning what you need to know to succeed? If the answer is yes, interview with companies that are growing and promote from within. Then, identify the types of jobs that will give you the experience you'll need to become a manager in that company.

If you want to be in sales your entire career, research industries and companies with the highest salaries, the best perks, and the most promising futures for their top salespeople. For instance, in the 1980s everyone wanted to get into real estate. In the 1990s, Enterprise software and Year 2000 software sales positions were most in demand. But what happened to Year 2000 software salespeople after the year 2000? Who knows...

> ### *Insider Tip*
>
> In upwards of 85 percent of all job interviews, you will be asked, "Where do you want to be in five years?" If you are not, you'll undoubtedly be asked a similar one. By determining your ideal career path now, you will be prepared when this question comes up in your interviews.

5. Structure

Although you know the type of job that you want, similar jobs can have totally different structures. For example, in sales you can have a job that is a part of a team or one where you are on your own. You can have compensation based on "management-by-objective" (MBO) or compensation based strictly on sales revenue or sales growth.

What kind of job structure is ideal for you? Do you want a job with set goals and objectives? Do you want a job where you are told exactly what to do? Or do you want one where you help in determining ongoing strategic decisions?

Maybe you want a job where you are part of a team and are compensated according to the *team's* successes. Conversely, you might prefer a situation where you work independently and are recognized solely for your own efforts. Do you want to work on short-term or long-term projects?

You've heard the expression "You can't place a square peg in a round hole." If you take a job that doesn't match the structure you are looking for, you will feel like a square peg. Typically, "square pegs" become disgruntled and end up always complaining about their jobs. You don't want that, do you? This is why it is so important to identify the kind of structure that is best suited for you.

6. Hours

Have you ever thought about how long and how hard you want to work? Do you mind working 50 to 60 hours per week? Or would you rather work only 40 hours? Do you want to work part-time or full-time? Many jobs today require far more than the traditional 9-to-5 schedule.

Often you could be required to work long hours, late at night, and sometimes on weekends. Is that a sacrifice you are willing to make? Examples of professions that require extensive hours are accounting, consulting, legal, healthcare, retail, real estate, and hotel management.

It is up to you. If you value balance in your life or if you have children, then work hours may be important to you. If you are one who wants to succeed and climb the career ladder at all costs, then work hours may not be a big deal. Either way, you need to decide how much you really want to work.

7. Travel

Another factor to consider when looking for a job is travel. Some jobs require extensive travel. Others demand little to no travel. If you enjoy traveling, then a desk job may not appeal to you. However, if you have a family you don't want to be away from, it may be best to have a job where you go to the same location every day.

As it turned out, one of the things I didn't like about day trading was that I had to go to the same place every day to trade. Some people like that concept. I'd rather be in a situation where I can have multiple working environments. What would you prefer?

8. Environment

Many people enjoy working because of the mental stimulation they get from being around other motivated people. If you like being around others, then a large office environment may be optimal. Some like the freedom of working on their own without the need for direct supervision. In this case, working out of the home may be more appealing.

Do you want to work at a corporate headquarters, a regional hub, or a remote office? A remote location is ideal if you want to remain independent. However, if you want to get promoted and be on the fast track, you may want to be at headquarters where you are visible to key corporate managers and your contributions can be seen first hand.

Do you want to work in an office building or out of your home? An office provides camaraderie and close proximity to your boss. However, working out of the home offers more autonomy. Perhaps best of all, because you don't have to commute, working out of the home allows you to have more time to yourself. But that comes at a cost. You lose the opportunity to meet as many new people as you would in an office environment. What aspects are most important to you?

Are you comfortable in a cubicle or do you need your own office? Some people enjoy working with background noise; others need the silence of an office. Often, people in jobs such as telemarketing, accounting, customer service, procurement, engineering, and administration are placed in cubicles. Whereas others such as lawyers, doctors, managers, and those in human resources personnel have their own offices.

Do you want to wear business casual or business formal attire? While I enjoy wearing casual clothing, other people enjoy dressing more formally. Which style is more comfortable for you? Clothing often can have a major influence on productivity. One of the reasons Southwest Airlines flight attendants are so chipper is that they wear fun uniforms.

The bottom line is your work environment, be it your office or your clothes, can have a major impact on job satisfaction and performance.

9. Location

In today's global economy, you could end up receiving job offers from all over the world. Have you ever thought about where you want to live? Often people have chosen to move to another city strictly for a job. Before you do that, you need to be honest with yourself about what is important in your life.

I used to think my career was the most important aspect of my life, that it didn't matter where I lived or worked, until I relocated to Raleigh, North Carolina, for a job promotion. Prior to my move, Raleigh was named the top region (to live) in the country. Thousands of people were flocking there. I took the promotion without having ever seen Raleigh. I was filled with excitement.

At the time of my move, I was single. I didn't know one person who lived in Raleigh, but that didn't matter to me. All I could see were the big dollar signs of a great promotion.

The first year, the job went fantastically well. I was earning more than ever before, had success and recognition within the company, and traveled to exciting places. But during the beginning of my second year in Raleigh, I started to question my decision. Even though I was earning a great income, I was not happy. I started to feel a void in my life.

At first, I had no idea why I was feeling so empty inside. After much introspection, I finally realized that I really missed my family and friends. I didn't recognize how important a local support structure was to me...until I no longer had it.

Until then, I didn't understand the importance of balance in my life. Finally, I understood that work and money were not the sole sources of happiness. I realized that health, love, family, friends, and spirituality were far more important to me than the job. Unfortunately, it took getting relocated to Raleigh for me to discover this.

Thankfully, I moved back to Chicago. Within a couple of months of my return, my mother became very sick. Ultimately, less than two years later, she passed away. Had I stayed in Raleigh, I would have missed out on the time I was able to spend with my dear mother during those final two years of her life.

If you are close to your family, you may want to live and work in the same metropolitan area as they do. If not, at least the Internet and phone provide ways to stay in touch.

Only you know where you want to live and how important it is for you to be near your family and friends. Every city has positive and negatives. I recommend that before you pick up and move for a job, ask yourself if you can still keep balance in your life. Then ask yourself if you can still live within the values of what is important to you. I'll bet you didn't realize how many dynamics you should consider when thinking about your ideal job.

10. Compensation and Benefits

The 10th and final element to consider is the one that pays your bills and puts a roof over your head: compensation and benefits. You might love your job, but if you are not making enough money to live the lifestyle you want, you won't be happy. When looking at compensation and benefits, there are several areas you should consider.

1. **Wages.** Wages are the first thing to consider when choosing an opportunity. After all, our wages pay the bills. Often, the lifestyle we live dictates how much we need to earn. How much do you want to make? How much do you realistically need to earn to live your ideal lifestyle? Do you want a salary or a pay-by-the-hour position? Some positions offer the chance to earn overtime. Is overtime important to you?

2. **Compensation structure.** There are many ways a company can compensate employees. Some firms pay employees hourly, while others pay a salary. Do you want an hourly job or one based on salary? Depending on the occupation, the compensation structure can include some form of leverage. This leverage can come in the form of a bonus or commission. The idea with leverage is that the better you perform on the job, the more money you make. Typically in leveraged positions, companies pay you less in salary, but the total you can earn can be more if you hit certain goals and objectives. Are you willing to risk a portion of your salary for the leverage to earn more if you succeed?

If you chose a profession that had leveraged compensation, do you want weekly, monthly, quarterly, or annual bonuses? Or do you want a commission-based job? If so, do you want a salary plus commission? Or are you willing to take a straight commission job where you can earn more money if you perform well?

The key is to decide what structure works best for you. If you expect to work long hours, taking an hourly job that pays overtime might be better for you than a salary job that doesn't pay overtime. If you expect to excel on the job, then perhaps taking a position in which a portion of the compensation is leveraged would be better for you than one without any risk. Either way, it is important to determine what structure works best for you.

3. **Profit sharing.** Profit sharing is when a company literally shares a percentage of its earnings with the employees. Many companies pay slightly lower salaries to their employees, but then allow their employees to receive sometimes significant bonuses based on the profit of the organization.

When the company is profitable, employees can make more total compensation than comparable ones in other organizations. Are you willing to risk a portion of your salary to earn potentially more money with profit sharing?

4. **Allowances.** Depending on the job and company, a position can come with an allowance or multiple ones. Allowances are a means, outside of salary and bonus, to compensate employees for expenses incurred while on the job. The most common allowances paid are for working out of the home (home office) and for doing extensive driving (car).

Do you want to work out of your home? If so, do you have room in your house to work? How much of a housing allowance would you need to make it worthwhile? What if the company will let you work from home, but they make you responsible for all expenses? Would you still take the job?

Does the occupation require you to drive frequently? If so, will you be compensated for the wear and tear on your car? Would you want a monthly car allowance or to receive payments by the mileage you drive? If you get a car allowance, are you willing to let the company dictate the kind of car you drive?

Maybe you want nothing short of being provided with a company car. But if that's the case, your choice of models will be quite limited. In any event, allowances can contribute significantly to your bottom line.

One of the reasons I chose to work for APC was that I received a $400 housing allowance and a $300 car allowance. That made a huge impact, because I still needed to pay for my car and housing anyway. To me, that was like found money and definitely had an impact on my decision.

5. **Stock options.** Stock options give employees the right to purchase company stock at a specified price, over a particular period of time. Some companies use options as a way of rewarding top performers, reducing employee turnover and increasing employee productivity. When a company's stock price goes up, options can be worth quite a bit of money. However, if a company's stock goes down, the options are worthless.

Many companies place restrictions on when you can exercise your options. I had a friend who worked for a wireless communications company. After joining the company, its stock skyrocketed and his options were worth more than $1 million on paper.

However, the company made him hold the options for an extended length of time before he could exercise them. Unfortunately, the stock crashed before he could exercise his options and his $1 million evaporated before he could cash in on even a single dollar.

Many companies offer stock options in lieu of higher salaries. Are you willing to sacrifice some salary for stock options? Is the stock likely to increase? What is an optimal vesting period? How long do you have to hold the stock before you can sell? These are all things to consider when comparing one job offer to another.

6. **Retirement plans.** Most companies offer some form of retirement program. But plans can differ significantly from company to company. Some offer a pension, while others offer deferred savings plans with matching funds. What type of plan do you want? There are pros and cons to every program.

As we saw in the late 1990s and early 2000s, many companies saw the funding for their retirement plans diminish. Thousands of employees saw their retirement savings vanish. When you are considering offers, you should look at the financial stability of each company and of their retirement plans. How is the plan funded? How secure is the plan? What is the likelihood that the plan will survive to pay the benefits you were promised?

7. **Medical benefits.** One area of the economy that has seen more inflation than almost anything else is healthcare. The costs of seeing a doctor have skyrocketed. Now more than ever, the type of health plan a company has can make a significant difference into your overall well-being and that of your family.

Many companies, as a way to reduce expenses, have significantly cut back on their healthcare benefits. In my opinion, this is a big mistake. Nothing is more important than healthy employees. Employees are ultimately what makes or breaks the success of a business. Some firms have either asked employees to shoulder a percentage of the cost of the healthcare plans or have reduced the quality of the programs. Several have even eliminated healthcare benefits all together.

I have a couple of friends who have a child with a preexisting condition that makes it very difficult to obtain medical insurance for the family. As a result, the quality of the healthcare program is one of the most important aspects of compensation and benefits that they consider. In fact, because their healthcare is so expensive, they have been sometimes willing to accept job offers for thousands less in salary, because the benefit of being covered by a good health plan far outweighs salary.

What is your situation? How important are healthcare programs? Do you have a family? Are you the main source of income for the family? If so, then healthcare may be very important.

Do you have a favorite doctor or are you willing to use a plan like an HMO that requires use of their doctors? Are dental and eye care important to you? If so, are you willing to accept an HMO, or pay a higher deductible to get the expanded coverage? Would you require disability and life insurance? For those of you who want to have children, would you need a plan that covers fertility options? Some plans actually will cover up to tens of thousands of dollars in fertility assistance.

I have yet to see a healthcare plan that wasn't explained in a book itself. Needless to say, these plans are complex. It's important to decide early on in your job search what kind of healthcare coverage you need.

8. **Raise policies.** Every company has its own rules for how much of a raise employees can get come review time. Some companies have very strict policies that limit the amount of a raise someone can get while others are more liberal. If you expect to be a top performer, a company's policy of giving raises can be quite important.

Will you tolerate a company that limits pay raises to 10 percent in exchange for more job security? Are you willing to work for a company where you have to "walk on water" to get a raise, but you get great perks? What is your expectation of a fair raise policy?

I can't overemphasize this point. If a company has a very strict policy on raises, then you had better hold out for more money up-front. However, if the company is more liberal and believes in significantly rewarding performance, then maybe you don't have to get such a high offer. Once you sign on at a company, it is usually very difficult to significantly increase your earnings without getting a promotion. So, that makes the initial job offer and the raise policies important elements of the decision-making process.

9. **Perks.** Some companies offer employees little extras that can make a big difference in job satisfaction. These perks can range from corporate daycare, to expense accounts, golf club memberships, and onsite exercise clubs, to discounts at local merchants and education reimbursements. What are the important perks for you? Are you willing to sacrifice some perks for more pay? Or would you sacrifice some pay for more perks?

Compensation Is the #1 Cause of Employee Dissatisfaction

Prior to jumping into your job search, you should develop a budget and figure out what you need to earn in order to be happy with your job. While compensation is not the sole determinant of job satisfaction, it carries significant weight.

If you are making less than you feel you are worth, or less than the lifestyle you want, odds are you won't be happy on the job. Many people don't take the time to determine what they are worth and what they expect to earn. This is a big mistake. By quantifying your expectations prior to starting your job hunt, you will be much more focused and successful in finding a job that excites you.

Consider All Aspects of Compensation, Not Just Salary

Often, some companies make up for lower salary and bonus earnings by providing phenomenal benefits and perks. Some companies have their own daycare and exercise facilities. Others provide benefits such as country club memberships, increased maternity leave, more vacation time, and even free lunches on Fridays. These perks can save hundreds, if not thousands of dollars every month. Everything doesn't just boil down to salary.

Once you know what you want, you will be much more focused, efficient, and successful in your job hunt. Also, you will convey the image of a goal-oriented person. That will come across loud and clear in an interview, and will rank you above your competition.

Define Your Ideal Job Using the 10 Elements of Job Satisfaction

While the 10 elements are fresh in your mind, list the characteristics you want in your ideal job. You can use the worksheet on page 64. Once you have identified your ideal job, try to summarize it in a one- to two-sentence personal mission statement.

If you read almost any corporate annual report, you will see a mission statement. This statement serves as the focus for the organization. When you articulate a mission for your job hunt, it allows you to be more focused and direct in your job-hunting efforts.

Once you come up with a mission statement, post it on your wall and in your notebooks and journals. By focusing on your goal, and not the process, you will succeed! Finally, using the worksheets in this chapter, come up with a list of potential companies you can target in your job search. It is always easier to get to your destination when you know where you are going.

Job Definition Worksheet 1

Type of job(s):

1. _____
2. _____
3. _____

Type of industry(s):

1. _____
2. _____
3. _____

Type of company:

Private: _____   Public: _____

Big: _____   Entrepreneurial: _____

Conservative: _____   Liberal: _____

High Growth: _____   Stable Growth: _____

Turnaround Candidate: _____   Established: _____

Desired career path:

Year 1. _____
Year 2. _____
Year 3. _____
Year 4. _____
Year 5. _____

Job Definition Worksheet 2

Ideal job structure: _____

_____

_____

_____

Desired work hours: Per day: _____ Per week:_____

Travel: Yes ____ No ____   If yes, how much travel: _____

Work out of home or office? _____

Type of office environment desired: _____

Attire desired...casual or formal? _____

City(s)/locations you can work in: _____

_____

Desired compensation and benefits: _____

_____

_____

_____

_____

Ideal Job Mission Statement: _____

_____

_____

_____

Job Definition Worksheet 3

Company brainstorm: (IBM, Procter & Gamble, Sony, Merck, Wal-Mart, Starbucks, etc.)

1. _____
2. _____
3. _____
4. _____
5. _____
6. _____
7. _____
8. _____
9. _____
10. _____
11. _____
12. _____
13. _____
14. _____
15. _____

Secret #3: Define the Job You *Really* Want
—Checklist Summary—

√ Dissatisfaction is caused by a mismatch between
   values and job.

√ Don't live to work. Work to live.

√ Almost half of your life is spent on work. Enjoy it.

√ Only you can determine where your passion resides.

√ Identify your likes and dislikes.

√ Explore your four P's of career alignment.

√ Before you search, define your ideal job using
   the 10 elements.

√ Create a personal job-hunting mission statement.

If you don't know what you want, how are you going to get it?

Secret #4

Justify Why You Should Be Hired

- The 7-Step Hiring Process.
- Predict the decision-making criteria.
- Create a business case to justify getting hired.

Congratulations! You're doing great! Thus far, you have already built a solid foundation for a successful job search. By believing in yourself, identifying your core strengths and competencies, and defining your ideal job, you are now well on your way towards getting the job you really want.

That brings us to the next phase of the job-hunting process: justifying why you should be hired. "Back in the good old days" it used to be that you could almost just show up for the interview and get the job. That certainly isn't the case anymore. Times are forever changing.

In today's challenging job market, you have to compete vigorously against many candidates. You have to earn each and every job offer. Sometimes you even need to convince a company to create a position that currently doesn't even exist.

Interviewers have to see more than just your smiling face. Hiring managers must be convinced there is a reason to hire you. They have to be shown that the *benefits* of hiring you will far outweigh the *costs* of doing so. To create a position, most managers go through a similar hiring process. I call this hiring methodology the 7-Step Hiring Process.

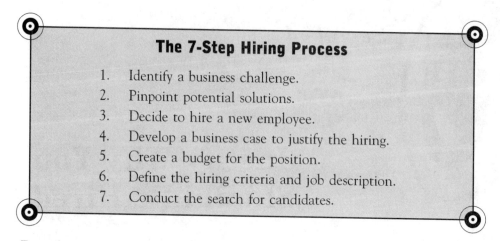

Every hiring manager has to go through a justification process in order to be able to hire someone for the company. Employers don't just hire people because it feels good. There has to be a business reason or a personal need to do so.

The following 7-step process is the hiring methodology I used as a sales manager for a large technology firm.

My goal in showing you this process is to provide you with insight into the mindset and perspective of a hiring manager. Armed with this knowledge, you'll be able to position your skills and talents to convince companies to hire you—even when no positions are currently available.

Step #1: Identify a Business Need

The first step of any hiring process is an acknowledgement that there is a particular business challenge or personal need. This could be anything from poor customer service to sluggish sales growth to the fact that the company's computer systems keep crashing. The bottom line is that there is something that needs to be improved or fixed in order for the business to operate more profitably or effectively.

Step #2: Pinpoint Potential Solutions

Once a challenge is acknowledged, managers have to ascertain all of the possible solutions for the given problem. Solutions can come in a variety of forms. Hiring, training, refocusing, and procuring are four of the most common ways to solve a problem.

Let's say a manager wants to improve customer service. Any one of the following scenarios could solve the problem.

Possible customer-service solutions include:

- Install new customer service software.
- Hire more customer service representatives.
- Fire the current customer service manager.
- Hire a consultant that can make recommendations.

- Give unhappy customers a coupon toward future purchases.
- Provide customer service training to the existing staff.
- Reorganize the existing customer service department.

In this scenario you can see that even though there is one problem (poor customer service), there are at least seven possible solutions. Any one of these solutions could potentially solve the problem. It is up to the hiring manager to determine which will be the most cost-effective and productive.

Step #3: Decide to Hire a New Employee

As you saw in the previous example on poor customer service, there are many ways to solve a business problem. Hiring more people may be one answer. Installing a new computer platform and training the existing staff are other potential solutions.

Managers must weigh all of the alternative solutions and decipher which is the most effective. They may ask others for advice as well. Ultimately, they will reach a decision. Often, this decision is to hire someone. However, many times it is not.

When trying to convince a company to create a position for you, one key is to quantify how you can provide a better return on their investment than other possible alternatives.

Companies Don't Hire People Just to Be Nice!

Companies expect to make a large return on their investment. Have you ever taken the time to figure out the dollars and cents of what kind of return you can provide to a given company? Companies hire people to either contribute towards revenues and profits, or to increase efficiencies.

Employees Must Consistently Justify Their Existence

Regardless of the position, when employees are not contributing in some way to the company's bottom line, they will be in jeopardy of losing their job. When companies lay off people, the first to go are usually those whose jobs are the most difficult to quantify and justify. Companies also lay off those employees who aren't the best fit for the position or the team.

The bottom line is companies don't lay off employees that are critical to the ongoing success of the business. A paycheck is not a birthright. Every day is a new day. In order to maintain employment, employees must contribute to the success of the organization each and every day.

Step #4: Develop a Business Case to Justify the Hiring

Once managers decide the best way to solve a business need is to hire someone, they put together a business case of why a position should be created. In their business cases, managers typically show how hiring someone will impact either productivity, revenues, cost structure, or profits.

Regardless of the justification, managers must demonstrate that hiring someone will provide a large "return on investment" (ROI) to the company. ROI is the benefit gained for the money invested.

For instance, if you are putting money into a savings account paying 5-percent interest, your ROI is 5 percent. Companies typically look for an ROI of at least 300 percent before they hire an individual. That's right 300 percent! Wouldn't it be nice to get that kind of return on your bank account?

This means that in order to justify hiring someone, managers have to demonstrate that for every $1 they invest in a new employee, that they will get at least $3 back in benefits to their line of business. Employees are expensive. Not only are there the base salary, there are also benefits and training costs. Benefits alone cost a company as much as 50 percent of any given employee's salary.

Let's say you are interviewing for a job that is paying $100,000 plus benefits ($150,000 total). You must demonstrate how you will positively impact a company's bottom line by at least $450,000 ($150,000 x 3). And, that doesn't even include training costs. Ideally, you want to be able to show an even greater impact because many companies have a much higher hurdle to jump than just a 300 percent ROI. Some are as high as 2,000 percent.

What Kind of Return Can You Provide to a Company?

If you can't answer this question you might as well stop job hunting. I don't care if you are an administrative assistant, an accountant, a lawyer, an architect, or a salesperson; If you have no idea how you can contribute to a company's bottom line, you are sunk! Focus on what you can do and the benefits you can provide.

Think about the results you can generate. Try to quantify some of those results. If you are in sales, show how you can add $500,000 in revenue. If you are a purchasing assistant, show how you can save a company thousands in expenses because of your ability to negotiate.

If you are a software programmer, show how you can reduce the amount of bugs in the software, saving tens of thousands of dollars in future support costs. If you are an accountant, show how you can find tax loopholes that can pay for your salary itself. Get the picture?

Step #5: Create a Budget for the Position

Once upper management approves the creation of a new position hiring managers are awarded with what is often called a "hiring ticket." That gives managers the approval to go out to interview people and ultimately hire someone. However, hiring tickets always come with stipulations and guidelines.

One of these guidelines is the budget for the position. Managers are usually given a "not to exceed" budget of how much they can offer new employees. This budget not only encompasses salary, but can also include items such as stock options, benefits, allowances and perks.

Insider Tip

Often, hiring managers will offer something less than the maximum budget in an initial job offer. Typically, they will leave some fudge factor for negotiations.

Let's say a manager wants to hire a new computer programmer. That manager may be given a *"not to exceed"* budget of $150,000 a year. As previously mentioned, often that budget includes the cost of benefits, so not all of that money can go towards salary. Benefits are typically assigned a value of anywhere from 25 percent to 50 percent. Thus, in this case, the manager can only hire someone for annual salary somewhere between $100,000 and $125,000.

Insider Tip

When you are negotiating for salary, if you are married, and covered by your spouse's healthcare plan, you may be able to negotiate for more money by offering your potential employer the opportunity to forgo providing you with health insurance. This could free up additional funding for your salary because healthcare is the largest component of benefit cost.

Step #6:
Define the Hiring Criteria and Job Description

Once the budget is set, hiring managers now have to decide what kind of person to hire. In order to do this, managers will put together a list of desired qualities and characteristics.

Hiring Criteria

- Work experience.
- Personality.
- Qualifications.
- Salary range.
- Background.
- Adaptability.
- Flexibility.
- Drive.
- Knowledge.
- Accomplishments.

Once hiring managers determine the hiring criteria for a given position, they will then rank the criteria by importance and relevance to the success of the position. Based on this prioritized list of criteria, managers then create a job description.

Job descriptions typically include an outline of the duties of the position as well as the qualifications needed to succeed. When you see a help-wanted ad or posting, that is the output of this step.

Insider Tip

Ideally, you want to influence a hiring decision before this step. Typically, once managers define the job, they already have an idea of who they want to hire. The key is to try to meet with the managers before they finalize the job description.

Step #7: Conduct the Search for Candidates

After determining the hiring criteria and creating the job descriptions, hiring managers are now free to initiate a candidate search. Depending on the position, managers may look at candidates inside the company, post help-wanted ads, or contact recruiters. Often, especially in more entrepreneurial firms, managers will search for candidates on their own.

In larger companies, this is the time managers may finally solicit the help of the human resources department (HR).

Interesting! Notice how HR doesn't get involved until this last step. Yet, how often do people focus strictly on HR during their job search? Focusing exclusively on HR is often futile because they are usually the last ones to know about a position. Managers typically already have someone in mind to hire, long before they contact HR.

When I was a manager, the only reason I had HR interview a candidate was to get a final blessing and to adhere to corporate guidelines. As a manager, I hired scores of employees over the years. I can tell you with complete certainty that HR introduced not one of them to me.

Certainly, in some larger companies, HR could help scour the field for potential candidates. However, they rarely will make the final hiring decision. The reason for this is that unless you are in the HR field, you will almost always be reporting to some other line of business. It is that manager, the one who you will report to, that will make the ultimate hiring decision.

Predict the Decision-Making Criteria

One of the best ways to accelerate your job search is to try to predict what will be the most important criteria to your potential employers. Using these predictions, you can tailor your message—be it in your resumes, cover letters, or job interviews—to ignite interest in prospective hiring managers.

So what will go on in the minds of interviewers when they interview you? One thing for certain is the fact that they want to be as sure as possible that the person they are hiring will solve their business needs and fit into the culture of their team and organization. When hiring managers interview you, there are many thoughts that go through their minds.

Typical thoughts of interviewers include:

- *How quickly can this individual contribute to my group?*
- *How much training is this person going to require?*
- *Can I believe what this person is saying?*
- *What salary will I have to pay this person?*
- *Does this person have the personality to fit our culture?*
- *Is this person qualified?*
- *Will this candidate make me look good?*

Interviewers Want to Look Good

That's right! Just as you like to look good in the eyes of your bosses, your family, and your friends, so do hiring managers.

Will the this candidate make me look good?

Do interviewers really think that way when they talk to candidates? You bet they do! Just like us, they want to look good. If it's not consciously, it's certainly subconsciously.

Regardless of what anyone tells you, interviewers look out for their own self-interests first. Then they consider the interests of the organization. After all, they are only human. It's human nature to want to look out for your own self before others.

When you understand how hiring managers think, you can best position yourself. After all, their time is valuable. Every moment they spend talking to candidates takes valuable time away from running their business segment.

Ordinarily, You Will Not Be the Highest Priority

If you wonder why interviewers don't return your phone calls, or why they take a long time to get back to you, it is because they are busy. Managers have a business to run. While the opportunity to interview for a job may be the most important thing for you, it may not be such a high priority for them. Somehow you have to create a sense of urgency.

There are ways you can become a priority. Imagine you have a perfectly good car right now, but eventually you would like to get a fancier one with more features. How much urgency will you put on buying a new one? Maybe you'll go online to compare specifications and cost. Perhaps you will even go to an auto show or test-drive some of them. It may take you anywhere from a month to several years to make a decision because there is no sense of urgency.

Now, imagine that your car just broke down and it's going to cost you $3,000 to fix it. On top of that, your car already has more than 125,000 miles on it. Do you think you will treat the car search with the same urgency? All of a sudden, there is a much more pressing need to do something.

The same holds true for managers. The greater their need and the more critical their problem is, the more time and energy they will spend on hiring someone. Thus, when interviewing, you need to demonstrate how you not only solve business problems but that there is an immediate need for the company to react quickly.

Convey an Image of Being in Demand

Just as in dating, one of the best ways to create urgency in interviewing is to show that you are in demand. Why is it that people often try much harder at the beginning of a relationship than later on? The beginning of a relationship is not exclusive and there is always that threat of being in competition with someone else.

How many times, when the relationship is new, does the guy buy flowers and dinners, versus later on, when the relationship is exclusive? Usually, it is a fact of life that people try harder when the stakes are higher.

Don't Act Desperate, Even If You Are

When you are in the job market, you never want to give the impression that you are exclusively dependent on any one opportunity. Instead, be confident and convey an aura that says many companies are interested in you.

It is human nature to want what is difficult to get. As much as I hate to admit it, when I dated, women always seemed to be more interested in me when I was already in a relationship then when I was completely unattached.

Somehow people can just sense when you are desperate. If interviewers are interested in you, they will react much quicker if they think you are in demand, than if they think you are desperate.

Insider Tip

Play "hard to get." When job hunting, the best way to create that "hard-to-get" or "in-demand" aura is to go out and have as many interviews as possible. Even if you go on interviews for jobs that aren't ideal, when you get one job offer, it is much easier to get others.

Create a Business Case to Justify Getting Hired

How do you demonstrate or quantify to a company that they will get a high return on hiring you? To do so you have to create a business case for yourself, much like managers do to justify hiring someone.

The first thing you need to do to create a business case is to equate work ethic and effort into monetary benefits. Let's say you are interviewing for an entry-level computer programming position and you are just graduating from college. How can you possibly demonstrate that the company will make a big return on their investment by hiring you?

One way is to show how you learn quickly and work hard. Being young and energetic, you can explain how you will put in the long hours and dedication necessary to get a job done right. You can also provide examples of how efficiently you developed applications in school and how quickly you can solve problems. You can provide examples of how you performed well under stress, and how you were able to balance many tasks simultaneously.

In fact, you can imply how a company would have to hire two people to replace the energy, enthusiasm, hours worked, and dedication that you will bring to the job. Ah, now that's the magic nugget. A manager would have to hire *two* people to get the same kind of work and effort you will provide.

By stating that a company would have to hire two people to get the same amount of results, you've just doubled your ROI perception in the eyes of the interviewer.

If You Have Experience, Quantify Its Value

Say you have several years of sales experience. Imagine hearing through the "grapevine" that one of your competitors is paying its salespeople 40 percent more than you are making. Their salespeople are happy and making tons of money. The problem is they aren't hiring. Should you give up? No! Instead, develop a business case.

Being a successful salesperson, assume you are currently servicing clients doing more than $3 million in business in an industry with a 28 percent gross margin. Well, what if you could generate the same kind of revenues for the new company?

Hmmm…$3,000,000 x .28 percent = $840,000. Wow! If your competitor hires you for a total package of $150,000 a year, they would make an ROI of more than 560 percent ($840,000/$150,000). That sounds like a good deal to me.

Create a Perceived Need

Just think, the $3 million in business you are currently selling is coming directly out of your competitor's potential client base. They are spending a great deal of time, money, and manpower on marketing and advertising to try to lure that business from you. Imagine if your competitor could get your clients' business without having to spend all that money on marketing and advertising. Not only is the company going to gain profits, they are also increasing market share.

Plus, as the company sells more, that is going to lower its overall cost of production through efficiencies of scale. How can your competitor afford not to hire you? They need you! Amazing! You actually can create jobs where they don't exist. The key is to equate the results you can provide into monetary benefits managers can relate to and enjoy.

To create a business case you need to show:

◉ How you can solve their business needs.
◉ How you can make an immediate contribution.
◉ Why hiring you is a better decision than any other option.
◉ The substantial ROI you can provide.
◉ How you will make anyone who hires you look good.

The concept of quantifying an intangible asset such as ROI can be challenging. Especially if you are going for a position that isn't as easily measurable as sales, marketing, advertising, or procurement.

When you can't specifically quantify in monetary terms the benefits you can provide, try to focus on other things. Improved efficiency, organization, response times, uptime, and morale are all potential benefits you can provide.

You Can Win Regardless of the Situation!

When you quantify what you can offer to an organization and justify why you should be hired, you will succeed in getting loads of job interviews and job offers. Going through this process will provide you with the foundation you need to go out there and market yourself.

Secret #4: Justify Why You Should Be Hired
—Checklist Summary—

√ Understand the hiring process.
√ Try to predict the decision-making criteria.
√ Create a business case to justify being hired.
√ Quantify your ROI.
√ Interviewers want to look good.
√ Interviewers will hire you...if they think you will
    solve a need and make them look good.

Companies don't hire people just to be nice!

Secret #5

Create Powerful Resumes and Cover Letters That Generate Interest in 15 Seconds or Less

- ◉ Five subjects every resume should contain.
- ◉ Two topics to avoid on resumes.
- ◉ Three types of resume formats.
- ◉ 10 laws of writing powerful resumes.
- ◉ Sample resumes.
- ◉ Five C's of creating compelling cover letters.
- ◉ Sample cover letters.

Job hunting, today, is far different from past years. It used to be you could mail a resume into human resources and wait by the telephone for an interview. Now, with the ever-present Internet, you could be competing against literally thousands of people. In fact, I know of a person who recently advertised a position for a financial analyst, based in Chicago, on a popular Internet job portal. He received more than 1,500 resumes in one day!

How can someone possibly get through 1,500 resumes? It is nearly impossible. Most likely an interviewer might get through 50 to 100 and that's about it. First, you have to be lucky to be in that first 100. Second, you have to have a message that really stands out from the crowd. The best way to change your luck is to bypass HR. However, there are many ways you can format your message so that it stands out from the crowd.

Resumes and Cover Letters Must Grab Attention Fast

With today's competitive job market, it is ever so critical to have a powerful message that grabs attention quickly. Otherwise you just won't get noticed. Believe it or not, interviewers only spend about 15–30 seconds initially reviewing a resume. If you don't catch their attention in that first 15–30 seconds, you lose!

You might think *15 seconds?* That's not fair. But before you get too upset, think about how much time most products and services get to capture your attention. Have you watched television lately? If so, I am sure you have seen a commercial for an upcoming movie. How long was that commercial? Movie studios typically get only 30 seconds to grab your attention…and to convince to go to the theater to see their movie.

Hmmm…30 seconds to sell a two-hour movie. How do they sell you on going to that movie? Do they show you the most boring and mundane scenes? Do they show you a detailed chronology of how the movie was made? Of course not. Instead, they show you the most exciting scenes and the best lines.

Resumes and Cover Letters Are Like Movie Commercials

You get only 15–30 seconds to sell yourself when trying to get an interview. Like a movie commercial, the only way to grab an interviewer's immediate attention is to show your highlights. If you bore an interviewer with mundane information and job history that they aren't interested in, you won't get the job.

I have seen thousands of resumes that have been littered with useless information and contained more bullets than the U.S. Army. Resumes with lots of garbage and bulleted information are tough to sift through. Subsequently, it is very difficult to find the golden nuggets on why a person should be interviewed. The key is to create resumes and cover letters that highlight your "best scenes" (strengths, competencies, and quantifiable accomplishments) so interviewers want to interview you.

Resumes and Cover Letters Are Your Advertisements

The primary purpose of resumes and cover letters is to sell your skills. *You* are the product being sold. To build your brand awareness, you must have a compelling message to advertise. But how do you know what you should focus on? What will generate the most interest? The best way is to imagine being in the shoes of the interviewer.

If you were looking at potential candidates for the position you are interested in, what qualities and characteristics would you look for? What expertise and quantifiable experience would you want to see? Once you come up with the answers to those questions, you now know what to put on your resume and cover letters.

Creating Resumes and Cover Letters Is Like Cooking

Regardless of what you are cooking, there are numerous ways to prepare a dish. When it comes to something such as pasta, there are literally thousands of recipes. You can have thick or thin noodles. You can prepare it with alfredo sauce or with a tomato sauce. You can add vegetables or keep it plain.

It's the same thing with creating resumes and cover letters. You can take your identical information and literally swizzle it into hundreds of unique styles and formats. It really is up to your taste and what you are most comfortable with.

In this chapter, I am going to provide you with suggestions, guidelines, tools, and samples that you can use to create your own recipe for great-tasting (successful) resumes and cover letters. However, just as with cooking, the best way to produce your own specialty is to try several different recipes and see which ones work best for you.

First, you'll review some generic guidelines that are applicable to both resumes and cover letters. Then, we'll explore each instrument in more detail.

I must note, however, it's impossible to give you all of the possible recipes for resumes and cover letters in this book. Nevertheless, I'll try to provide you with what I feel are the most important guidelines. For more information, you can find literally thousands of free recipes and ideas for resumes and cover letters on the Internet. Just go to your favorite search engine and type in phrases such as "sample resumes," "free resume samples," "sample cover letters," "free sample cover letters," and "sample resumes and cover letters." There are also entire books dedicated just to writing resumes and cover letters. However, you can find more than enough information and ideas in this book and for free on the Internet.

General Guidelines

Like most ads, the more copy (words) you have in your resumes and cover letters, the less people will remember them. Some of the most popular ads have been those that are simple. One of my all-time favorite ad campaigns was Nike's "Just do it!" It was a simple but powerful message.

Nike's campaign did a great job of creating excitement for its products through using candid and forceful simplicity. Even though the campaign originally ran years ago, I still remember it like it was yesterday.

For you to excel in the job hunt, you need to have a short, but powerful message. Your resumes and cover letters should contain just enough information to make companies remember you and want to interview you. On any given day, human resource departments can receive hundreds, if not thousands, of resumes and cover letters. Your resumes and cover letters have to stand out.

The sole purpose of the resume and cover letter is to get you the interview, not to get you hired. A *powerful* resume and cover letter will not land you a job, but a *weak* combination will cost you one!

Customize Your Message to Each Opportunity

To create a powerful message—one that will secure you an interview—you need to tailor your resumes and cover letters to each opportunity. Every job and company is different. On clothing, a label may read, *"One size fits all."* When trying to get an interview, rarely is that the case.

You have to tailor your message to the opportunity. Use your resumes and cover letters as advertisements of your success. Include information and vocabulary in your message that is appropriate for your target audience.

Use Industry-Specific Language

If you want a job in information technology, you will want to include phrases such as "network management," "systems optimization," "increased uptime," and "relational database." If you were seeking an accounting position, you would want to use items such as "ledger," "receivables," "bottom line," "return on investment," and "inventories."

It is important to convey, on your resumes and cover letters, both your experience and accomplishments, as well as your knowledge of the industry. You want to demonstrate that you have the necessary expertise.

Keep Your Message Short but Sweet

Many people make the mistake of having multipage resumes, and cover letters that are full of needless information. Typically, multipage resumes and cover letters are inundated with opinions, lack the facts, and are flat-out boring! As an interviewer, I have read hundreds of resumes that literally put me to sleep. When that happened, I guarantee you—once I woke up—I immediately rejected that person and tossed it into the circular file. Do you think I'm being harsh? Well, this is reality.

Convey a Professional Image

When you create resumes and cover letters on your computer, print them out using either a high quality laser printer or a "laser quality" ink jet printer. If you do not have a high quality printer, create the resume, save it to your favorite software media, go to a local copy shop, and print your resume using their computer network and high quality printers.

How else can you create resumes and cover letters that will get read, not tossed? Stay tuned! In the pages that follow, I will first show you how to create a powerful resume. Then, I'll show you how to create cover letters that will get you noticed!

Having a powerful resume is critical to any successful job hunt. When creating a resume, the most challenging tasks are determining what details to include and how to organize the information on the page. Unfortunately, there are no "industry standards" on how to write a resume. In fact, "job-hunting experts" typically differ in their viewpoints.

Note that I am basing this on my personal experience (both as a hiring manager and as an advisor to many clients). Because there is no one right way of writing a resume, ultimately, you have to choose what you are most comfortable with.

My goal is to provide you with the information you need that will make your resume stand out from the crowd and get you interviewed! In creating a resume, there are certain main components that every resume should contain, as well as others that should be avoided. Let's first look at what should be included.

Five Subjects Every Resume Should Contain
1. Profile or summary.
2. Accomplishments or achievements.
3. Expertise or skills.
4. Education.
5. Work experience.

1. **Profile or summary.** When creating a resume, the first thing you should put on the top of the page is a one- or two-sentence description providing an overview of your personality and experience. This is the most important piece of the entire resume. If you don't capture your interviewers' attention here right away and show them that you are the most qualified candidate for the position, your resume will be tossed faster than a hot potato.

    By including a few tidbits about your personality and expertise, rather than an objective statement (as many suggest), you are not limiting yourself to one specific position. Instead, you are opening the door to multiple opportunities.

    An opening sentence such as, "Driven, competitive, and dynamic individual known for consistently exceeding expectations..." is a much stronger opening to a resume than something such as, "I am interested in a position that is challenging and capitalizes on my strengths and expertise."

2. **Accomplishments or achievements.** The second part of your resume should include a bulleted section of quantifiable accomplishments and results. This is your personal "highlights" section. Remember when I used the analogy of a movie commercial that shows the best scenes and lines from the movie? This is the section of your resume where you want to list your best highlights.

    Nothing makes for a better highlight than a juicy, quantifiable accomplishment. Rather than hide your best stuff throughout the litany of information on your resume, it's much better to show it up front. When the interviewer can see highlights such as "Reduced expenses by $100,000," "Increased customer satisfaction by 20 percent," and "Increased year-over-year revenues by 35 percent," it will grab their attention big time.

3. **Expertise or skills.** The third section of your resume should include a summary of descriptions, one to three words in length, demonstrating your core expertise and experience. Depending on the job you are trying to get, you may want to further break it down into subcategories such as, "Technical Expertise" and "Management Expertise," or "Administrative Skills" and "Organizational Skills."

    For this section, as well as the others, think what criteria would be important to the person doing the hiring. Many times, you can get some great clues from job descriptions. If an ad specifies that a company wants someone who is proficient in Microsoft Office, Excel, and PowerPoint, you'd better show that expertise on your resume (assuming you have those skills).

4. **Education.** For this section, you want to include all of the pertinent education you have received that is relevant to the job opportunities you desire. If you lack significant work-related experience you may want to expand on this section. However, those of you who have good work experience, should limit this section to what is important.

Unless you don't have a college education, putting stuff on your resume such as where you went to high school is not necessary. However, if you have taken some continuing education courses at a local community college or university relevant to the job you want, then that is something you might want to include. Again, think about what your potential bosses would want to see.

5. **Work experience.** The fifth component to your resume is the section that outlines in more detail your specific work experience. This segment is where you list the different jobs you have had and provide objective details about your duties while in these positions.

As you will see, you can organize your information either by category or by date. The key is to include only relevant information and highlights that will make potential hiring managers want to interview you. Relevant information should include the company(s) you worked for and any main responsibilities that demonstrate your aptitude to succeed in the job you are trying to get.

Two Topics to Avoid on Resumes

You'll notice that when I discussed the five subjects every resume should contain, I left out two big ones that many "experts" often recommend: The "objective statement" and "references." Why would I suggest that? Do you have any ideas? Let's look at each one individually to understand why.

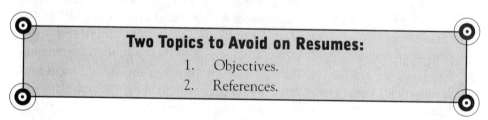

Two Topics to Avoid on Resumes:
1.   Objectives.
2.   References.

1. Objectives.

Although many people recommend opening a resume with an objective statement, I am adamantly against this concept. In my mind, having a specific objective statement limits your scope of opportunities. If you start your resume with a statement such as, "A product manager position in the consumer industry," you have eliminated all of the other industries and positions for which you might be qualified. Why limit the field of opportunity? It's not necessary.

When you are too specific to what you want, you put a lid on the opportunities. You don't want to limit your possibilities by saying you are only interested in one type of job. Most companies keep resumes for at least 90 days. Often, if managers see a great resume, yet the candidate isn't quite the right fit for their specific opening, they will pass the resume onto someone else. It pays to *not* be too specific.

Starting your resume with a profile or summary instead of an objective is a great way of demonstrating your interests and abilities, without specifically stating that you will only work in one specific type of position.

2. References.

Many people make the mistake of putting references directly on the resume. How do you know what references to include? Different interviewers will want to speak with various kinds of references. Others may not request references at all. There is no need to volunteer the information unless you are specifically asked to do so.

Rather than including specific references on your resume, I recommend on the bottom of your resume to either include, "References available upon request," or just don't put anything at all.

Create a Separate Reference List

While I don't recommend putting references on your resume, I highly recommend you create a separate list of references for those instances when you receive a request. Save it as a separate document. Then you can pick and choose from your list the references who are most appropriate for each request.

To compile your list, try to get a combination of both work and personal references. Two or three of each is sufficient. Have accurate information for each reference including name, address, phone number, position, employer, e-mail, and length of time you have known the reference. It is common practice to only list references that you have known for at least one year or more.

Call Your References Before Your Interviewer Does

Make sure it is okay with your references to use them. Also, be certain that they will be a great reference. Many a good job opportunity has been lost because candidates did not contact their references before listing them. The last thing you want is someone to be surprised by a phone call from an interviewer or recruiter and then give a negative reference.

Inform each of your references to the type of positions you are seeking and why you feel you will succeed in those positions, so that they will be more prepared if someone calls. In fact, you may want to even prepare a "cheat-sheet" for your references stating your key selling points. Also, make sure each of your references have a copy of your most recent resume and cover letters.

Three Types of Resume Formats

They are chronological, functional, and what I call "hybrid" formats. Each format has its strengths and weaknesses. The key is to understand each one and determine the optimal format for you.

1.   Chronological.
2.   Functional.
3.   Hybrid.

1. Chronological

A chronological resume is structured by the date(s) you were employed, from your most recent job to your least. Over the years, this has been the most popular resume structure. However, just because it is the most popular, doesn't necessarily mean it is the best for you.

For those who have had a strong and logical employment history, this format works perfectly. However, for others who have had large lapses of time where they were unemployed or those who want to switch industries or careers, the chronological style may not be the best format to use.

A chronological resume is constructed by listing date, job history, and accomplishments. In this format, in the left-hand column, there are categories such as, "Profile," "Accomplishments," "Expertise," "Work Experience," and "Education." On the right side of the resume is where you fill in the details such as job description, quantifiable accomplishments, and time frames of employment.

Basically what makes a resume chronological is when you list your experience and accomplishments based on time, rather than on relevance.

If your most recent experience and accomplishments are the most relevant to the position you are trying to get, and you have a good work history, then the chronological format is a fine structure to use. However, if not, you may want to use one of the following two formats.

2. Functional

The second way you can organize your resume is by function. Here, you list your accomplishments by job description or job function instead of by date. The functional resume may be more useful if you have lapses in time where you were unemployed, or if you chose not to work. Large lapses in time can be a "red flag" or a cause for concern to an interviewer. If this is your situation, you may be better suited with the functional approach.

With a functional resume you organize your job history based on relevance and experience, rather than by time. Instead of listing each job by the date you worked, you consolidate the jobs you worked and your experience into categories. A functional resume still contains the same core information; however, your expertise is highlighted, not your chronological history or timeline.

With the functional resume, instead of having one broad category called "Work Experience" you might break it out into separate categories such as "Accounting Experience" and "Controller Experience." This way you are putting the focus of your resume on what you have done...not when you did it.

3. Hybrid

The third way you can structure your resume is to use a "hybrid" layout. Hybrid incorporates the strengths of both the functional and chronological formats. You provide the information in an order of relevance to the interviewer, however, within each category, you also structure the contents by date. This makes it very easy for interviewers to find the information they are most interested in, yet it shows you have had a consistent work history.

I find the hybrid format to be optimal for those who have extensive and relevant work experience. When you have had more than 10 years of experience, it's important to include only the most relevant information on your resume. It's possible a job you had eight years ago may have more relevance to a given situation than a job you did only five years ago. By using the hybrid format, it gives you the flexibility to highlight the most relevant information, yet keep a logical flow.

I know some of this may sound a bit confusing, but don't worry. Towards the end of this chapter I will provide you with samples of each of the three formats of resume, using my own career as an example. Again, as I mentioned before, there is no *one* right format. The key is to choose the format that is right for you.

10 Laws to Writing Powerful Resumes

Now that you know the subjects that every resume should contain and avoid, and the different ways you can format your resume, it's time to discuss the 10 Laws to Writing Powerful Resumes.

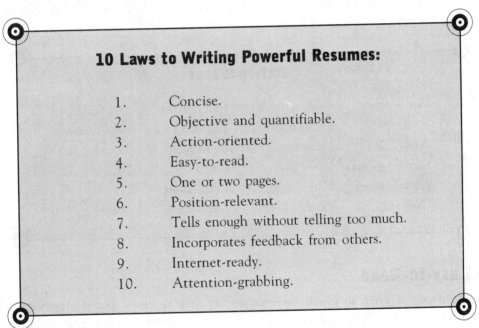

10 Laws to Writing Powerful Resumes:

1. Concise.
2. Objective and quantifiable.
3. Action-oriented.
4. Easy-to-read.
5. One or two pages.
6. Position-relevant.
7. Tells enough without telling too much.
8. Incorporates feedback from others.
9. Internet-ready.
10. Attention-grabbing.

1. Concise

In as few words as possible, make your points short and concise. The fewer words the better. Instead of saying something verbose and opinionated such as, "I am the best procurement manager that ever walked the face of the earth." State something such as, "Reduced procurement expenses by 15 percent." Now that is short and sweet! It's also much more objective!

2. Objective and Quantifiable

Nothing will turn off interviewers more than a resume besieged with opinions and essays. Stick to the facts. If you were tremendously successful in eliminating wasteful spending in your previous job, then state something such as, "Reduced expenses by 35 percent." This comes across as powerful and factual. Showing a quantifiable result such as, "Reduced overhead by X%" is the best way to advertise, loud and clear, that you are a great cost-cutter.

If you are in sales perhaps you want to convey that you are the world's greatest salesperson. Maybe you believe that you are so good, you can sell sand in the desert. If so, give them some great impressions with something such as, "Exceeded quota every year," "Grew year-over-year sales by over 65 percent," or "Won three corporate management awards." Now those are some powerful and factual statements. Wouldn't you be impressed?

3. Action-Oriented

The best resumes contain action words. Action words bring your experience to life and get you noticed.

Action Words

Achieved	Customized	Evaluated	Strengthened
Authored	Demonstrated	Featured	Supervised
Awarded	Developed	Generated	Trained
Collaborated	Directed	Grew	Utilized
Coordinated	Eliminated	Implemented	Won
Created	Established	Improved	Wrote

4. Easy-to-Read

Often people cram so much information on their resumes that the reader has no clue where to start. Some candidates put so many bullets on their resumes that the interviewer can't possibly tell what is important. The reader should be able to find relevant and interesting information quickly.

Interviewers will only spend 15–30 seconds to initially scan your resume. If, in 15 seconds, they cannot find what they are looking for, most likely your resume will be wadded up and tossed with a bank shot off the cubicle wall and into the wastepaper basket. (Interviewers get so much practice...they just hate it when they miss the basket!)

Interviewers want to quickly discover what you will bring to the job and company. Make it easy for them to see why they should interview you and what makes you different than other candidates.

5. One or Two Pages

I am a big advocate of a resume being curtailed to a maximum of two pages in length. Why? Because I can't scan a resume longer than two pages in 15–30 seconds and neither can anyone else. (The only value of a multiple-page resume is that it weighs more when wadded up, thus providing a better chance of making the basket into the garbage can on the first try.)

The resume is an advertisement that creates interest in you. Your resume should create just enough curiosity for the reader to want to interview you. This can easily be accomplished in one or two pages.

The key here is to place the most recent and relevant information on the resume. Quite honestly, it typically doesn't matter what you did 15 or 20 years ago. Most likely, you have forgotten much of that knowledge anyway. What is important to interviewers is, "What you have done lately?"

6. Position-Relevant

Many resumes are muddied with personal items that have no relevance to the reader. As a result, people often put themselves at a disadvantage before they get the chance to interview. If something personal needs to be said, say it in the interview. People have been known to put interests, hobbies, political ideology, and even religious beliefs on the resume. This is unwise.

Why give interviewers information that could get you rejected even before the interview? Interviewers like to hire people with interests and basic values similar to their own. If you volunteer interests or beliefs that are different, you'll get bounced. Why take that chance?

When you keep the information on your resume strictly business, you will have more room on your resume for what is really important: position-relevant information.

Position-relevant information (PRI) is the information that has a significant impact in the decision-making process for job selection. The best way to test each statement in your resume for PRI is to ask yourself, "So what?" Put yourself in the interviewer's shoes and, with the desired position in mind, ask this question regarding each statement you want to include on your resume.

Let's say you want to put on your resume, "Proficient at Microsoft Office." So what? Well, if you are interviewing for a secretarial position, this could be useful. However, if you are interviewing for a sales position selling surgical instruments, it may be less relevant. PRI is what interviewers care about.

Imagine Being the Interviewer

You can determine the appropriate PRI by putting yourself in the position of your potential boss. Suppose you were the person evaluating your resume. What would be important? If the position was for product management, then an MBA, prior experience, and communication skills may be the PRI. If you are interviewing for an engineering position or a project manager position, then the PRI might be project history, significant outcomes, and timely completion of projects.

When putting statements into your resume, ask yourself, *"Is it PRI?"* Does the information pass the *"So what?"* test? If so, use it, otherwise leave it out. Sometimes, by saying too much, you can buy back a sale.

7. Tells Enough Without Telling Too Much

Don't tell more than you need to when creating a powerful resume. A great resume should contain only sensible information. The following are some of the things to avoid putting on your resume.

Don't Ever Put Salary Information on Your Resume

You will put yourself at a great disadvantage. It can only hurt you. If your compensation is too high, you will be rejected without even having the chance to sell the company on why you are worth it. If your compensation is too low, hiring managers will not think you have the skills or confidence necessary for the job, and reject you. If you are in the ballpark, then you have placed a cap on what your job offer can be.

No company will offer you more than 15–20 percent more than what you are currently making. Why limit your potential? There is absolutely *no* need to put compensation history in your resume!

Do Not List Weaknesses on Your Resume

I know this sounds crazy but many people unknowingly list weaknesses on their resume. They then wonder why they can't get interviews. Weaknesses include jobs where you unintentionally lasted only a short time (less than three months) and any other information that could negatively reflect on you as a person. Keep the resume focused on business.

Do Not Give Away *All* of Your Best Information

Save some great zingers for the interview! The resume is the advertisement that gets you the interview. Just as most people don't buy a product solely because of its ad, you will not get the job just because of your resume. However, if you have a powerful resume, you will certainly get many more interviews.

8. Incorporates Feedback From Others

The most important thing you can do before you distribute your resume is to proofread it. Use your word processor's spelling and grammar check. Then, have others critique it. Sometimes you can get too close to your creation and miss obvious mistakes that your software does not catch.

I know in writing this book my spelling and grammar check missed several mistakes that only others could detect. The more people who critique and review your resume, the better! I am always amused and amazed at how many people have mistakes in their resumes.

For example:

- Reason for leaving last job: maturity leave.
- I have lurnt the Microsoft Word Computor Progrom.
- Received a plague for Salesperson of the Month.
- I require a salary commiserate with my extensive expertise.

Again, make sure you stick to position-relevant information. Some of the things people have included in resumes are unbelievable. Job-hunting professionals like me have seen it all.

Examples of Irrelevant Information

- Note: Please, don't misconstrue my 10 jobs as 'job hopping,' I have never quit a job.
- It's best for employers that I not work with people.
- I was working for my dad until he decided to move.
- I have a fantastic track record, although I am not a racehorse.
- I am loyal to my employer...feel free to respond to my resume on my office e-mail.
- Personal interests: Donating blood. Fifteen gallons so far.
- Marital status: Often. Children: Various.
- Reason for leaving last job: They insisted that all employees get to work by 9:00 am.
- My boss made me a scapegoat, just like my three previous employers.

The bottom line is, make sure your resume only contains information that is relevant to the position. Otherwise, your resume will be a waste of paper and a waste of the interviewer's time.

9. Internet-Ready

More and more companies are asking for resumes to be sent electronically (via e-mail). Others are creating standard electronic forms that can be filled out on their Websites or at kiosks in their facilities.

When a company requests that you send in a resume via e-mail, often it is scanned for keywords. As I mentioned earlier, human resources can get inundated with literally thousands of resumes for a posted opportunity. Typically it is physically impossible for them to wade through each and every submission.

To maximize efficiency, many firms use a computer to read resumes first. Computers decipher which resumes should be reviewed by using pre-selected criteria based on a defined subset of keywords and phrases.

So, how can you create a technology-friendly resume?

Use Industry and Job-Related "Buzzwords"

Because computers often scan resumes before humans do, it is important to use industry buzzwords or keywords on your resume. Examples of keywords for computer industry professions are "operating system," "network management," and "uptime." Examples of "buzzwords" for legal professions are "litigated," "class action," "awarded," and "negligence."

Determine the most common phrases for your targeted industry and include them where appropriate. Action words, as mentioned earlier, are also critical, because computers will look for those as well. Believe it or not, computers can scan resumes in a very similar fashion as humans.

Create a PDF of Your Resume

One of the most difficult things about sending your resume online is to maintain the formatting that you intended. I have always been amazed at how the same file will look one way on one person's computer and totally different on another's.

The best way to get around this problem is to convert your resume into an Adobe PDF file format. When you convert a document file into a PDF format, it basically captures an image of your document exactly as it shows on your word processor. What you see is what you get.

Most everyone who uses the Internet has Adobe's Acrobat Reader on his or her computer. If not, they can download a copy of it right from Adobe. By having your resume in a PDF format, regardless of the type of computer or operating system the company uses, your resume can be read and printed exactly as you intended.

To create a PDF version of your resume, you can do it one of many ways. The most cost effective is to go to Adobe's Website and use the tool that converts most any document into a PDF file. In addition, there are many places where, for a small fee, you can convert your document.

Create an Unformatted, "Text Only" Electronic Resume

I also recommend creating a version of your resume where all you have are carriage returns, blank lines, and space bar blanks that replace tabs (text format). That way you can send an electronic resume to a company that might not have Microsoft Office or Adobe Acrobat Reader. Also, some older or more limited e-mail systems can't handle more than 79 characters on a line.

Granted, most companies will have the ability to receive a Word or PDF file. However, having an unformatted, electronic resume can be especially helpful when filling out forms through a company's Website. This way, you can cut and paste information right out of your resume into the form so you don't have to "recreate the wheel" every time.

Creating an unformatted version is very easy with most standard word processing packages. Typically when you go to save a file, you are given an option as to what type of file.

Create a different name for your text resume to prevent losing your formatted version. A name such as "Todd_Bermont_Resume" saved as a "text-only" file makes it compatible with any e-mail system.

Once you save a text version of your resume, then go into your operating system's notepad and open the document. Clean out any miscellaneous characters that were created as a result of the document being formatted in a "text-only" format, and re-save the document.

Create Public Versions of Your Resume

When most people think of job hunting as it relates to the Internet, they immediately think of trying to find a position through an online portal such as *Monster.com*, *CareerBuilder.com*, or *HotJobs.com*. These sites store your information online in a database with thousands of others so potential employers can scan them.

While in concept these portals are a great idea, the reality is that as few as 5 percent of all jobs are actually found this way. Thus, I don't recommend spending more than 5 percent of your time focused on these sites.

With that being said, if you are out of work, you have nothing to lose by posting your credentials online. You never know what might happen. I am a big believer in using all of the job-hunting resources available. Just be judicious with your time and spend it appropriately.

Some job sites utilize standardized forms into which they have you enter your information. Others allow you to post your resume as is. The online forms can take quite a bit of time to complete. This is why I recommend you focus mainly on the "top three." There are many other sites you can use. But remember if you spend more than 5 percent of your time filling out these forms, you are most likely wasting your time.

The best way to quickly fill out these standardized forms is to have your unformatted, "text-only" resume readily available in a window on your computer screen. Often you can cut and paste parts of your Internet-ready resume right into their online forms.

Also, as you are entering new information on each site, cut and paste that information into a word processing document. Most sites ask for similar information. So by keeping the information from one site, you can save a lot of time and energy by reusing.

In summary, not only should you have printed versions of your resume, you should also have your resume in at least one or two electronic formats that can be used for online distribution as well.

10. Attention-Grabbing

As in an advertisement, your resume must look good to immediately grab the attention of interviewers. Have others read your resume and give you pointers. See if it grabs their attention. Look at your resume a day or two later to get a fresh perspective of it. Then, if after a few weeks you still haven't gotten a job yet, review it again.

With the passing of time you often gain different ideas on how you can make improvements. I also suggest looking at other people's resumes. The best way to do this is to go to networking events and swap resumes with others.

Whether you are creating a hard copy or online resume, use a layout that is easy-to-read and professional. For your formatted versions, use a variety of fonts, **boldface**, *italics*, and · bullets to make your important points stand out.

For printed resumes, use only high quality (heavier bond) paper—not copier paper. There is something to be said for paper with a substantial feel—it conveys a good image. Use fonts (such as Arial, Courier, Garamond, or Times New Roman), colors (such as blue or black ink on white paper), layouts, and words that create uniqueness without compromising professionalism.

For both printed and online resumes to be powerful, they need to be creative. In addition to the action words described earlier, use words that express strength and confidence. For example, the phrase "proficient at" is far stronger than "learned." Proficient means that not only did you learn something, you know it inside and out.

The most effective way to grab the attention and interest of interviewers is to put some of your best selling points right near the top of the resume. For years, people have unintentionally hidden their finest accomplishments in the job experience section of the resume. Sometimes, interviewers never make it that far. If you have some solid, quantifiable results or accomplishments, don't hide them. Move them to the front.

I recommend right below your personal summary, or profile (on the top of your resume) you insert a separate section either called "achievements" or "accomplishments." In this section put some of your best highlights. These should strictly be your sensational, yet objective and quantifiable accomplishments. Strong statements such as "Saved $1 million in expense," "Increased productivity by 22 percent" and "Increased sales for XYZ by 45 percent" will grab the attention of interviewers and make them want to interview you.

Resume Summary

A powerful resume opens the door to many interviewing opportunities. However, customizing your resume for each situation can be very time consuming. This is why cover letters exist. Cover letters are an excellent means to customize your message for each opportunity. It is much easier to change the wording of a cover letter than it is to change an entire resume. Shortly, I'll show you how to write dynamite cover letters that will command attention.

Thus far, we have discussed suggestions and guidelines on how to create a winning resume that can have the broadest possible appeal. However, if you would like more guidance and ideas, do not despair.

There are many "how-to" books dedicated to writing resumes. You can find these books in the same section of the library or bookstore where you found this book. Also, there are thousands of free and fee-based Websites that can help you out.

In addition, there are several computer software applications that can help you create a winning resume. Some are specific to resume generation. Others, such as word processing applications, include resume templates you can use.

Sample Resumes for Each Format

On the following pages, I have provided you with examples of resumes in the three main formats we discussed: *chronological, functional,* and *hybrid.* I have also provided you with a sample chronological resume in an online, "text-only" format. To help better illustrate which format you should use, I have chosen to use my own career progression as an example.

The chronological resume is a snapshot from earlier in my career, when I went from IBM to APC. The functional example is taken from later in my career, when I decided to leave APC. The third sample, the hybrid format, is a resume I would use now to try to get a position with another organization. You'll notice as the more experience and accomplishments I gained, the more I move more towards the hybrid format.

This is not to say that you, too, should choose a hybrid format. Only you can determine what format is best for you. The key is to choose one that best fits your career accomplishments, experience, and timeline.

As you are looking at each sample resume, notice how I locate accomplishments right at the top of the resume to immediately grab the interviewer's attention, and how the content in each of the Five Components changes, as I progress throughout my career.

Finally, take note on how I use a variety of fonts, bullets, and character formatting to make certain points stand out This is your commercial, and you want to grab the attention of the interviewer in the first 15 seconds or less. I formatted these resumes with this goal in mind.

Sample Chronological Resume

Todd L. Bermont

555 N. Chicago Way, #253, Chicago, IL 60610
(555) 555-5500 tbermont@10stepjobsearch.com

Profile

Driven and results-oriented sales representative, known for generating new business and consistently achieving sales objectives throughout his career in selling information technology solutions.

Accomplishments

IBM Corporation
- Won five "Branch Manager Awards" and the "General Manager's Award"
- "100% Club" every year on quota
- Ranked in the "Top 10%" of all IBM employees in 1992

NCR Corporation
- Sold First NCR PC Solution to IL. Dept. of Public Aid
- Represented sales force in development of a new Unix workstation

University of Illinois
- Graduated with Honors

Expertise

- Large account selling
- Territory management
- Lead generation
- Cross-selling
- Resource coordination
- Business development
- Cold-calling
- Direct-response marketing
- Negotiation
- Sales of high-tech solutions

Education

- University of Illinois, Urbana (1986)—Bachelor of Science, Marketing
- IBM and NCR sales education programs

Experience

Account sales representative, IBM Corporation (1989–1992)
Sold PS/2, AS/400, RS/6000, and consulting to a *new-business, financial* territory. More than doubled territory sales each year on quota. Sold the first RS/6000 minicomputer in the Chicago Finance Branch of IBM. *Won* five "Branch Manager" awards and one "General Manager" award.

Territory sales representative, NCR Corporation (1986–1989)
Sold UNIX Towers and DOS Personal Computer solutions to a F1000 and State/Local Government, new-business territory. Sold first NCR PC solution to the Illinois Department of Public Aid. Chosen as the only sales representative in St. Louis to provide input on a new Unix workstation under development.

References are available upon request.

Todd L. Bermont   Sample Functional Resume

51 N. Parkway, Chicago, IL 60610

(555)555-5400 tbermont@10stepjobsearch.com

Profile

Results-oriented and accomplished sales executive with a proven track record of achieving significant revenue growth in domestic and global F1000/OEM accounts.

Accomplishments

American Power Conversion
- Met and exceeded 100% of sales quota each and every year on quota
- Won the 1998 "Top Team Award" in North America
- Named "Top Presenting Partner" at 1997 IBM Europe Sales Meeting
- Voted "Top Trainer" at 1994 APC Europe Sales Meeting
- Awarded "Top Fortune 1000 Salesperson" in 1993

IBM Corporation
- Won five "Branch Manager Awards" and the "General Manager's Award"
- Attained the "100% Club" every year on quota
- Ranked in the "Top 10%" of all IBM Employees in 1992

Expertise

- Sales management • Compensation planning • Territory planning •New-business generation
- Interviewing and hiring • People development • Global business strategy •Market Analysis
- Project Management • Product Development • Customer Satisfaction •Negotiation

Education

- University of Illinois, Urbana, IL (1986), Marketing, Graduated w/Honors
- IBM and NCR educational sales programs

Sales Management Experience

- **Director, OEM, American Power Conversion**
- **F1000 Channel Manager, American Power Conversion**

  In charge of managing a sales force focused on generating significant revenue growth in both new and existing, strategic accounts. Responsibilities included hiring, managing, budgeting, forecasting, funnel development, training and mentoring of salespeople. Consistently exceeded corporate objectives of increased revenue, profit and market share.

Corporate Sales Experience

- **District Manager, American Power Conversion**
- **Account Sales Representative, IBM Corporation**
- **Territory Sales Representative, NCR Corporation**

  Sold computing solutions to *F1000* and *State/Local Government* accounts. Developed new business and generated significant revenue growth in new and existing accounts. Consistently achieved and exceeded sales objectives.

Todd L. Bermont

51 N. State Parkway, Chicago, IL 60610
(555) 555-5400; tbermont@10stepjobsearch.com

Profile

World-renowned author, speaker, and consultant known for consistently exceeding expectations throughout his career in coaching, sales, and executive management.

Accomplishments

10 Step Corporation

- Featured: CNN, FOX, Monster.com, CareerBuilder.com, radio, *and* newspapers
- Authored three books: one ranked #1 "Most Popular" on Amazon.com
- "National Leadership Award," Small Business Advisory Council
- As a lecturer at the University of Chicago, received rating of 4.5/5.0
- Awarded "Certificate of Merit" by Writer's Digest
- Named to the "Leadership Committee" at University of Chicago
- Developed online, job-hunting course offered by 500-plus colleges and universities

American Power Conversion

- Met and exceeded 100% of sales quota each and every year on quota
- Won the 1998 "Top Team Award" in North America
- Named "Top Presenting Partner" at 1997 IBM Europe Sales Meeting
- Voted "Top Trainer" at 1994 APC Europe Sales Meeting
- Awarded "Top Fortune 1000 Salesperson" in 1993

IBM Corporation

- Won five "Branch Manager Awards" and the "General Manager's Award"
- Attained the "100% Club" every year on quota
- Ranked in the "Top 10%" of all IBM Employees in 1992

University of Illinois

- Graduated with honors

Expertise

Keynote speaking	Sales training
Career coaching	Sales management
Compensation design	Resource coordination
Territory planning	Business development
Interviewing	Personnel
Global strategy	Hiring
Project management	Product development
Customer satisfaction	Cross selling
Market analysis	Negotiation

Education

- University of Illinois, Urbana, IL (1986)—Bachelor of Science, Marketing
- Miller Heiman: Strategic Selling, Conceptual Selling & LAMP
- Acclivus—Coaching and Base Training
- Rodger Dawson—Power Negotiating
- IBM—IBM Advanced Sales School
- NCR—Sales School

Todd L. Bermont (Page II)

Executive Management Experience

PRESIDENT, 10 Step Corporation (2000–Present)

Founded company focused on sales training, consulting, and career coaching. Authored several books including one ranked "most popular" in the category by Amazon.com. Guest lecturer at the University of Chicago's Graham School. Instructor and developer of an online, job-hunting course available to over 500 U.S. colleges. Trained and coached scores of individuals and companies on improving productivity, enhancing selling skills, and improving results.

DIRECTOR, OEM, American Power Conversion (APC) (1995–1999)

In charge of *OEM* division focused on global, strategic partnerships with leading computer manufacturers such as Dell, Gateway, HP, IBM, and Sun. Managed more than a dozen employees in U.S. and coordinated additional indirect staff in Europe and Asia.

Grew revenue more than 1000% from 1995 to 1999 while only increasing the number of direct reports by 200%. Additional achievements included increasing attach rates, profitability, customer satisfaction, and market share.

CHANNEL MANAGER, F1000 ACCOUNTS, APC (1994–1995)

Managed a *Fortune 1000* Channel, responsible for growing the APC presence in large accounts. Key accomplishments included more than tripling the average territory sales while simultaneously increasing customer satisfaction and APC market share. Contributors to this success included: revamping the sales compensation plan, extensive sales training, joint territory customer calls, creation of a vertical channel support team, development of a select major account program, and enhancing sales tools including creating proposal and presentation databases.

Corporate Sales Experience

DISTRICT MANAGER, MIDWEST REGION, APC (1992–1994)

Sold power protection equipment to a Midwest, *F1000* territory. Increased territory revenues by more than double in 1992 and triple in 1993. Secured the largest, single sale in the history of the Midwest Region at that time.

ACCOUNT SALES REPRESENTATIVE, IBM Corporation (1989–1992)

Sold PS/2, AS/400, RS/6000 and consulting to a *new-business* territory. More than doubled territory sales each year on quota. Sold the first RS/6000 minicomputer in the Chicago Finance Branch of IBM.

TERRITORY SALES REPRESENTATIVE, NCR Corporation (1986–1989)

Sold UNIX Towers and DOS Personal Computer solutions to a *F1000, new-business* territory. Sold first NCR Personal Computers to the State of Illinois Department of Public Aid.

References available upon request.

Sample Text-Only Resume

TODD L. BERMONT
51 State Parkway
Chicago, IL 60610
(555) 555-5400
tbermont@10stepjobsearch.com

(Profile)

Driven and results-oriented sales representative, known for generating new business and consistently achieving sales objectives, throughout his sales career.

(Accomplishments)

IBM

– Won Five "Branch Manager Awards" and the "General Manager's Award"
– "100% Club" every year on quota
– Ranked in the "Top 10%" of all IBM Employees in 1992

NCR Corporation

– Sold First NCR Personal Computer solution to the IL Dept. of Public Aid
– Chosen to represent the sales force in the development of a new Unix workstation

University of Illinois

– Graduated with honors

(Expertise)

–Large Account Selling—New Business Development—Territory Management
–Cold-Calling—Lead Generation—Direct Mailings—Cross Selling—Negotiation
–Resource Coordination—Selling IT Solutions—Selling Consulting Services
–Project Management—Selling to F1000 Accounts—Selling to Government

(Education)

–University of Illinois, Urbana, IL (1986)—Bachelor of Science, Marketing
–IBM and NCR advanced selling programs

(Work Experience)

ACCOUNT SALES REPRESENTATIVE, IBM Corporation (1989–1992)

Sold PS/2, AS/400, RS/6000, and consulting to a new-business, financial territory. More than doubled territory sales each year on quota. Sold the first RS/6000 minicomputer in the Chicago Finance Branch of IBM. Won five "Branch Manager" awards and one "General Manager" award and was the first sales representative to bill out his own time as a consultant in the entire branch.

TERRITORY SALES REPRESENTATIVE, NCR Corporation (1986–1989)

Sold UNIX Towers and DOS Personal Computer solutions to a F1000 and State/Local Government, new-business territory. Sold first NCR PC solution to the State of Illinois Department of Public Aid. Chosen as the only sales representative in St. Louis to provide input on a new Unix workstation under development.

References available upon request.

Five C's of Creating Compelling Cover Letters

Once you have created your resume, the next step is to have an outstanding cover letter that will convince interviewers to look at your resume and consider your credentials. You can have the world's greatest resume, but if you don't have an eye-catching cover letter to go with it, don't bother sending it. The cover letter explains why you are the right candidate for a given position.

Wait...isn't the resume supposed to do that? Well, in a way yes, but the resume is more of an overview of *who* you are, where a cover letter answers the question, "Why you?" Imagine you are a product. Your resume describes what your product is. The cover letter is the salesperson that says why someone should consider purchasing.

I'm sure you've heard the saying, "You can't judge a book by its cover." Don't believe it! The flashier and more exciting a book's cover is, the more it sells. Cover letters provide the same function for your resume that a book cover does for the contents of the book. The more interesting your cover letter, the better your chances of getting your resume read.

The cover letter is the "tickler" advertising that gets the reader to want to look at your resume. There are Five C's you should remember when creating your compelling cover letters.

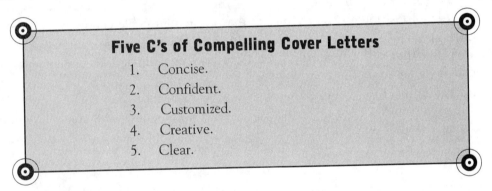

Five C's of Compelling Cover Letters
1. Concise.
2. Confident.
3. Customized.
4. Creative.
5. Clear.

1. Concise

Much like the resume itself, the cover letter should be short and to the point. Like a powerful advertisement, the copy should be dazzling and grab the attention of the reader.

2. Confident

Don't be shy with your cover letters. Strut your stuff! After all, if you aren't confident in your abilities, how do you expect the interviewer to be? Your cover letter should be written in a very positive tone that conveys that you know you are the best candidate and you are confident that you should be considered.

Like an assumptive close in selling, when you assume you will get the interview odds are you will. Just be careful to balance your enthusiasm. There is a very fine line between confident and cocky. Hiring managers like confidence.

3. Customized

The main difference between the cover letter and the resume is that you add more custom tailoring to the cover letter. In the cover letter you should include references to the company you are interviewing with and how you will be a great asset to them. Stress how your experiences make you the *best* candidate for their job.

Each interviewer is going to want a different type of candidate. When you are writing your cover letters, try to, once again, put yourself in the shoes of the interviewer. Ask yourself, *If you were the interviewer, what would you want in your ideal candidate?* Then ask yourself what you can say about your career that is relevant to the opportunity at hand. That is what you should include in your cover letter.

If you are responding to a specific job posting or advertisement, make sure you reference it in your cover letter. Then, as concisely and confidently as possible, state your case on why they should interview you before anyone else.

4. Creative

For a cover letter to be successful, it must be creative. Think about your key selling points and how they can benefit the company(s) you are targeting. If you are a comptroller and you successfully reduced expenses by 35 percent at your current job, then that may be of real interest to a company that is having trouble containing its costs.

Look at what makes you uniquely qualified. What qualities or achievements can you mention that will differentiate you from your competition and make someone want to interview you?

As you know, hiring managers get flooded with resumes and cover letters. The ones that will stand out are those that have something unique about them. Often, it's your creativity that differentiates you from your competition.

5. Clear

A successful cover letter will always be crystal clear about what the objective for the letter is. In essence, your cover letter has to go for the close. What do I mean by that? In sales, going for the close means asking for the order. The objective of the cover letter is to get you an interview. Hence, be absolutely clear in your cover letter that you are the best person for the job and that you want (and expect) an interview.

Your cover letters should be concise and personalized, create interest in you, and ask for the interview. Your cover letters must also convey an understanding of the company and the opportunity, and how you will succeed in the targeted position. The key is to provide enough golden nuggets about your personality and experience that will make someone want to grant you an interview.

Following are two examples of effective cover letters. If you would like more specific guidance, there are many books written on how to generate winning cover letters. Also, as in resumes, you can find a wealth of information and sample cover letters on the Internet. Just go to your favorite Internet search engine and type in one of the following key phrases "free sample cover letters," "sample cover letters," or "cover letters."

Mr. I. M. Hip
Vice President, Customer Service
Rye Bread Company
1 Interviewing Blvd. Suite 310
Danville, CA 94526

Dear Mr. Hip:

I am applying for the position of Customer Service Manager at Rye Bread Company. With my experience and background, I am confident I can make an immediate contribution to your team. Enclosed, please find a copy of my credentials.

Currently, as Assistant Customer Service Manager for Baloney Industries, I helped increase customer satisfaction by 40 percent and reduce product returns by 33 percent. Amazingly, we were able to achieve this while simultaneously reducing headcount by more than 10 percent. This was accomplished through fostering teamwork, creating an innovative organization, and maximizing call-routing procedures.

I look forward to having the opportunity to meet with you to discuss how I can be an asset to your company. If you have any questions, please feel free to contact me at (555) 555-1212. I will follow up on this correspondence next week to schedule a time to meet at your convenience.

Thank you for your time and have a great day!

Sincerely,

Vernon L. Dent

Sample Cover Letter 2

Ms. Jane Interviewer
Vice President, MIS
Joe IT Company
1 Interviewing Blvd. Suite 400
New York, NY 10036

Dear Ms. Interviewer:

I am applying for the position of Website Developer at Joe IT Company. With my unique ability to combine technical skills with marketing aptitude, I am confident I can make an immediate contribution to your team. Enclosed, please find a copy of my credentials.

Although a recent graduate of TLB University, I am not your typical new graduate. I have put myself through school by helping small businesses develop and maintain their Websites. As a result, I bring a unique perspective of the most current classroom education…along with real-world experience.

I will be in Manhattan on Tuesday and Thursday of next week. I'd like very much to have the opportunity to meet with you. I will follow up this letter with a phone call to see if there is a time that would be convenient for you. If you have any questions, please feel free to contact me at (555) 555-1212.

Thank you for your time and consideration.

Sincerely,

John Q. Public

Secret #5:
Create Powerful Resumes and Cover Letters
That Generate Interest in 15 Seconds or Less
—Checklist Summary—

√ Resumes and cover letters are your personal advertisements.

√ Know what to say...by imagining yourself as the interviewer.

√ There are five subjects every resume should contain.

√ Two topics to avoid on resume are "objectives" and "references."

√ You can format your resumes three different ways.

√ There are 10 laws to writing powerful resumes.

√ Develop a separate list of references and ask permission.

√ Use the Five C's to create compelling cover letters.

√ Use industry "buzzwords" that grab attention.

You only get 15-30 seconds to sell yourself!

Secret #6

Network and Market Yourself

- ● Where to start.
- ● Who to call.
- ● Three *surefire* methods to market yourself.

Where Should You Start?

The most common dilemma people ask when being faced with the daunting task of finding a new job is where to start. Unfortunately, most people start their job search by spending time on the least effective means of finding a job: Sunday's classified section and the Internet.

Forget the Internet!

Do you have any idea how many people find jobs using the Internet? Most studies show that as few as 5 percent of all jobs are found through the Web. What a pathetic number!

But, think about it, if someone can post a position and in one day get more than 1,500 resumes…realistically, even if you can walk on water, what are the odds your resume will be even read, let alone get you the interview.

That is not to say the Internet is useless. In fact, quite the contrary is true. The Internet is a tremendous resource for finding sample resumes, interview questions, and cover letters. The Internet is also a fantastic tool for doing research for interviews and getting directions on how to get to them. The problem is that the Internet is just *not* a very good tool for actually *getting* interviews.

If you are on a pier with 30 other fishermen, what are the odds of you catching as many fish as if you found a secret place that no one knew about? Help-wanted ads and the Internet are where everyone goes to fish for a job. You won't catch much fish in those spots. Instead, find the little "secret" places that few people know about or are willing to try.

Unfortunately, doing so requires effort. No one said this was going to be easy. Nothing worthwhile in life ever is. By virtue of the fact you have already invested in this book shows you have what it takes to succeed!

If Something Is Too Good to Be True, It Probably Is

At first the Internet seemed to be the nirvana of the job hunt. What a great concept, just post a resume on the Web, respond to online help-wanted ads, and just sit there and wait for your phone to ring. I wish it were that easy.

When the Internet first gained popularity and the economy was booming, it actually was a good way to get interviews. But just like the gold rush of the 1800s, by the time everyone learned of this great concept, there was very little gold remaining to be mined.

Of course I am being a bit facetious in saying, "forget the Internet." Certainly, I am not saying you should completely ignore your Internet options. Just keep in mind that if only 5 percent of all jobs are found through the Internet, you shouldn't spend more than 5 percent of your time trying to find an opportunity there.

Start by Networking

Networking is the most effective means of finding a job. I know, I know, networking is so cliché. It is probably the most overused term in the entire job-hunting vocabulary. I wish I could come up with a better term, but networking is truly the most effective way to find a job.

Studies show that somewhere between 80 and 90 percent of all jobs are found either through networking or personal marketing. With that being the case, common sense says that you should focus the majority of your job search on these activities.

Merriam-Webster defines networking as "the exchange of information or services among individuals, groups or institutions." In basic job-hunting terminology, networking is the act of personally contacting all of your friends, relatives, previous coworkers and acquaintances to tell them you are in the job market and to actively solicit their help.

There is no better way to broadcast your message for wanting a new job. You will be amazed at the number of people you already know who may be aware of potential opportunities. If they are not, many of them will be able to give you names of people, at their companies, who may be interested in you or able to help you.

Don't Ask for a Job

Asking someone for a job is like a salesperson at a department store going up to you and asking, "May I help you?" Ooh...that phrase is like hearing nails on a chalkboard. Even if you want to be helped, we are programmed to say, "No thank you. Just looking."

When you call someone and ask for a job, the programmed response is to say, "Sorry, I can't help you."

Don't put pressure on your friends and acquaintances by asking them for a job. Instead, describe to them the type of position you are looking for and the skills you possess. Ask them if they know of anyone to whom they can refer you. Ask them if they have any ideas on how you should approach your job hunt.

By the way, always ask people if they can *help* you. Yes, use the word *help*. Most people get a natural high from helping others. When you call someone and ask for *help*, instead of asking for a job outright, you are playing off of one of the positives of human nature—the desire to help. Who is going to say, "No, I don't want to help you"?

Call Everyone You Know

You never know who might know of a job opportunity. If you have held previous positions, gather all of the business cards you have filed away in a drawer and start calling these people. Call your old customers or vendors. Contact all of those people you've met over the years at conferences, trade shows, and golf outings. Also, don't hesitate to call your friends and relatives.

There is absolutely *no* shame in having someone help you get a job. That is how the real world works and you might as well play along.

I have found that by far the best people to network with are those whom you have had some sort of positive working relationship with in the past. If you were an advertising account executive who just got laid off, try calling people at your previous accounts and media outlets. If they liked your work, they may want to hire you internally. If you were a procurement manager, call all of the vendors you used to work with.

Don't hesitate to call your old bosses either. Several times, after I started my own business, ex-bosses have called me, unsolicited, about job openings. People rarely stay at the same company forever anymore. One of your old bosses may be working for a different company that could use a person like you.

Prior coworkers are also great people to network with. If your prior work experience is limited, that is okay, there are plenty of other sources of people you can network with. Other professionals to contact are your insurance agent, your accountant, your doctor, your dentist, and even your hairstylist or manicurist. These people talk to dozens of people every day and may know of something. Also, college friends and acquaintances are great sources of job leads—especially those from the same area of study as you.

You have helped many of your friends and acquaintances out in the past...in part by giving them business. The least they can do is help you in your time of need. Try to provide copies of your resume to each person you contact. If you aren't comfortable giving a resume, then create a one-page summary that details some of your capabilities and accomplishments and provides guidance on why someone would want to hire you.

People Can Make Money by Helping You

Many companies offer employees cash rewards for referrals. One company I worked for gave a $500 reward for referring a person to the company who got hired. So, your friends and associates might not just be doing you a favor; they may be helping themselves.

Police departments and the FBI have used bounties or rewards for centuries to get people to provide information that can help in the solving of a crime. Guess what? It is pretty effective. Otherwise they wouldn't do it...right?

Make it worth their time. I have had friends and clients in the past that have given people a very tangible reason to help—money! That's right, I have known people to put out a "bounty" of anywhere from $500 to $1,000 to anyone that provides them with a lead or information that turns into a job.

I am not saying you have to do this. It is up to your comfort level and your pocketbook. This is just another tool you can put in your toolbox.

Church or Synagogue?

These organizations are a great way to network. Any given church or temple will have potentially hundreds of members...who just might be able to help you out. I have found that people in a given community are very receptive to helping others out within the same community. Most religions put a large emphasis on helping others in their time of need.

Also, don't be afraid to approach your clergy to ask them if they know of anyone who could use your talents. Clergy have the opportunity to interface with the entire community. It is quite possible that they may know of someone who could have a job for a person like you.

If you belong to a church, temple, or other faith-based organization, you have probably paid dues or volunteered in the past. So it is perfectly okay for you to ask your clergy for help in your time of need. That is one of the reasons faith-based organizations exist—to help the community they serve.

What other organizations have you belonged to? When you were in school, were you in a fraternity or sorority? Did you play any sports? If so, call your former fraternity brothers or sorority sisters. Contact your former coaches and teammates.

Professional Organizations

I have spoken in front of groups such as *"Women for Hire"* and *"Women in Direct Marketing."* Most industries have organizations tailored to their field. These are great ways to network. If you don't already belong to a group in your field of interest, it may be a great idea to join one; not just for the job hunt, but for your long-term success.

Tools

Many companies have *internal bulletin boards* with job postings. On their lunch hour, your friends and associates can take a quick scan of the board to see if there are any openings that fit your interests.

Even better, most companies now have *online databases* or *online bulletin boards* that list open positions. In fact, one company I worked for had an *"Open Positions"* database that you could search by position type and expertise. It only takes a couple of minutes for someone to scan a company's database, to see if there is anything that might be a good match for you. Plus, if you have friends and contacts that are in management, they may be able to do internal networking for you with other managers in their organization.

Many positions are in a developmental stage where funding has not yet been approved. If your contacts are at the managerial level, they may have access to *position approval databases* or they may know of other counterparts who are looking for people.

If you can get in before the position is posted, you may have a great chance at getting that job. At the very least, you may have an edge over future candidates.

Other Networking Resources

In recent years, there have been several different groups that have come into existence that provide excellent networking opportunities for job seekers. As mentioned earlier, faith-based organizations have become very active in providing facilities to help job-hunters. However, you don't necessarily have to belong to a church or synagogue to use these services.

In Chicago, several churches got together to form a separate entity called the Career Transitions Center. This center has offered regularly scheduled meetings where outside experts come in to offer counseling and advice. Typically these meetings have also allowed people to network and share ideas with each other.

Also in Chicago, a group of synagogues funded an organization called Jewish Vocational Services. They, too, have offered placement services and numerous networking opportunities outside the synagogue.

If you are not comfortable utilizing faith-based organizations, there are many others from which to choose. Again, in Chicago, one of those has been YoPro (short for Young Professionals). It has provided an innovative way to network called "Speed Networking." Here people rotate from table to table and get a couple of minutes to articulate who they are and what job they are looking for.

While I have given you some examples from Chicago, these types of organizations exist in every major metropolitan area. If you want help finding these organizations, go to your favorite search engine on the Internet. Type in your city, along with keyword phrases such as "networking groups" or "career transition." When you visit one of these networking groups or events, bring several copies of your personal business cards and resumes.

Write a Script

Every person you talk to represents a potential opportunity to find a job. You never know who might be able to help you find a job. Before you start networking, write a script of what you want to say. Ideally, create a script for different circumstances. For instance, what you would say to a friend could be totally different than how you would approach your family doctor.

For your doctor you might want to say something such as:

Hello Dr. Quackinbush, how are you doing? (Pause) I just wanted to touch base to see if you might be able to help me on something. (Pause) Currently, I am in the process of looking for a new job as an executive assistant. I have had a great track record but recently, was laid off. I was wondering if you had any ideas of people whom I should contact about a potential position.

Keep your script casual, yet to the point. Again, don't be afraid to call professional people whom you have given business to in the past. You have helped put food on the table for insurance agents, stockbrokers, lawyers, hairstylists, manicurists, and many others. There is no shame in asking them to help you in your time of need, so you can eat.

For friends, you could say something such as:

Amy, how's it going? (Pause) Remember that great job I had as marketing manager for Disco Dave's? Well, they just went bankrupt and I am now looking for a new job. I was wondering if you knew of any opportunities at your company or anyone I could contact about finding a new position? I'd really appreciate your help.

The key is you don't want to make anyone feel threatened, burdened, or obligated to help. You want people to help you from the heart. I am sure you have been a good friend to many people. You have always been there when friends have needed you. There is no shame in asking your friends to return the favor.

Surround Yourself With Positive People

When networking, it's always more comfortable to be surrounded by other people who are out of work. Let's face it...most of us like to commiserate with others from time to time. However, while it may feel good at the moment, complaining about life with others who are out of work is not the healthiest activity you can do for your job hunt. Instead, try to network with people who are upbeat and positive and, ideally, people who are employed who can help you.

Create a List of Companies to Target

Bring several copies of that list along with several copies of your resume and business cards to your upcoming networking events. When your contacts go through the list, they may see a name of a company at which a friend works. Now you have a great reference and starting point to use when you call into that company.

Some networking forums are better than other ones. Don't go just to go. Make sure your time is productive.

Have an Objective

Before networking, have in your mind what you want to accomplish for each activity. Set a quantifiable goal. When you go to an event with an objective such as, "I want to meet at least three people who are in my industry and get a minimum of two contact names that I can call," you will be more focused and likely to succeed.

Insider Tip

Be willing to help others. Don't be afraid to share your advice and ideas. There is a saying that goes "what goes around comes around." If you are helpful to people, eventually someone will help you too.

Networking Works

As painful as networking can be, it still is by far the most effective way of scouting out job openings. The more people you meet, the greater your chances of finding an opportunity. Job-hunting is a numbers game. Every person you talk to gets you that much closer to someone who has a job for you.

Market Yourself

By now, I am sure you realize that rarely do job opportunities just drop in your lap. You need to go out and earn them. Getting the job you want takes time and dedication. It also often requires doing things that aren't comfortable or natural to do.

Besides the traditional forms of networking discussed earlier in this chapter, there are three methods that you can use to go out and *market* yourself, so you can start landing those interviews. Some of these techniques may fit your personality, while others may not. Try them all and see what works best for you.

3 Surefire Methods of Marketing Yourself

1. Cold-call for *known* job opportunities.
2. Cold-call for *informational* interviews.
3. Direct response mailings/"blasts."

1. Cold-Call for *Known* Job Opportunities

The first method of personal marketing is making cold calls, over the telephone, for *known* job opportunities. A *known opportunity* is an actual job opportunity that you have identified either through a help-wanted ad, a posting, or through networking. A *cold call* is calling someone, "out of the blue," who is not expecting your call. This can be an acquaintance, friend, ex-manager, or a complete stranger.

Don't Call HR!

If you have identified companies that have a current job opening, try finding out the name of the person who would be your boss. Most people waste their time by just focusing on human resources. Well, guess what? There are many other fishermen also fishing off of the human resources pier. Instead, call up the receptionist and ask for the name of the person who would be your potential boss. To get that name, think of what the most likely titles would be for your potential boss. Then, call and ask the receptionist for the person that has that title. If you get a recording, hit 0 and # until you reach a living breathing person.

Don't Be Afraid to Make Cold Calls

People can't bite you over the phone (and they rarely do in person). Call and introduce yourself. How you introduce yourself is up to you. The key is to relate to the person on the phone with some sort of common ground.

When making cold calls over the telephone, call from your home phone. Turn off the caller ID-protect feature, if you normally have your name blocked. Most companies have caller ID. If the receptionist sees your name on the caller ID, or he of she is more likely to answer the phone than if he or she sees "unknown" or "private" on their display.

Before Calling, Practice Your Script

You will find that by having a script and practicing it, you will be much more comfortable making the call. Making a cold call for an interview is just like making a sales call. The best salespeople always prepare for their phone calls and meetings. If you are prepared, you will be successful.

Your script should be very similar to your cover letter. Introduce yourself as concisely as possible, create interest in you, and then close them for the interview.

Demonstrate Knowledge

Include in your script hot buttons (areas of interest), and the language or lingo of the company and industry. The best place to find initial hot buttons are in company mission statements and company annual reports.

When you make your calls, try placing a mirror in front of your phone. While you are gazing at this mirror, see if you are smiling while talking. People can hear a difference in your voice if you are smiling. People can tell if you are happy, scared, insecure, or somewhere in between by your tone of voice and your energy level—all of which are affected by your nonverbal expressions.

Your energy level will be higher when you are smiling and your tone of voice will be more positive. People like talking to positive and energetic people, not those who seem depressed.

Example script for responding to a help-wanted ad:

Good morning, my name is _____ and I am hoping you might be able to help me. I noticed your ad for a brand manager position and I was wondering if you are the correct person with whom to schedule an interview.(Pause for their answer)

If you found the correct person say something such as:

I currently work for _____company and I have a fantastic track record in bringing new products to market. I saw your opportunity and immediately thought that I could be a tremendous asset to your company. How would I go about scheduling an interview?

If not, then say something such as:

Who would you recommend I speak with about this opportunity? (Pause for their answer)

Getting Rid of the Cold-Calling Jitters Is Easy

Are you still afraid of picking up the phone and making a cold call? You don't believe it's easy? What do you have to lose? The worst that can happen is that the person you are calling can't help you. So what? What is the big deal? If someone says no, are you any worse off than before you asked for help? Of course not! It's not like you have to walk on hot coals. The worst that happens is that someone says no.

When making cold calls, nine out of 10 people may not be able to help you. Don't get frustrated! Look at each individual who can't help as getting you one step closer to a person who can. Be glad they said no. They just got you that much closer to someone who can say yes. Don't take rejections personally. Making cold calls is a numbers game. There are supposed to be rejections. The more people you call, the greater your chances are of reaching someone who might be able to help you.

Cold-Calling Really Works!

But you have to call the right person. When you are making cold calls, call decision-makers. Recently, a client of mine, Dave, called me because he was all frustrated. He was trying for weeks to respond to what he thought was the ideal help-wanted ad. But he wasn't having any luck. Discouraged and down, he finally called me. This was the conversation I had with Dave:

Dave: *Todd...for weeks I have been calling the HR department of this company that has been advertising a sales position in my local newspaper. This job is ideal because it is only 15 minutes from my home and they want someone with the exact type of experience that I have. But, no one will return my phone calls. What should I do?*

Todd: *Come on Dave, you are in sales. When you call on customers, who do you try to contact?*

Dave: *The decision-maker, of course.*

Todd: *So...would you be reporting into the HR department? Would HR be your boss?*

Dave: *No. I would be reporting into a sales manager.*

Todd: *Exactly! So why are you wasting time with HR...they aren't the decision-maker, the sales manager is right? (I paused) Why don't you call him instead?*

Dave: *You're right. Let me get off the phone with you and call them right away.*

Indeed, just like he said, as soon as Dave got off the phone with me, he called the company's receptionist and said to her, "I was wondering if you could tell me the name of the sales manager who covers the South Suburbs?" Without hesitation she gave him the name and transferred him directly to the sales manager.

Dave then went on to say to the sales manager, "Hello, my name is Dave and I'm your man." The sales manager was dumbfounded. Dave went on to explain why he was calling and by the end of the phone conversation, he got the interview.

Now I am not saying that you should be so bold when you cold-call prospects. That was his personality, so it worked for him. What you should take from this story is that cold-calling can and does work. So don't be afraid to use it.

2. Cold-Call for *Informational* Interviews

An informational interview is where you meet with a person who can help you in your job search, but may not be in a capacity, or have an opening, to hire you. The best people to conduct informational interviews with are people at your targeted companies who are either at the same level as you would be (who can recommend you to their boss) or people who would be at the level of your potential boss.

For instance, if you want a position in network administration, try contacting other network administrators who are already employed, and try calling the MIS directors or whatever the titles du jour are. If you would like a position in accounting, then try to meet with other accountants as well as partners. If you want a job in marketing, try calling similar level marketing professionals as well as product managers.

Typically, your counterparts at other organizations can relate to what you are going through and are usually more than happy to help you. In addition, even managers who do not have openings are often willing to meet with potential candidates. Finding good people is always difficult. By talking to you now, managers have another prospect to add to their funnel when a position opens up.

Develop a List of Prospects

Look at directories of your graduating classes and social organizations you belonged to such as fraternities or sororities. Many of these directories list what people are currently doing. Scan through the directories to see if anyone may be in a capacity to help you. Also, gather up all of your business cards and contact files. You can use these connections when trying to line up some informational interviews as well.

Write down a list of companies that you are interested in. Then go to their Websites and call their receptionists to get the names of people you should call. Finally, pick up your local phonebook and come up with a list of prospects from there as well.

Don't meet with people just for the sake of meeting with people. Focus your efforts on informational interviews with people who may be in a capacity to help you either because they are in the same industry or because they may have potential opportunities.

One More Time, Create a Script

Once you collect a list of prospects, develop a script and start calling these people. While calling, don't put people on the spot. Just ask them if they can assist you. Tailor your script to the method of how you got the person's name.

If you are using a scholastic list, introduce yourself as a graduate of the university or high school, or, if you are contacting a member of an organization you belong to, introduce yourself as a fellow member.

Cold-calling an organization to which you belong:

My name is _____ and I am graduating from _____. The reason for my call is that I have an interest in consulting. With the success you have enjoyed in your field, I would greatly value your opinion. I was wondering if you might be able to help me by giving me an honest assessment about what it takes to succeed in your industry. (Pause) When would it be convenient for me to meet with you?

Cold-calling outside your industry:

Good afternoon, my name is _____ and I am currently a top producer at_____ with expertise in _____. Would it be possible if I could get your feedback for a few minutes to see if someone of my background and skills would be a good fit in your industry.

Cold-calling example inside your industry:

Good morning, my name is_____ and I am currently in the market to change positions. I have demonstrated a consistent ability to reduce costs and improve productivity. I was wondering if you had a few moments where I could meet with you and get your feedback on whether or not there would be a fit for a person like me in your company.

Informational Interviews

You never know who might be able to help you. Even though there may be no positions open, when managers spot a great talent, they often create a new position just to get that person into the organization. I have done that myself.

Once I hired someone from a competitor, even though I didn't have an opening, because he was a great talent and I knew he would be a terrific addition to the team. Plus, he always seemed to beat my team when we competed with him in the field. I figured if I couldn't beat him, I should hire him.

If the manager can't create a position for you, he or she may refer you to counterparts who do have openings for someone with your talents. Plus, remember that people can make money from internal referrals. So they may be more than willing to help you out.

Prepare for Informational Interviews

Just like regular interviewers, the people you meet with for an informational interview value their time too. Treat them with gratitude and respect. After all, they are going out of their way to help.

Your goal for the informational interview should be to learn as much as possible and to identify at least one additional person who can help you. At the beginning of the informational interview, present a brief overview about yourself and your career objectives. Then, for the rest of the interview, soak in as much as possible. Ask lots of questions.

Sample Questions You Can Ask on Informational Interviews

- What do you enjoy most about your current position?
- What do you like least about your current job?
- What made you decide to go into this industry?
- Why did you choose to work with this company versus others?
- What are the qualities and characteristics of successful employees?
- How much experience do you need to succeed?
- What is the best piece of advice you can give someone like me?
- Can you recommend anyone I should introduce myself to?
- Is it okay if I use your name when calling that person?

3. Direct Response Mailings

In addition to making cold calls over the phone, you can do targeted mailings to companies in your field of interest. Here you need an aggressive cover letter that clearly states your desire, your skills, your accomplishments, and your credentials. As mentioned earlier, your letter has to be short, to the point, and it has to generate interest in 15 seconds or less. The more creative your message is, the better off you will be. With the cover letter, include a copy of your *powerful* resume.

Try Using Overnight Packages

To really get the package noticed, send your information using an overnight or messenger service. Most executives and managers get hundreds of pieces of mail every day, and the only mail that sometimes gets by the gatekeeper (secretary or administrative assistant) is a package that shows urgency: an overnight package. Priority-mail from the post office also works very well and is less costly.

If you do not have the money to send an overnight or priority package, you can improve your chances of getting past gatekeepers by putting a "Personal" and/or "Confidential" sticker on the envelope containing your credentials. You can find these at your local office-supply store or at many post offices.

Faxes

Another effective way to create urgency is to send a fax to targeted companies. Here you want to try to get attention without advertising to the secretary or administrative assistant that you are looking for a job.

Insider Tip

A trick I learned to get a fax by the gatekeeper is to have a cover sheet that does not mention the purpose of the fax. Then, on the final page of your fax transmission include a mostly blank page that just says, "Thank you for your time." This way your resume and cover letter will be sandwiched in the middle of the transmission and may not be as obvious to the gatekeeper.

E-mail

One other way for you to direct market yourself is to use e-mail. If you are lucky, you may find the name and e-mail address of the proper contact person right on the company's Website. More often than not, you will have to send your credentials to a general e-mail address such as info@xyz.com or human.resources@xyz.com.

E-mail is effective because it costs you nothing to send your information, and you can blast out your credentials to hundreds of companies at the same time. The downside is that when you send your information to a general address, it often gets deleted.

Another drawback to e-mail is that with spam and viruses becoming more and more of a problem, many people are deleting all e-mail they get from people they don't recognize. However, don't let that discourage you from at least trying.

> ### *Insider Tip*
>
> To get your e-mail noticed, use a title/header that states a benefit. Put something such as "Cost Reduction," "Increase Your Productivity," or "Increase Your New Business" in the title. That way it is not so obvious you are looking for a job and they may actually read your e-mail. Or you can use an e-mail header such as, "Proven copywriter looking for work" or "Results-oriented management opportunity."

Online Resume "Blasts"

Another tool that is available to you is the online resume "blast." There are many services that for a small fee offer to blast your resume out to thousands of companies and/or recruiters. Typically, the cost for such a service is about the same as the cost for two people to go out to dinner at a restaurant.

The jury is out to the effectiveness of these services. If you have the money, my feeling is why not try it? I certainly wouldn't risk my last dollar on these services. But if you can spare the cash, then by all means, try one of these services. You can find these resume-sending services either through search engines or any major job portals such as *Careerbuilder.com* or *Monster.com*.

Market Yourself to People Who *Need* You

Don't waste your time and money sending out mailings and faxes to just anyone. Make sure you are targeted. Limit your efforts towards strictly people who would need your expertise or services.

If you are in administration, send your credentials to the director of administration or the administrative manager. If you are in sales, send the resume directly to the sales manager of your local area for that company.

To find out the names of the people you should send your credentials to, just call your targeted companies and ask. Ask who is the sales manager, administrative manager, human resources manager, etc. You would be surprised how helpful receptionists can be.

Start out by being really friendly and respectful to the receptionist. Most people treat receptionists rudely. If you treat receptionists with respect, they will relate to you better and want to help you more.

Be personal. Get the name of the receptionist and call that person by name. People respond much more when called by their name. Thank people very much for their assistance. You may need their help in the future, so you don't want to take them for granted.

Sample script for getting a contact name:

Good morning, how are you today? Who am I speaking with? (Pause)
My name is _____ and I was wondering if you might be able to help me. (Pause)
You wouldn't happen to know the name of the sales manager in charge of the Southern region, would you?

It is always a good practice to be cheerful and nice to everyone you meet. You never know who might be your ticket to success.

Network and Market Yourself: Summary

In this chapter, we discussed the importance of networking and covered ways for how to go about doing it. Additionally, we identified three "surefire Methods" you can use to *sell* yourself and *find* job opportunities. In personal marketing, just like in sales, it is impossible to close every deal.

The most successful people view each *no* as getting that much closer to a *yes*. Finding interviews is just a numbers game. The more you go out and sell yourself, the greater your chances of success. Once you finish this book, go out there and network and market yourself. You will be well on your way to getting the job you want.

Personal Case History: Career Overview

There is no better way to prove the effectiveness of networking and marketing yourself than to show you my own personal career progression. I am going to take you all the way back in time to when I was in high school to illustrate the value of these activities. In the following chart, you can view *every* job that I have had throughout my entire career and how I found each one.

In fact, out of 15 different jobs I have performed over the years, only *one* was ever found through using either the help-wanted ads or the Internet! That was my first job, as a busboy for a banquet hall. Obviously, that job wasn't the most rewarding position I have ever held. In fact, I hated it. The only thing I learned from that job was how to make a tasty mint parfait.

I did find *two* other jobs through tools we will talk about in the next chapter. However, a whopping 80 percent (12 out of 15), of all of the jobs I have ever gotten, were obtained through networking and marketing myself. Need I say more? This stuff works!

Personal Overview

Job	Company	How I found the job	When I got it
Busboy	Heights Banquet Hall	Help-wanted ad	High School
Telemarketer	Farmers Insurance	Teacher: *Networking*	High School
Salesperson	Alice in Videoland	Teacher: *Networking*	High School
Salesperson	Alice in Videoland	Old Boss: *Networking*	College
Salesperson	Video King	Old Boss: *Networking*	College
Summer Intern	Royal Dutch Shell	Resume Blast: *Marketing*	College
Sales Rep.	NCR Corporation	College Placement Office	Post-college
Account Mgr.	IBM Corporation	Dad's coworker: *Network*	Post-college
District Manager	APC Corporation	Recruiter	Post-college
F1000 Manager	APC Corporation	Called VP: *Networking*	Post-college
OEM Director	APC Corporation	Called VP: *Networking*	Post-college
Guest Lecturer	University of Chicago	Religious org.: *Network*	Post-college
Keynote Speaker	Numerous Clients	*Networking* and *Marketing*	Post-college
Sales Trainer	Numerous Clients	*Networking* and *Marketing*	Post-college
Career Coach	Numerous Clients	Speaking: *Networking*	Post-college

Secret #6: Network and Market Yourself
—Checklist Summary—

√ Call everyone and anyone who can help you.

√ There is no shame in asking for help.

√ Don't rely on the Internet to get you interviews.

√ Cold-call for *known* opportunities.

√ Cold-call for *informational* interviews.

√ Proactively market yourself using blasts, faxes, and mailings.

√ Create scripts for each method of networking.

√ More than 80 percent of all jobs are found by networking and marketing.

The more you go out and market yourself the greater your chances of success.

Secret #7

Utilize Available Tools and Resources

- ◉ The 10 best job-hunting tools and resources.
- ◉ A complete job-search guide

Networking and marketing your skills is tough work. At times, it's natural to feel a bit discouraged. When you get frustrated in your own personal efforts, don't despair, there are many other tools and resources you can use to find a job.

Do you have a toolbox in your home? What are the tools you use the most? I use my hammer and screwdriver most. In your toolbox, you probably have many more tools than just a hammer and a screwdriver. You might have a drill, a saw, and a wrench. Even though you might not use those tools on a daily basis, it is still good to have them. You never know when you might need them.

In the previous chapter we talked about the two *job-hunting tools* you should use the most: networking and marketing. However, as with your toolbox at home, in job hunting, there are many other tools at your disposal.

Like your drill, saw, and wrench, most likely you won't use these tools on a daily basis. However, you will want to utilize them at different times throughout your job search to maximize your efforts. Especially when you want to take a break from networking and making cold calls.

The 10 Best Job-Hunting Tools and Resources

In this chapter, I am going to share with you 10 of the best job-hunting tools and resources that, when all else fails, you can use to find additional job interviews. As you saw in my personal case history, there were a couple of times throughout my career where some of these tools really helped!

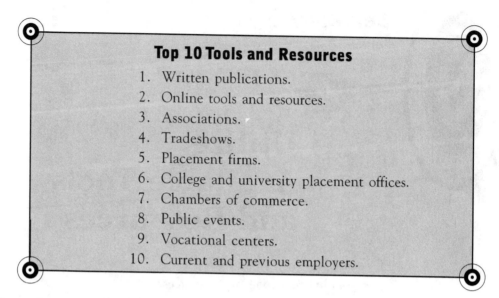

Top 10 Tools and Resources
1. Written publications.
2. Online tools and resources.
3. Associations.
4. Tradeshows.
5. Placement firms.
6. College and university placement offices.
7. Chambers of commerce.
8. Public events.
9. Vocational centers.
10. Current and previous employers.

1. Written Publications

Most people typically start their job search by looking at help-wanted ads in the *classified* section of their local daily newspaper. However, there are other written publications that can provide excellent leads too. Let's look at each type of publication in more detail.

Local Daily Newspapers

Local newspapers are great resources for finding job opportunities. Newspapers are especially helpful for people who want hourly and entry-level positions. On any given day, a newspaper can contain hundreds, if not thousands, of opportunities.

Higher-level positions can also be found in the classifieds when companies are rapidly expanding or relocating. When companies need to hire a lot of people quickly, classified ads help them get the word out fast.

The most prominent days for help-wanted ads in your local newspaper are Thursdays and Sundays. Usually, these ads are found in the *Classified* or *Job* sections of the paper. Typically, most of the ads are placed in the Sunday paper.

The daily *Regional* and *Business* sections of your local newspapers are also excellent resources to use throughout your job hunt. You will discover many opportunities by reading stories about your area's economy. Many times you will find stories about a company expanding or relocating. When you see stories like this, get on the phone and make some calls.

If a company is building a new office or store, most likely they will need new employees. Don't be shy; call them. The worst that happens is you are told there are no openings. At least you'll have tried.

Articles about start-up businesses and new locations usually appear far sooner than the help-wanted ads themselves. If you read about a company moving to your city, be proactive. Contact them before they place help-wanted ads. This will give you an edge over your competition.

Weekly Business Publications

Crain's is an example of a publisher of weekly business publications. They have publications in major cities such as Chicago and New York. These business publications are great resources because they list lucrative job opportunities and provide a wealth of information about the region's local business climate.

To find the weekly business publications in your area, check your local bookstores, convenience stores, newspaper stands and kiosks at train stations and bus depots, and as always, check the Internet.

National Business Publications

Publications such as *The Wall Street Journal, Barron's, and Investor's Business Daily* often contain at least a couple of pages of help-wanted ads for higher-level positions. Some national business publications come out on a daily basis, while others are weekly.

Typically, the cost of advertising a position in a national periodical is much more expensive than a local newspaper. As a result, companies tend only to post their highest-level positions in national periodicals. Usually, the higher paying the position, the more difficult it is to find a qualified candidate. Because of this difficulty, companies will often resort to placing national ads to find the best talent.

National periodicals sometimes have regional editions that will list local job openings as well. *The Wall Street Journal* and *Investor's Business Daily* are two such publications.

I recommend subscribing to at least one or two of these national publications during your job hunt. Outside of the classified ads, they provide great insight into the economy as well as new industries and businesses.

Industry Publications

Most cities and regions have local publications that are dedicated to different industries for that area. In Chicago one example is *ePrairie*, a newspaper dedicated to the information technology industry. In St. Louis, the *St. Louis Small Business Monthly* is a publication written for entrepreneurial companies and small- to mid-sized businesses.

Companies with targeted needs often place job advertisements in these publications. Determine what industries interest you the most and focus on the appropriate publications. In addition to local and regional publications, most industries have national and global publications as well.

Phonebooks

Perhaps one of the oldest yet most effective written publications still available to the job-hunter is the good old-fashioned phonebook. Many a job-seeker has found out about an opportunity by just picking up the Yellow Pages and calling companies about job openings.

As crude as this may sound, it can still be effective. If you know what type of company and industry you want to work in, it is very easy to get a targeted list in the phonebook. This is also a good place to find some of the other resources that I will talk about in this chapter, such as recruiters and vocational centers.

2. Online Tools and Resources

One of the earlier chapters had a very strong quote: "Forget the Internet." This was to make a point that you remember not to solely rely on the Internet to get a job. I can't tell you how many people have failed in their job search because all they do is sit at home and surf the Internet or waste a ton of time in chat rooms.

With that being said, it doesn't hurt to have the Internet in your job-hunting toolbox. Just remember that only about 5 percent of all jobs are found through the Internet. So, don't spend much more than 5 percent of your time utilizing this tool.

Company Websites

One of the best ways to use the Internet in your job search is to go directly to the Websites of companies that you are interested in. Let's say you want to get a job as a software developer. There are hundreds of thousands of companies that could use a software developer, from banks, to software companies, to manufacturers. What type of company do you want to work for?

Let's say you want to work for either a bank or an insurance company. You can go to your favorite search engine and come up with a list of potential targets. In this case, all you would need to do is type in search phrases such as "top 50 banks," "Top 25 insurance companies," or you can get geographically specific such as "insurance companies Denver" or "top banks Milwaukee."

Go to the home page of each of your target companies' Websites. On most sites, companies will have a section called "Career Seekers," "Jobs At," "Job Seekers," "Human Resources," or "Employment Opportunities." Even during challenging times, many jobs are posted right on company Websites.

To find a specific company's Website, just type in the company's Internet address on the address line of your browser. Often, a company's Internet address is either its name, or its stock symbol, followed by an extension such as .com, .org, .biz, or .net. In the case of Dell, it is both the name and the stock symbol, *www.dell.com*.

If you don't know the Internet address of the company you are interested in, just go to your favorite search engine and type in the name of the company. In fact, some of these same search engines have their own sections for job openings and postings.

Use Company Websites to Create Your Own Opportunities

Responding to posted job opportunities is just one of the ways you can use company Websites to get interviews. However, not all companies advertise open positions on the Web and not all companies will post every open position, either.

Believe it or not, you can actually use the Internet to uncover opportunities that aren't publicized. But how do you do that? It's easy!

Let's say you want to work in the finance department of a major manufacturer. Go directly to the Website of your targeted companies. On almost every public company's Website they have an online version of their annual report. You can bring up that annual report and identify the "Controller" and/or "VP of Finance." Then you can go to the "contact us" section of the company's site to get the company's general phone number.

Call Your Potential New Boss

Develop a script for what you want to say. In that script, generate interest for why that person would want to talk to you. And (hint, hint) don't call and ask for a job. Instead, call, introduce yourself, and ask if you might be able to have a few minutes of that person's time to talk about improving their area of interest.

What if you want to work in some other line of business? Well, what would the title of your boss be? Go to company Websites and do a search on that title. If you can't find anything, at least get the company's general phone number and make a quick phone call.

Be proactive. Rarely do even posted jobs just fall into your lap. As the famous motivational speaker Les Brown would say, "To succeed, you have to be hungry!"

Online Career Portals

There are many online bulletin boards, job portals, and career networks on the Internet where you can electronically view job openings, post resumes, and chat with other job seekers. Some of the most popular sites have been *Monster.com*, *Hotjobs.com*, and *Careerbuilder.com*.

In addition, there are many "headhunters" and job placement agencies on the Internet. As always, the Internet is dynamic and always changing. The best way to find online job bulletin boards and portals is to go to your favorite search engine and type in the phrase *"job search."* You'll see hundreds listed.

Just remember, there are so many of these sites that you could spend eight hours a day just surfing them. Prioritize your time and focus on the ones that are most likely to help you. Again, I don't recommend spending more than two hours a week (5 percent of a 40-hour workweek) on these sites.

Newspaper Websites

Many local newspapers have their own Websites that provide you with the ability to search online for jobs. You can search by job category and job location. Additionally, many of these newspaper Websites allow you to post your resume online. Also, these sites provide recent articles and sections on job hunting that give fabulous advice.

3. Associations

Joining an association in your field of interest is a great way to meet the "movers and shakers" in your field. Most have monthly meetings or conference calls. Many of these organizations bring in high-powered speakers who may know of openings in your field of interest. Besides monthly meetings, most associations have member lists and job opportunity exchanges.

Depending on your field, there may be one or more organizations that you could join. The only downside is, these organizations are sometimes costly. With that knowledge, you can learn a tremendous amount about your field of interest just by joining an association. Also, through networking, you may discover some great opportunities. Examples of associations include the American Marketing Association, American Medical Association, and the National Restaurant Association.

By joining an association, you will learn about the latest trends and movements in your industry. Armed with this knowledge, you'll be much more articulate about your field of interest and prepared for your upcoming interviews.

Insider Tip

If you can't afford to join an organization, sometimes you can go to one or two meetings for free. Just say that you are considering joining their group and you would like to be a guest at their next meeting to check it out. Most associations will let you come to at least one session for free.

4. Tradeshows

Tradeshows are one of the most effective ways to leverage your time and money to find job opportunities. In one day you can meet literally dozens of people from the best companies in any given industry.

You can learn much about potential employers just from what they are displaying in the booth. You will also enhance your knowledge because at tradeshows, you are exposed to the latest industry news. Best of all, you will be one of the only job seekers at the show.

Most industries have both local and national tradeshows. The banking industry has national shows such as the Banking Automation and local shows such as the Texas Banker's. The restaurant industry has national shows such as the National Restaurant Association Food and Beverage Show and local shows such as the Florida Restaurant Association Show.

The computer industry has national shows like COMDEX and local shows such as TECHXNY. Perhaps the most renowned industry shows are the Consumer Electronics and Auto shows.

Prepare for Every Show You Attend

Bring a stack of resumes with you and try to meet as many people as possible. Go to each booth and ask for someone who can give you guidance on job opportunities at their company. Leave a resume whenever possible and get a business card from everyone you meet.

After the show, call them or the people to whom they referred you and mention the show. People are much more apt to talk to a referral than to a complete stranger. You might get lucky and actually talk with someone…right at the show…that can hire you. You never know until you try.

Develop a Script and Dress Appropriately

Prepare in advance what you want to say as you walk into each booth. Typically, you will only have about 30 seconds to generate interest in yourself. Be prepared and dress appropriately. If the show is a casual show, such as the auto or restaurant shows, then business casual is fine. However, if you are attending a banking show or a healthcare show, you should definitely go with business formal, as dress in these industries tends to be more conservative.

Go to Shows When They Are Slow

Typically, at most tradeshows, there are slow periods where the people working the booths don't have much to do. These are the best times to conduct your job-hunting efforts. Slow periods are usually between 8:00 a.m. and 9:00 a.m. or between 4:00 p.m. and 5:00 p.m. Other slow periods include the final hours of the last day of a show and the times when there are breakout sessions.

Insider Tip

Sometimes, going to the show during the booth setup can be advantageous. Often, tradeshows do not charge an attendance fee during this time. Here you can meet the people setting up the booths. Shows can be quite expensive to get into, and admittance is often limited. So, this is a way of accomplishing some of what you want to do without the cost and limitations. During setup, there are no potential customers in the booth, so people are often more willing to spend time with you.

Don't bother people at tradeshows when they are busy and their booths are crowded. You don't want to interrupt them while they are conducting business. This will irritate your potential prospects and limit your chances of success.

However, if you go when it is slow in the booth, people are usually much more eager to talk to you (if for no other reason than to stay awake). Sometimes, working a tradeshow booth can be a lonely and boring experience. During these times, prospects will be much more receptive to what you have to say versus when they are busy.

5. Placement Firms

Job placement firms are services that help to bring hiring managers together with potential candidates. Their employees are often called "headhunters," "recruiters," and "search consultants," and these firms are great places to find interviews.

In addition to placement services that focus on placing people for *full-time* employment, there are also firms out there that can help you find *temporary* or *part-time* positions. These are typically called "temporary agencies" or "employment agencies."

Usually when a firm uses the word *agency* in their name or description, it means that the firm focuses on placing *temporary* positions. Firms that use the term *recruiter* usually focus on *full-time* employment. Let's first take a look at recruiters.

There are Three Different Kinds of Recruiters

1. **Employer compensated:** This first type of recruiter is one that is paid solely by the employer. In this case, to locate potential candidates, employers pay anywhere from 25 percent to 100 percent of the first year's salary to the search firm. This is the only type of recruiter I recommend. They are the only firms who won't charge you to help. They receive their compensation strictly from the companies instead of you.

   There is only one downfall to using these firms: Because the hiring companies are paying them, they have to keep the employer's best interest in mind more so than yours.

2. **Compensated by you:** This second kind of placement firm is one who charges *you* for the job search. Many of these firms focus on higher-level executives. Typically, they can charge a lot of money. Sometimes it can cost thousands of dollars to use this type of recruiter.

3. **Compensated by both you and the employer:** The third type is a hybrid that charges both *you* and the *employer* for their services. Again, I recommend only using the type of recruiting firm that solely charges the employer for their services. Quite honestly, most recruiters that charge a fee typically do not do a better job than those whose services are free. Before you meet with recruiters, ask them up front how they are compensated.

Employment Agencies

The opinion of many "experts" in the field is that one of the best ways to find a *full-time* job is to first work in a *temporary* or *part-time* position. The thesis is that once you prove yourself in a temporary position, a company may see how good you are and want to hire you for a full-time job. Additionally, the theory is that the part-time job will help you pay your bills while you are searching for a full-time job.

While these are indeed benefits to getting part-time employment, there are also many drawbacks. First, it takes focus away from your main objective: finding a full-time job that you *really* want. Second, if you are accustomed to earning a high income, and you settle for a part-time job for significantly less money, it can be a real blow to your ego, which can be a significant setback to your job search. Only you will know what is best for your situation. But if you want to try this route, then employment agencies can be very helpful.

There are both national and local agencies. These agencies specialize in placing temporary workers in everything from the plant floor to administration, accounting, and sales. You can find these firms by looking them up either in your local phone book or the Internet. Whether you use recruiters or agencies, make sure you are prepared.

Have Your Resume Ready Before Contacting Placement Firms

Your resume should be tailored so that recruiting firms or agencies can market you and your skills to their clients. Often a good recruiter or agency will offer suggestions for your resume. Listen to them because they understand the type of person their client wants to hire and the type of resume that their clients expect.

Schedule Appointments With the Top Firms in Your Industry

Recruiters and agencies may have dozens of clients looking for employees just like you. However, the top industry specialists may not be located in your city. To find out who these specialists are, and where to find them, look in industry trade publications, talk with friends in the industry, and don't forget the old standby: the phonebook.

You can also find them on the Web by going to your favorite search engine and typing in phrases such as "recruiter" and "employment agency" along with the name of your hometown or a large city near you.

Develop and Practice a Script

A prepared script is essential because job placement professionals are busy. Typically, you will have about one minute to sell yourself. If you don't present a compelling case in the first minute, then they will just say, "We have nothing for you." The more prepared and exciting you come across, the greater your chances of being invited to an interview.

Just as I strongly urge you not to rely solely on the Internet to find a job, don't exclusively depend on recruiters or agencies, either. While they tend to be a bit more effective than the Web, networking and direct marketing yourself are still the best ways to find opportunities.

6. College and University Placement Offices

Another place to find out about job openings is at the job placement office of the college or university you attended. Even if you graduated years ago, don't hesitate to call the placement office to see what companies are interviewing for positions.

Either you or your parents paid a lot of money for your degree. Make the school do something for you. Use the potential of future donations as a carrot. Sometimes you can even get a slot on the interview schedule when companies visit campus.

If you are still in school, the job placement office is a primary source of opportunities for you. Many schools allow you to submit your resume and bid for interviews. Some hold a lottery and some allow the interviewing firms to preselect the people who will interview based on resumes (again, this emphasizes the importance of a great resume).

Go to Open Houses

Whether or not you are still in school, a great way to meet companies is to attend open houses that are often held prior to a company interviewing. When I was a student at the University of Illinois, companies such as IBM and Procter & Gamble held open houses the evening before they interviewed.

If you are a graduate, or a student who didn't get on the interview list, don't hesitate to drop in on the open house. Open houses are advertised on campus kiosks, bulletin boards, and in school newspapers.

While you are at it, go to other colleges and universities in your area even if you never attended those schools. Placement offices are open to the public, so walk in and ask for the schedule of companies coming on campus to interview. Then, look for bulletins on kiosks and in the student newspapers to see which companies are holding open houses.

You have nothing to lose. The worst that can happen is you get kicked out of the placement office or a company says they are interested only in current students from that school. But if you are convincing enough, who knows what can happen? They might respect your spunk and tenacity.

Once again, I cannot stress enough the importance of creating a script for these scenarios and practicing it. You will only have about 30 seconds to make your impression count.

7. Chambers of Commerce

Your local chamber of commerce is another resource you can use in your job search. Here, you can find companies that are relocating to or expanding in your area. These companies hold tremendous opportunity for job-seekers.

People at the chamber of commerce work with local companies all the time. They just might know of an opportunity suited for you. Also, some chambers hold job-hunting events as well.

8. Public Events

There are many public events available today that offer a wealth of opportunities for job seekers. Some of these events are free. Others charge a small fee. Often these events are held at a hotel, restaurant, or local convention center.

Job Fairs

Perhaps the most prevalent are events called job fairs. At a job fair, multiple companies send representatives, each searching for candidates for a wide variety of positions. Usually, job fairs are advertised in your newspaper's *Community* or *Business* sections and are typically sponsored by either the local newspaper or chamber of commerce.

While often catered towards more entry-level positions, job fairs can still be a very productive way to network even for people with several years of experience.

Pink Slip Parties

These are public events that came into being during the tech bust. The goal of these events was to match job-seekers with possible employers through a more casual means than the more formal job fairs.

Pink slip parties typically allot a couple hours for power networking. Afterwards, food and beverages are often served and the networking turns into a social event.

Although these parties started out in the technology field, they have since spread to other industries. They are usually held once every couple of months at a local restaurant or nightclub. Check your local newspapers and Websites to find out the next party near you.

"Speed" Networking Events

Similar to pink slip parties, these events are also more informal and are usually advertised in local media outlets. These events are designed to foster communication, learning, and networking among a particular industry or age group.

Speed networking events can provide many job opportunities. Held in a casual place such as a restaurant or upscale bar, you have the opportunity to meet counterparts from your age group, your industry, or both. Here, you get the opportunity to meet several potential decision-makers, all in one room. Often companies go to these events specifically to look for potential candidates. Other times, hiring managers attend just to put their feelers out.

When attending these events, I recommend either dressing in business casual or business formal attire. Bring with you several copies of your resumes and business cards. Don't be shy or afraid to attend these events. Usually everyone wears name badges and you can just go up to people and introduce yourself. You will find this environment to be friendly, upbeat, and a great place to find job opportunities.

9. Vocational Centers

As I mentioned previously, there are many vocational centers available to you that offer free job-hunting services. Many of these centers are funded either by faith-based organizations or a local municipality. These centers are great because they often offer free use of computers and other valuable job-hunting tools. In addition, these centers typically provide counseling on your resume and offer regular networking events where you can identify potential job opportunities.

To find the vocational center closest to you and most appropriate for you, again, look to the Internet. Go to your favorite search engine and type in your city along with the phrases such as "vocational center" or "career assistance."

10. Current and Previous Employers

Have you had a good track record? If so, your past and present employers could be a fertile ground for finding new job opportunities. Many people don't realize that sometimes the best opportunities for jobs are often within their own company. You might be thinking, "Come on, I want to get the heck out of here. Why would I want another job at the same place?"

Often, people become dissatisfied in their jobs, not because they dislike the company or what they are doing, but because of their boss or situation. Maybe your job just isn't the right fit anymore. Maybe the job is stale and you just need a change of pace.

If you have never before taken the time to define your ideal job, you may not be in the best job; however, you may be in the right company. You would be surprised at how much better things can be with a change in management or responsibilities.

Plus, if you find a job within your company, you don't forgo the vacation time you have earned and the vested time you have accumulated in your retirement and stock option plans.

One of my previous coworkers at APC left the company around the same time I did. He thought the grass was greener elsewhere. But after four years of jumping from one floundering company to another, he realized life wasn't so bad at APC after all. He had a great track record there and when he contacted the company, they welcomed him back.

Now he has a completely different position than the one he had left four years earlier. He is rejuvenated and thrilled that he rejoined the company. You just never know.

It Pays Not to Burn Your Bridges

Unfortunately, at times, I not only burnt my bridges, I torched them. Getting the last word can feel good at the time, but rarely does it provide you with any long-lasting benefits. I've learned the hard way that it always pays to treat everyone with respect, regardless of how you feel. It is a small world out there and you never know who may hold the keys to unlocking your next opportunity.

Don't Rule Out Your Current Employer

You can find out about internal job openings in human resource databases, on corporate bulletin boards, and by talking to fellow employees and managers. Sometimes, if you have a good rapport with your current managers, and they want to see you succeed, you can ask them if they know of any new job opportunities within the company.

Call Your Previous Managers and Coworkers

Rarely does someone stay at the same company his or her entire career. If you have had good working relationships with coworkers and managers in the past, call them. It's very possible that if a previous manager liked you before, he or she may want to hire you again.

In college, I landed two summer jobs by working for previous bosses who jumped ship and went to a different company. Given the opportunity to do so, and with the knowledge of my track record, they hired me again.

Twice, since I quit APC to start my own business, previous bosses have contacted me to see if I was interested in working for them at a new company. Although, I cordially declined, it was nice to know those opportunities were there. So, as you can see, it is very possible that if you have been a solid performer, you may be able to hire on with a previous boss or coworker.

Secret #7:
Utilize Available Tools and Resources
—Checklist Summary—

√   There are 10 great resources you can use to find a job.
√   You should try every tool at your disposal…you
         never know where your next opportunity might be.
√   Don't forget your previous coworkers and bosses.
√   Treat everyone with respect because you never
         know who might hold your future keys to success.

When you get frustrated, don't despair.
There are many other tools and resources you can use to find a job.

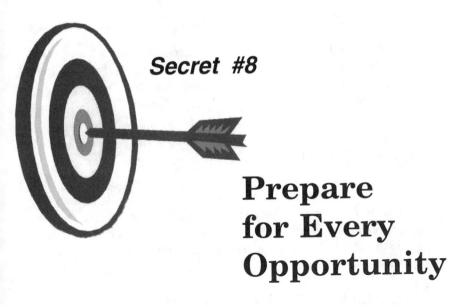

Secret #8

Prepare
for Every
Opportunity

- ◉ Learn the eight characteristics of ideal candidates.
- ◉ Research prospective companies and industries.
- ◉ Answer 65 of the most common job-interviewing questions.
- ◉ Practice, practice, practice.
- ◉ Go through a final interview checklist.

Prepare for Every Opportunity...Not Just Interviews!

Every person to whom you talk throughout your job-hunting process represents a potential opportunity. You never know who might be able to help you in your endeavors. Whether you are networking with a friend, talking to a recruiter, calling a receptionist, attending a job fair, or even having a cup of coffee at a local coffee shop, be prepared.

Job opportunities can pop up at any time. Recently, I was at a local coffee shop and a woman started talking to me. She said, "Just last week I was sitting in the very chair you are sitting in and I got a new job." I said to her, "No kidding, I am actually writing a book on the topic...how did you do that?"

She said, "I sat down as I normally do, just having a cup of coffee, and I started talking to another woman. She mentioned she worked for a local school in the area. The next thing you know we started discussing my current situation and by the end of the conversation, I had a new job. I wasn't even trying...it just happened."

You just never know who you might run into during your job search. A complete stranger might just hold the keys to your next job. It pays to prepare for any opportunity, not just your interviews. Treat each person you meet as if that person could hire you on the spot. Your dream job may just be a cup of coffee away.

In this chapter, the main focus will be to show you how to prepare for your job interviews. However, you can pretty much apply any of these principles, techniques, and tips to any job-hunting situation that might arise including an innocent conversation in a coffee shop.

Regardless of the opportunity, the best way to prepare is to imagine being in the shoes of the other person. If you were on the other side of a networking conversation, what would motivate you to help a person find a job? If you were the receptionist on the other end of the telephone, what could a person say that would make you want to provide assistance?

As I have suggested numerous times throughout this book, one of the best ways to prepare for any opportunity is to develop a script and practice it. No two situations will be the same, but the more you prepare and practice, the more you will know what to say and the better off you will be. For situations where you just bump into someone on the street or in a café, put together a little 30-second pitch you can use to sell yourself.

Preparing Is as Important as Playing the Game

Sports teams prepare for hours, sometimes days, watching films of the previous games of their upcoming opponents. A football team will prepare and practice an entire week for one, three-hour game. That is the kind of effort you want to bring into your job hunting.

Athletes study their opponents' strengths, weaknesses, and strategies. They practice how to minimize their competition's strengths while exploiting their weaknesses. They tirelessly prepare a strategy of how to win the game.

To win at interviewing, you too must develop a winning strategy (prepare). Regardless of what opportunity you strive for, you are going to come up against stiff competition. The more you prepare, the better you'll be able to compete.

Insider Tip

When I interviewed candidates, the most important question I asked was, "With all of the great candidates that I am interviewing for this position, why should I hire you?" When answering this question, you need to show why you're better than your competition, otherwise you won't get hired.

Throughout your job search, no matter to whom you are talking, you need to be able to articulate why you should be hired. There will always be people who have more experience. You are going to have to know how to combat that. In some cases, you may actually be accused of having too much experience. You need to be able to address that as well.

No person is perfect. Your competition is no different. They will have weaknesses that you can exploit. Maybe someone hasn't developed as much expertise as you have. Or perhaps someone's track record isn't as good. Without being arrogant, prepare how you will convey your strengths and experience to combat any competition that may arise.

In both sports and interviewing, preparation is typically the single most important factor in separating those who succeed from those who fail. Only with preparation can you reach your potential.

Toot Your Own Horn, But Stick to the Facts

If you don't "toot your own horn" and sell yourself, nobody else will. As we talked about in Secret #4, one of the most important aspects of preparation is to articulate your strengths and competencies and bring them to life. But whatever you do, **don't make things up or lie.** Doing that will always come back to haunt you.

Insider Tip

My mother had a saying I still live by today:
"When you tell the truth, you never have to remember what you said."

When I hired employees, I looked for a particular personality, competitiveness, drive, and spirit. Even if a candidate had less experience, if he or she fit the personality I desired, I was often willing to take a chance on hiring him or her. Many times, I have took risks believing that, in the long run, a better personality and drive will overcome any shortcomings in experience.

The First 90 Seconds Are the Most Important

Regardless of whether you are meeting a stranger for the first time, you're networking, or you're interviewing people know within the first few moments of any conversation whether they are interested in what you have to say or if they would rather watch bubbles in a fish tank. It is critical to make a powerful and lasting first impression.

The best way to create a captivating impression is to prepare for every possible job-hunting situation from meeting a stranger on the street, to networking, to making cold calls, to the interview itself as a sports team would prepare for a championship game. One of the first steps to take in that preparation is to learn the eight characteristics of winning candidates.

The 8 Characteristics of Winning Candidates!

Companies spend tremendous sums of money conducting market research before coming out with a new product. One of the purposes of that market research is to understand what consumers want so companies can tailor their products towards those desires. If a product doesn't contain what consumers want, nobody will buy it.

In this segment, I am going to save you all of the time and expense of conducting your own market research and tell you exactly what your interviewers will want. There are eight characteristics that hiring managers expect in their ideal candidates. Just like a company has to fulfill consumer wants you have to give interviewers what they desire otherwise they won't hire you.

8 Characteristics of Winning Candidates:

1. Confident.
2. Organized.
3. Personable.
4. Conscientious.
5. Efficient.
6. Creative.
7. Goal-oriented.
8. Problem-solving.

1. Confident

Interviewers want people who are confident about themselves and their skills. If you don't feel confident and excited about yourself, then how are interviewers supposed to? Experience breeds confidence. But, if you lack experience, you can make up for it in preparation, enthusiasm, and drive.

Envision going to a restaurant and asking the server if the fish is good. If he says, "Well, some people like it, but I've never tried it," you may be hesitant to order the fish. However, if he says, "The fish is fantastic and it's one of our most popular dishes," you may be more inclined to order because of the server's confidence in this dish.

Interviewing is much the same. Be confident in what you are serving: you! Confidence instills excitement in you and in your skills. If you are excited about yourself, you will convey that enthusiasm. Everyone wants someone who is enthusiastic.

Once or twice a day, remind yourself that you are *fantastic!* Tell yourself that you have qualities that no other person can match. We are all human and no two people are exactly the same. So celebrate! You have something no one else has: *your unique individuality.* You have to believe that only *you* can be hired for the job. With your qualities, experience, individuality, and enthusiasm, how can any company go wrong?

Most people look at life as if the glass is "half empty," rather than "half full." Life is full of opportunities. I know you can have the right perspective. A positive attitude will help you not only in interviewing, but also in life. Again remember, *you are great!* You have a tremendous amount of talent and enthusiasm. You will succeed!

2. Organized

Nothing is more annoying to interviewers than a person who is disorganized. Once again, you need to be prepared. Plan to show up early to your appointments. The quickest way to appear disorganized is to be late for an interview. That will get you rejected every time.

Prior to your interviews, jot down some topics you want to cover and questions you want to ask. An interview is like an open book test—you will not be thrown out of the interview for looking at your notes. Notes are perfectly acceptable. In fact, bringing notes shows forethought and preparation.

Insider Tip

One trick I use for interviews is to write (in small print on a top corner of the page) a few important notes on topics and questions to discuss along with the names of the company and people with whom I am meeting. That way, if I get nervous, I won't forget what I want to say, or to whom I am talking.

It is perfectly acceptable to take notes during the interview. If the interviewer says something important, by all means write it down. Taking notes shows your interest in the position—just do so in moderation. No one expects you to have a perfect memory. And if they do, then who wants to work for a company like that anyway? Note-taking can be useful, as long as it doesn't distract from the interview.

Besides taking notes, other things that demonstrate your organization include how you dress, how well you can articulate your goals and objectives as well as your strengths and competencies, and the quality of your supporting materials including resumes, business cards, and project portfolios, when appropriate.

3. Personable

Smile. There's an old saying: "When you smile the whole world smiles with you." This popular sentiment is so true. In smiling, you create a friendly atmosphere that is more pleasant for both you and the person to whom you are talking. As a result, people will be more attentive to your message. The more you smile, the more you will succeed.

Again, think of going to a restaurant. Imagine one day you have a waitress who is a grouch, and everything she does seems to be an effort. Then, another day, you have a different waitress who is cheerful and concerned about how you enjoyed your meal. Which meal would you enjoy more? To whom would you give a better tip?

Interviewing is similar. Interviewers are inundated with prospects. They remember people who smile, who are genuinely pleasant, and who enjoy the interview. If you are not friendly and personable during the interview, your chances of getting the job will be slim. Who wants to work every day with a grouch? I sure don't. Not being friendly is the quickest way to get an interviewer's heel on your behind.

4. Conscientious

I have never met an interviewer yet who wanted to hire a lazy bum for a job. Do not, I repeat, do not go into an interview and say, "I am looking for a 9-to-5 job." Forget it. Everyone wants a hard-worker. Even if you don't want to work long hours, please don't say that in the interview. Interviewers want to hear that you are flexible and that you are willing to work the hours necessary to get the job done.

Interviewers might ask, "Are you willing to work long hours?" To answer, you might want to say, "I am willing to spend whatever time it takes to finish the job. In some cases that might be accomplished in a normal work week, and in other cases, it might take longer."

Or interviewers could ask, "Are you looking for a straight 9-to-5 job?" A response to this question would be, "I am looking for a position that is challenging and best utilizes my skills—more than a position that is just a 9-to-5 job. I'm willing to put in whatever effort it takes to succeed!"

The point I am trying to get across is that employers want employees that will give 110 percent. You will be able to decipher on your own, how long and hard you will have to work in a particular job. If the position is not for you, then you can always turn down the offer.

In today's job market, you will be competing with aggressive and motivated people who are enthusiastic and willing to work long hours. You need to convey these same traits. Because if you don't, your competition will.

5. Efficient

In addition to wanting conscientious employees, employers want employees who will work smart and efficiently. Some people will take 10 hours to complete the same amount of work that others might complete in two. Employers want people who will put in a full day's work. But they do not want people who will work hard and get nothing accomplished. They want efficiency.

An old saying goes "It's better to work smart than to work hard." Well, employers want it both ways. They expect you to work hard, but they also want you to work at peak productivity.

6. Creative

Whether you are interviewing for a position in marketing, accounting, computing, or for a job on the plant floor, interviewers favor people who show some form of creativity. Creativity demonstrates the ability to think on your feet and dream up better methods of accomplishing objectives.

When you look at the companies that are market-leaders in their industry, typically they got there because of their creativity. They developed a better and more creative solution to a given problem, need, or desire. Anyone can follow orders. However, not everyone can think above and beyond that.

You might be thinking, *I'm not a creative person. Does that mean I can't get a job?* No! First of all, everyone is creative in some way. Secondly, creativity is not a "show stopper" in itself, but expressing creativity sure helps.

Some vocations require more creativity than other ones. Certainly creativity is more important in a position such as advertising than it is in administration. However, even in administration a boss will still prefer that an employee demonstrate some sort of creativity.

Anyone can look at a position from its job description alone. One way you can differentiate yourself and demonstrate creativity is by changing the rules of the game. Explore areas of the position to which you can add your own definitions and perspectives.

For example, let's say that you are interviewing for a claims adjuster position at an insurance company. The standard job description is that you inspect cars that were in accidents, assess the damage, and negotiate a settlement with the customer. You, being the creative person you are, could demonstrate creativity by *expanding* the job description.

You could say something such as, "Not only am I qualified to process claims, but, with my background, I can also help you streamline the process, improve customer satisfaction, and save the company money."

Super! By being creative, you have just eliminated half of the people interviewing for the position. You demonstrated a talent that others did not. You showed an ability to understand and streamline processes as well as a desire to make the customer happy. The previous candidates did not demonstrate the expertise you just stated. Now, everyone who interviews after you must articulate that they, too, have these qualities.

You just "raised the bar" on your competition!

Even Superstars Have to Be Creative

In basketball, Michael Jordan succeeded because of his drive, tenacity, and, yes, his creativity. Early in his career, he became known for his relentless attacks to the basket, his dunking skills, and his power. As he got older, Michael realized the competition was starting to get wise to his moves and that he no longer had his former speed and stamina.

Instead of relying on his old tactics, Michael reinvented himself by developing an incredible fade-away jump shot that was almost impossible to defend. Michael's creativity allowed him to excel against the toughest competition in basketball.

As you are preparing for your opportunities, think of ways you can redefine job requirements or activities. Think of areas where you can add value that interviewers might not have thought of. But be creative without going overboard. Having a good balance will help you interview to win.

7. Goal-Oriented

Today's labor force is better trained and more productive than ever before. One trait that separates the superstars from the rest of the pack is goal-orientation.

What does it mean to be goal-oriented? It means you have a reason for existence. You aren't following the pack, you are leading it! Having goals means you know what you want out of your career, your relationships, and your life.

When you set goals, you know where you want to go and how to succeed. Ask the top performers in any profession and they will tell you that the main reason for their success is that they set aggressive, yet achievable, goals.

In your interviews, you will be asked questions such as, "Where do you want to be in five years?" and "What are your career aspirations?" Questions such as these differentiate one candidate from another. If you are wimpy with your answer and another candidate knows exactly what he or she wants, you lose!

It's much better to figure out what you want now rather than in the pressure of the moment in a job interview. Without set goals and objectives, you will be relegated to the second team!

Do you want to go into management? Do you want to earn big money? Do you want to travel? Do you want to help others? What are your goals and aspirations?

Take a few minutes now to write down a couple of ideas. Don't worry. You don't have to solve all of life just yet. You could come up with something as simple as "I want a job where I can travel" or "I want a position that will continue to challenge and motivate me."

When you stop looking forward, you have no reason to live. I have known of many people who died within weeks of their retirement! Scary, huh? Why would that happen? Most likely, because they couldn't envision life past their retirement. Don't let that happen to you. Life has so much to offer! Now is the time to lay the foundation for your dreams.

What makes your life a nightmare is when you fail to invest the time to dream and fail to take ownership for your happiness. By having specific goals that are aggressive and rewarding, you will not only be viewed more positively by those who are interviewing you, but you will have a much richer outlook on life.

8. Problem-Solving

Companies want more from their employees than people who show up just to punch a clock. Employers expect their workers to be both doers and problem-solvers. Whether you are an assembly-line worker, a supervisor, or a vice president, managers want employees that solve problems and come up with new ideas.

Some employers even offer incentive bonuses to employees who generate recommendations that save the company money. Demonstrating qualities in the interview that show you are a problem-solver will give you an edge in your interviewing. Managers want people who solve problems instead of creating them!

Thus far, we have discussed the importance of preparation for every opportunity and identified the eight characteristics interviewers want in their ideal candidates. Now, it's time to go into detail about how you can best prepare for perhaps the most important job-hunting opportunity of all: the job interview!

4 Steps to Winning Preparation: Job Interviews

For the remainder of this chapter I am going to share with you four of the best ways to prepare for your interviews. If you follow these steps, you will interview to win and get the job of your dreams!

1. Research prospective companies and industries.
2. Answer 65 of the most common job-interviewing questions.
3. Practice, practice, practice.
4. Review a final interview checklist.

1. Research Prospective Companies and Industries

When countries go to war, one of the first things military leaders will do is to learn the enemy. They study their strengths, their weaknesses and their surroundings. Then, they develop a plan of attack. The goal of the battle plan is simple: to win!

Many of these same principles can be applied to your job search. To win, you need to learn the strengths and weakness of your targeted employers and understand their surroundings (industry). Armed with this knowledge, you can develop a winning plan of attack for your job interviews and any other job-hunting opportunity that might arise.

There are multiple resources you can use to get as much information as possible on the companies and industries in which you are interested. The more you know about the company and its industry, the better you will perform when it comes to crunch time.

Start Your Research By Using the Internet

The Internet is timely, easy to use, and makes information very accessible. There are many places you can visit on the Web for free to find information that will be helpful in your research.

Company Websites: Most major companies provide a wealth of information on their company Websites. Typically, they provide information such as their mission statement, financial results, products and services, company history, and as mentioned before, sometimes, they even post employment opportunities.

Yahoo.com: On Yahoo.com there is a link called "Finance." This link takes you to an awesome part of their site that provides recent news and financial information about *public* companies and their competition. They also offer extensive information about stock performance and analyst recommendations. They even have a message board that often provides valuable insight into the company that is not found anywhere else.

Vault.com: On Vault.com there is both general and financial information about most large companies. It also has a message board that employees use anonymously. Employees either vent frustrations or give compliments on this board. I have found many of these conversations on *www.vault.com* to be pretty accurate.

There Are Plenty of Other Resources

Your local library: There you have access to company annual reports, *Moody's, Standard & Poors, The Wall Street Journal, Barron's,* and *Investor's Business Daily.* These are all excellent resources to find information about your prospective employers.

Company receptionists and investor kits: Besides the Internet and library, the company itself is a great place to find valuable information. I always find secretaries and receptionists to be extremely helpful. They usually have plenty of company information right at their fingertips.

If the company is publicly traded, an even better resource is the investor relations department. Just call and ask them to send you an investor's kit. This kit typically contains the most recent financial reports, press releases, and new product brochures, all of which provide valuable information to use in establishing rapport during the interview.

Full-service stockbrokers: If you can't get through to a company's investor relations department, then full-service brokerage houses are also fantastic places to get information. If you have an account with a full-service broker, just call him or her and ask that he or she provide you with research reports about the company interviewing you.

These reports usually contain detailed information about the company's financials, products, and competitors.

Company advertisements: Advertisements show how companies position themselves in the market. Some companies focus on being the cheapest price while others tout their quality and customer service. Advertisements also provide valuable insight into company products, services, and culture.

Newspapers and other business publications: As we discussed earlier in the book, publications such as your local newspaper and business publications may have articles highlighting your prospective employers. Not only can you use these articles to identify job opportunities, you can also use them to come up with questions and comments for your interviews. Often, mentioning a recent article is a great way to break the ice in an interview, especially if it is positive news.

One Goal of Research Is to Know More Than Your Competition

Whether you actually use all of the previously mentioned sources of information or a small subset, the knowledge you gain will help you succeed during your interviews. One of the keys to researching the company is to be able to position how you can help the company achieve its business goals and objectives.

When you can tie together your strengths with your knowledge of the company you are interviewing with, you create a knot that will be very difficult for your competition to untie.

Focus on What Is Important

With all of this information in mind, what should you know and remember? Focus on company financials, products, target markets (customers), challenges, competition, and industry trends.

Is the company a leader in the industry? Have sales increased year to year? Is the firm profitable? What are its best-selling products? What are the profit margins? Is the company conservative or a risk-taker? Does the company have a lot of long-term debt, or do they have cash in the bank? Are there recent government regulations or actions that may have affected the industry?

This information will be extremely useful throughout the interview and makes a great rapport builder. For instance, if you are interviewing for a position at a bank, you could start out the conversation with, "How has the Federal Reserve's action to change the discount rate affected your deposits?"

If you are interviewing for a computer company, you could ask, "In such a highly competitive market where computers are becoming more of a commodity, how has your company continued to grow profits while others have failed?"

Every Annual Report Has a Mission Statement

Companies conduct their operations and form their corporate culture based on the philosophies found in the mission statement. By showing how your skills and talents can help the company achieve their mission, you will convey the message that you will be a valuable addition to the team.

Mission statements also provide great insight into a company's values and beliefs. You can incorporate into the interview how you complement these values. This will also help you establish rapport with interviewers.

Identify Company Strengths and Weaknesses

When you can relate how your skills can augment a company's strengths and how your expertise can help them overcome their weaknesses, you become a much more valuable commodity.

For example, the company interviewing you may be successful because of its team approach. People may be compensated by profit sharing to increase productivity and cost-effectiveness. In this case, you could focus on how you are a great team player and how you have led teams to success in your previous job.

Conversely, a company may have weaknesses in certain areas. Perhaps they are interviewing you to eliminate one of these weaknesses. Maybe they need more expertise in selling to large accounts and you have Fortune 1000 experience. Focus on how you can help them by bringing new experience and proven success to the table.

2. Answer the 65 Most Common Job-Interviewing Questions

You have studied the company and you have convinced yourself that you are the most qualified person for this job. You are now ready for the interview, right? No, not quite. You're only halfway through the preparation phase. The next area of preparation is to anticipate and prepare answers for the most commonly asked job-interviewing questions.

Brainstorm on all of the possible questions you think hiring managers will ask you during your interviews. Once you have a list of possible questions, then jot down how you should answer them.

Shortly, I will share with you 65 of the most prevalent questions interviewers will ask, along with some sample answers. When you do your brainstorming session, include these questions. Then, use my mock-up responses as a guide for coming up with your own answers to these questions. Tailor your answers to *your* strengths. After all, interviewers will be interviewing *you*, not *me*. Let's dive in!

1. "Why are you interested in this position?"

Example:

The job description is a perfect match for my skills and aspirations. This is a win-win opportunity. I know I can be a great asset to your company and believe that my successes will be rewarded.

This question separates the contenders from the pretenders. Here, a boss wants someone enthusiastic and who is a go-getter. If candidates answer this question without conviction, then most likely they will not perform well on the job. However, if they are energetic and give a well-thought-out response to the question, they are well positioned to succeed.

2. "What are your greatest strengths?"

Example:

One of my best strengths is that I am a team player. Whether it takes a willingness to learn or a willingness to work until 10 p.m. to complete a project, I am going to do what it takes to make the company successful.

This answer should be tailored toward the interviewer's ideal candidate. If the interviewer is looking for someone who is competitive and street-smart, then list those as key strengths. If the interviewer is looking for a team player with proven experience, then focus on those strengths.

At the beginning of every interview you should either ask, "If you had the ideal candidate for this position, what kind of qualities and characteristics would you look for?" or "What are some of the qualities of your top performers?" By asking one of these questions early on in the interview, you will know the areas you should focus on.

3. "What is your biggest weakness?"

Example #1:

Because I am a team player, I can sometimes work too hard. There have been times when I had to step back and relax a little more.

Example #2:

Being too hard on myself when I fall short of my own expectations...even though they are typically higher than what others expect of me.

This question helps interviewers determine how you will handle difficult situations. It also provides insight both into the candidate's weaknesses as well as the candidate's integrity.

You would be amazed at how many people air dirty laundry when faced with this question. I have had people tell me their biggest weaknesses are "dealing with pressure" or "dealing with colleagues"—both of those are no-no's. Every job has pressures and difficult situations.

In addition, the intent of this question is to make you think and to demonstrate your ability to turn a negative into a positive. No boss likes negative feedback. The way this question is answered can tell a great deal about you and whether you could be positive employee or a potential problem.

Notice how in the previous answers, I turned negatives into *positives* for the company. I know everyone has weaknesses. I have plenty myself. But I didn't want to hear about these in the interview and neither will your interviewers. Instead, interviewers want to hear a positive response such as working too hard. If you demonstrate the ability to think positively, even in a negative situation, you will score valuable points in the interview.

4. "Why do you feel you are right for this position?"

Example:

You mentioned you are looking for someone that is motivated with a proven track record. With my tenacity and previous experience as _____, I can step in and make an immediate contribution.

This is the ultimate question for you to be able to sell yourself. If you did a good job probing into what the interviewer is looking for in the ideal candidate, you can tailor your answer, go for the close, and get the offer.

The interviewer expects you to be confident in answering this question and wants to be sold on *you*, so I recommend being assertive—even borderline aggressive—and proud of your efforts. This is where you can really snag the job.

5. "Can you give me the highlights of your resume?"

Example:

During my years as an accountant, I have consistently helped the company reduce expenses, make deadlines, and increase efficiencies.

Many interviewers don't have time to study resumes. Sometimes, they spend as little as 15–30 seconds. Typically, the interviewer will have seen at least 20-30 resumes before getting to yours. At this point, the interviewer's brain starts to feel as mushy as instant oatmeal.

By asking you for the highlights of your resume, the interviewer is most likely admitting that he or she didn't have the time to read your resume. But that's okay. This is a great opportunity to sell your talents.

You can use the resume as an outline of your credentials. Just like overhead slides help a professional speaker stay on track during a speech, your resume can keep you focused on what it is you want to emphasize during the interview.

This question also allows you to provide editorial on the most salient points on your resume. Prepare to discuss the key items you think would be most beneficial. Be sure you translate how your key selling points will benefit the company. Only comment on those areas of your resume that are most relevant to the opportunity at hand.

6. "Tell me about yourself."

Example:

I am a motivated person who always gives 110 percent and strives for success. I enjoy challenges. With my personality you won't have to waste a lot of management cycles micromanaging me: I tend to always be harder on myself than any boss.

This is the ultimate cop-out question! Interviewers use this question when they are not prepared and can't think of anything else to ask. Basically, in asking this question, interviewers are trying to figure out how similar you are to them. When I interview people, I look for people who were the most similar in *personality* and *drive* to me. So in answering the question, provide information that interviewers can relate to and find interesting.

One way to stimulate the attention level of interviewers is to look at the things they have in their offices. If they have certificates and awards hanging on the walls, most likely they are very confident and competitive and are looking for someone similar. People like this have egos the size of Texas. It is a good idea to stroke those egos a bit.

If they have subtle furniture and pictures of their family on their desks, they may be more down-to-earth and looking for someone with solid values and a strong work ethic.

Is the office decor modern or old fashioned? Are there fish plaques, sports trophies, or article reprints on the wall? These kinds of things give insight into the types of people interviewing you. People hire candidates with similar values, viewpoints, and motivations as themselves.

Keep your answer to this or any question to 90 seconds or less!

To answer the "Tell me about yourself" question, use the first few seconds to provide some of the personal background strengths that you identified in your personal strength worksheet. Then, in the next several seconds, focus on your personal skills and experiences; in the final 20 seconds, summarize your personal attributes with your work-related strengths and relate that to a tangible benefit interviewers can digest.

7. "Why did you choose your major?"

Example:

I chose marketing because I enjoy working with others. I have always been fascinated by how different companies position themselves and their products. Marketing allows me to capitalize on my unique blend of creativity, hard work, and ability to relate.

This is an interesting question because it gives insight into how a person thinks. Some have said, "Well, my parents were in this field, so it seemed right." I have also heard answers such as, "I wasn't sure what I wanted, and this sounded good." I am constantly amazed at the terrible answers I hear in response to this question.

Interviewers want someone who put thought into this decision and looked years into the future. Have a well-thought-out answer to this question. Otherwise, you could knock yourself out of the running.

8. "What are your interests?"

Example:

I enjoy playing and watching competitive sports such as baseball, football, and golf.

As a sales manager, I asked this question because I wanted people who were competitive. I looked for people who thrived on competition for their interests. Competitive individuals usually made very good salespeople. If the person played sports, I asked them if they played for fun or if they played to win. I always looked for someone who competed to win.

Other interviewers may look for totally different interests. One interest that is good is traveling, because jobs often entail that. Even casino gambling is acceptable if the interviewer is looking for a risk-taker. The key is to be honest but share only relevant interests.

While sales managers like risk-takers, administrative managers or plant-floor managers may not. Thus, make sure your interests are in line with the opportunity. Like so many other questions, interviewers ask this question to see how similar you are to them.

If the interviewer has a golf-ball paperweight on the desk and a picture of Arnold Palmer on the wall and you like golf, then mention that golf is one of your passions. If the person has several pictures of family on the desk, declare how one of your interests is doing things with the family.

Answer this question in a way that demonstrates that you've got a lot in common with the person interviewing you. However, be honest! If you don't play golf, don't say that you do. Lying in an interview will always backfire.

9. "What are your short- and long-term goals?"

Example:

My short-term goal is to obtain a position with a company that will challenge me and allow me to grow. One of my long-term goals is to grow with the company and move into management. I feel that in order to be a successful leader, I first have to start out in the trenches.

This question elaborates on your thought process and whether or not you are an employee who can be counted on for the long haul. If your ultimate goal is to become a doctor, but currently you are interviewing for a paralegal position, you probably won't get the job.

However, if you are interviewing to become an accountant and your short-term goal is to perfect your accounting skills while your long-term goal is to be a partner, that makes sense.

You don't have to say that you want to go into management. It is perfectly okay to say, "My long-term goal is to remain in a position where I can best contribute to the success of the company while being motivated, challenged, and rewarded." However, you'd better have a darned good idea about what you want and why you want it.

A few months ago, a potential client approached me and asked for help on her resume. I looked at her resume. But I couldn't tell by the resume what kind of job she wanted. So I asked her what she wanted to do for a living.

She said she wanted to go into insurance. I said, "Okay. What do you want to do in insurance?" She said, "I am not sure...perhaps to process claims." This was strange because on her resume it said she just completed law school.

I said to her, "Please don't take offense, but why would you want to go into claims processing when you just spent all of that money on a law degree? That job pays a fraction of what a lawyer can earn." She said, "I am not sure I want to be a lawyer. I don't think I like law. I just want a job right now."

I was incredulous. I wanted to do what Moe of the Three Stooges did in so many episodes...bang my head against the wall. I couldn't believe what I had just heard. This person just wasted all that time and money getting a degree in a field she didn't like...and in which she didn't want to work. In reality, she had no idea what she really wanted.

Needless to say, I tactfully told her that I couldn't help her with her resume until she figured out what she really wanted to do. I would have been happy to help her explore her options but before I had the chance, she stormed out in tears. She left so fast that the wind she created caused papers to fly off my table.

Was I too critical with her? Many would think so. However, I will tell you right now: I was not. When you are in an interview, you had better be able to articulate your goals and objectives and how your prior experience and credentials will be of benefit for you in achieving those goals.

If she told me she had always wanted to process claims, and that her law degree would be helpful in determining the legal legitimacy of claims, that would have been a different story. Then, she could've articulated how she could help save an insurance company thousands of dollars by being able to spot potentially fraudulent claims. Instead, she had no idea why she got her degree and was not interested in figuring out how she could use her degree to her advantage.

Don't find yourself in this situation. Have some idea of the direction in which you want to go. Don't expect interviewers to help you figure out your goals and desires. Only you truly know what you want to do.

10. "Tell me how your friends/family would describe you."

Example:

They would describe me as a competitive person who has a unique ability to succeed. Whether in school, sports, or on the job, they would describe me as a person upon whom you could always depend to give 110 percent and come out ahead.

This is a great way for people to describe themselves from a unique perspective. This question gives valuable insight into how candidates feel others perceive them. How you answer this question demonstrates how you truly feel about yourself.

11. "What interested you in ____(chemical engineering)?"

Example:
I have always enjoyed the thrill of solving complex problems and discovering new solutions.

Every profession has unique and exciting facets. What motivates a chemical engineer can be totally different from what inspires a teacher or police officer. The key is for you to be able to articulate why you chose your vocation and to show passion for your choice.

Having been a sales manager, in interviews I looked for people who said that they were stimulated by money, competition, and the thrill of victory. If they didn't say one or more of these things, I would not hire them. Any good salesperson is motivated by money and shouldn't be in the business if they are not.

However, if you are interviewing for a position other than sales, you may need a totally different response. If you interviewed for a nursing or teaching position and you said that money and competition motivate you, most likely, you would be bounced immediately. Customize your responses to the interviewer and targeted position.

12. "Using single words, tell me your three greatest strengths and one weakness."

Example:
Competitive, successful, creative, and workaholic.

This question forces candidates to be concise and think quickly on their feet. Again, this provides valuable insight into the mindset of the individual. This question is also a great test of your listening skills. If you answer this question with multiple-word descriptions, it signals that you did not pay attention to the question, and demonstrates that you don't listen very well.

It is my belief (and most interviewers will agree) that if someone is not a good listener, that person will not be a good employee. So if someone asks you to describe yourself using one-word adjectives, answer in single words only.

13. "What motivates you to succeed?"

Example:
Seeing a challenge and conquering it.

Motivation is key to success for any job. If your motivation does not fit what the type of motivation for which the interviewer is looking, then there is a mismatch and you'll be kindly escorted to the door. Make sure your motivation is in line with what the interviewer would expect for the job.

If the tables were turned and you were the interviewer instead of the interviewee, what kind of motivation would you expect in the ideal candidate? For a research person or a scientist a great motivation would be something such as, "I love the thrill of solving tough problems...it's almost like a game to me." What would be the proper motivation for the position you are interviewing for?

14. "What is your ideal job?" or "Describe your ideal job."
Example:

My ideal job is one that utilizes my talents to the fullest and allows me to grow and be rewarded as I contribute to the success of the organization.

Here, the candidate should state aspects of the job at hand. If the candidate's concept of the ideal job does not match the job at hand, then the interviewer will think that the candidate will not work out and move on to the next interview.

When stating your ideal job, make sure you include items from the job description of the position you are interviewing for. It's hard to hit a bull's-eye when you can't see the dartboard. The job description gives you a good target for which to aim.

15. "Describe traits you want in an ideal company and job."
Example:

I want to work for a company that does not tolerate mediocrity and one that is growing, profitable, and an industry leader—such as yours. I want a job that is challenging and where I can make an immediate contribution.

To answer this question, again, relate qualities of the company and position that you know to be true for the opportunity at hand. If there is a match, then that is great. If not, it's on to the next candidate. Use the job description for guidance and also look to the company's mission statement. The mission statement often offers valuable insight you can use to answer this question.

16. "What qualities do you feel are important to be successful in _____?"
Example:

A successful customer service representative has to be resourceful, a quick-thinker, and a problem-solver.

Here, you want to be able to articulate what the interviewer feels is important to succeed. There are many right answers to this question. It depends on the job and the personality of the interviewer. Be truthful with yourself and your interviewer.

Believe it or not, interviewers can usually see right through fabrications. If a shy and reserved person told me the keys to success were to be outgoing and gregarious, I immediately flushed the candidate because they did not exemplify what they were saying. Don't ever lie!

17. "What previous experience has helped you develop the skills necessary for this job?"

Example:

On my previous job as _____(an administrative assistant), often I had to work with irate customers when my boss was not around. As a result, I was pushed through the school of hard knocks to learn how to ease customer tension and make quick decisions to protect valuable customer relationships.

If you do not have previous *position-relevant* experience, then relate some other experience that could demonstrate skills necessary for the job. An example could be as farfetched as convincing a date to go to a hockey game over a movie. That would demonstrate selling skills. For an accounting job, you could mention how you were the treasurer for a club at school or that you handled the finances of your condominium association.

When I interviewed candidates, I immediately disqualified anyone who admitted that they had no position-relevant experience and could not come up with any experiences that could somehow relate to the opportunity at hand. Good employees have to think quickly on their feet. If a candidate did not provide an answer to a question in a timely and sincere manner, I immediately rejected that person.

18. "Give me an example of your teamwork and leadership."

Example:

As project leader for _____(final assembly team) I held a contest to see who could come up with the best idea to improve quality. This resulted in employees providing valuable feedback and feeling they were a part of the team. Perhaps most importantly, as a result, we reduced defects by 15 percent.

In most positions, teamwork is critical to success. Typically, interviewers want team players. In fact, when I hired employees, I usually wanted the best of both worlds. I looked for team players. However, I also wanted people who competed to win on an individual basis.

Be careful in your answers. You need a delicate balance. You don't want the interviewer to think you are too dependent on others. Yet, you don't want them to think you are too independent or a "wild duck" either. The key is to demonstrate that you possess both talents and that you can go with the flow.

19. "What was your greatest challenge and how did you overcome it?"

Example:

My greatest challenge was handling a very emotional employee. I overcame this challenge by finding out what motivated her and discovered how to channel her emotions into positive results. As it turned out, all I had to do was to simply tell her each day how much I appreciated her efforts and how valuable she was to the team. As a result, her performance substantially improved and she became one of my best employees.

This question provides insight on how tested a person has been, and what that candidate perceives to be a big challenge. This question really separates the winners from the losers. Poor candidates have a tough time of thinking of a challenge and are feeble in their answers.

I looked for tough and thought-provoking challenges—ones where the person had to think beyond the bounds to solve. If someone brought up a weak challenge as being a big deal, I lost interest quickly.

20. "Have you received any special recognition?"

Example #1:

I won an internal quality award.

Example #2:

I made the dean's list.

As a hiring manager, I did not settle for mediocre people. I expected someone to have received some sort of recognition. Good employees usually strive for recognition. If not, there is something wrong.

Recognition can be anything from making the dean's list to winning a contest to receiving a plaque in honor of raising money for a charity. If someone can demonstrate an ability to achieve recognition, most likely, that person will be a strong and hard-working employee.

If you have not yet been formally recognized for your efforts, then do something to gain some sort of recognition. This can be as simple as helping with a charitable function or mentoring a child. One activity I have done in the past is to call a local school district and offer to be a guest lecturer or teacher. Teaching kids is fun and rewarding.

I have developed a tremendous respect for teachers after volunteering to be a guest lecturer. Plus, volunteering is a great way to give back to the community.

21. "Why should I hire you over other candidates?"

Example:

Because of my competitiveness, proven success, and unique ability to learn, I will make an immediate contribution to the continued success of your organization. Your company already has enough risks every day—why risk hiring someone who is less than the best? I know I will make you proud to have hired me.

When I asked this question, I wanted the person to be a bit cocky. This is where the person can really go for the close. (Because I hired for sales, I looked for people who knew how to get the order.) I also looked for them to repeat some of the traits I noted were important during the interview. That, again, showed good listening skills.

Other managers may have different "hot-buttons." Put yourself in the shoes of the person interviewing you. If you were the interviewer, what would you want to see in an ideal candidate? What is it about you that would cause an interviewer to want to hire you versus someone else? What qualities and characteristics really define and differentiate you?

22. "Do you have any questions?"

To answer this question you should ask questions that demonstrate thought and creativity. You also want to ask assumptive questions. Assumptive questions are questions that convey a message that you expect to be hired and that you expect to be a major contributor to the team.

Example #1:

How do you reward top performers?

Example #2:

Is there a cap on earnings for top performers?

Example #3:

Looking out a year from now, if you were to give me a perfect review, what will I have accomplished?

Questions like these exude confidence. These assumptive questions illustrate that you are a positive individual and demonstrate that you are confident you will get the job. Top candidates always ask at least a couple of assumptive questions.

If candidates didn't ask assumptive questions during the interview or asked ones that were not thoughtful, I usually rejected them. I expected thought-provoking questions about company strengths, employee turnover, raise policies, and visibility for top performers.

Don't ask questions about benefits. Save that for when you get the job offer. You can ask HR those types of questions. You don't want to ask questions that say "what's in it for me." Instead, you want to ask questions that show "what's in it for them."

23. "What did you earn last year?" or "What are your compensation expectations?"

Both of these are very difficult questions to answer. You must be very careful. If you give too much information, you will paint yourself into a corner and limit your potential salary. To answer these questions, use either a categorical response or a "ballpark" figure. Personally, I prefer a categorical response such as the following.

Categorical Example:

I am confident that I will be a top performer for your company. I expect to be compensated at a level equivalent to other top performers in your organization.

Ballpark Example:

Last year, I was in the ballpark of the mid-100s.

Notice that in the categorical response, not only was I somewhat evasive (so I didn't limit my options), I demonstrated confidence that I expect to be a top performer. Now, that's a much more powerful way to answer the question!

Additional Commonly Asked Questions

What follows are some additional questions you will likely see in your interviews. There are no example answers to these questions because I want you to exercise your mind. There is an old saying that is quite appropriate here: "If you give a man a fish, you feed him for a day. If you teach a man to fish, you feed him for a lifetime."

Taking this into account, I want you to learn how to fish and start preparing on your own. Answer these questions positively...and with confidence. Following, I'll give you an example to show you how.

24. "Why are you looking to leave your current position?"

Example of a *good* answer:

I am at the stage in my career where I want a job that is more challenging and rewarding.

Example of a *bad* answer:

I am leaving because I hate my boss and my company is full of losers.

Do Not Provide Proprietary Information

Unfortunately, sometimes companies interview people from the competition just to gain proprietary knowledge, not because they are actually considering hiring someone. Plus, most interviewers look negatively upon individuals that provide information that they shouldn't give.

Providing confidential information is unethical. Proprietary or confidential information can be something as simple as telling them how many shifts a factory is running...to the cost of goods...or the number of people in your division.

Instead of giving exact figures, try to use percentages. If you saved more than $50,000 in expenses, if that is proprietary information, then say something such as, *"Reduced expenses by 15 percent."* Rather than providing specific numbers, try to focus on percentages such as, *"Increased sales 120 percent in my territory"* or *"Reduced the cost of production by 33 percent."*

General Questions

25. Why are you looking to leave your current position?
26. What was your greatest accomplishment at _____ company?
27. How does your company compete against ours?
28. Have you ever been asked to do something unethical? If so, how did you handle it?
29. What would your last boss say were the areas that you needed to improve upon the most?
30. What de-motivates you or discourages you?
31. What is your definition of success?
32. What was your biggest disappointment?
33. What do you feel it takes to have a successful career?

34. What do you like the most about your current position?
35. What do you like least about your current position?
36. What is the toughest decision you have ever made? Tell me about it.
37. Can you explain why you were not employed during _____ period of time?
38. Why did you choose to go into _____ industry?
39. Why did you choose to work for _____ company?
40. Is there ever a business situation where it is okay to lie about something?
41. Are you willing to accept a lower salary?
42. Why would someone with your knowledge and expertise want to interview for this job opportunity?

Leadership Questions

43. When in a group setting, what is your typical role?
44. Have you ever had to fire anyone? What caused you to take this action? How did you handle it?
45. Have you ever held a leadership role? How did you motivate people to succeed in that role?
46. What was your most difficult situation? What did you learn from it?

Teamwork Questions

47. How do you feel about working in a team environment?
48. Can you describe how you helped the morale of the team and motivated them to succeed?
49. Have you been in team situations where not everyone carried their fair share of the workload? If so, how did you handle the situation?
50. How would you handle a situation where the boss asked you to do something that you did not agree with?
51. Which do you enjoy more: working as a part of a team or by yourself?

Problem-Solving Questions

52. Can you give me an example of a difficult work situation and how you handled it?
53. How do you prioritize when you are given too many tasks to accomplish?
54. Can you give me an example of a time when you had to conform to a policy you didn't like? How did you handle it?
55. Can you tell me about a time when you went above and beyond the call of duty to get a job done?
56. Why are manhole covers round?

I know this question sounds crazy, but one of my previous managers used to always ask it. Later in this book I will tell you how to handle this question, but first, try it on your own.

Drive and Motivational Questions

57. Tell me about one of your most significant accomplishments.
58. What was your favorite job and why?
59. What have you done to make yourself more proficient in X?
60. Can you give me an example of when you showed initiative?
61. Can you give me an example of a time when you motivated others to succeed?

Organizational and Strategic Questions

62. Do you set goals for yourself? How often?
63. Tell me about an important goal you set for yourself and how you accomplished it.
64. How do you start your workday?
65. What do you want to do in five years? Ten years?

Now Comes the Fun Part

You need to answer each of these questions in your own words, along with any other questions you might have come up with in your brainstorming session. I have given you examples and techniques to answer these questions. Tailor your answers to your areas of interest, to your personality, and to your strengths.

The questions I shared with you are based on my own personal and real-life experience. They are either questions I have been asked myself or questions I liked to ask when I interviewed people. Ultimately your experience may differ, but these questions will give you a great head start in your preparation for winning job interviews.

Questions will vary from interviewer to interviewer, industry to industry, and company to company. But I guarantee that you will hear at least a couple of these questions in your next interview.

When you write down answers to these questions, I suggest that you jot down a couple of keywords that will help you remember how to respond to each inquiry. Finally, if you want even more potential interview questions, once again go to your favorite search engine on the Web. Type in search phrases such as "free sample job interview questions," "sample interview questions," and "job interview questions."

Preparing in Advance

Preparing in advance will help you in almost any situation, be it interviews, networking, or making cold calls. So, spend a few moments taking another look at the questions I provided. Answer them as if you were in an interview. Mold the answers to your skills, experience, and personality. And, if you haven't already done so, take the time to come up with some additional questions and answers on your own.

Adapt your answers to any situation. People hire people whom they like and those like them. You want interviewers to be able to relate to you on both a professional and personal level. That is why it is so important to develop a strong rapport with interviewers. By having flexibility in your answers, you are better able to relate to anyone you meet and interviewers will be much more inclined to offer you a job.

3. Practice, Practice, Practice!

There's an old story about a tourist who asks a stranger on the street, "What's the best way to get to Carnegie Hall?" The stranger answers, "Practice, practice, practice."

At this point you may be feeling a bit overwhelmed. I know that seeing all of these questions can be somewhat intimidating. But you will be surprised at how easy it is to prepare once you just dive in and do it.

The more prepared you are, the more confident you will be, and the better you will perform in the interview. However, before I leave this topic, I cannot neglect to mention the most crucial part of preparation—practice.

Role-Play With Your Friends

Have friends play the role of potential interviewers. Do not use your family. They will be too easy on you. You want the role player to be someone who will not hesitate to provide objective feedback and criticism when necessary.

Give the role player the list of possible job-interviewing questions. To simulate spontaneity, you can write down questions on index cards and put them in a large bowl. You can then have the person playing the role of the interviewer randomly pick questions out of the bowl to ask you.

When practicing, act out the interview as if it were for real. Afterwards, get feedback. Tell your friend not to be afraid to be critical. Better you bomb out with your friend than the interviewer!

Practice the interview until you are confident you can get the job. Start the role-play by knocking on the door and entering the room. Do not break out of your role—this will hurt your concentration and will not properly simulate the interview. After the interview, you can discuss how you performed. But try to complete the simulated interview first.

Record Your Performance

Another great way to review your practice is to record yourself using audio or video. By listening to yourself on audio or viewing yourself on video, you can really identify your strengths and weaknesses. Maybe you say the word "um" once every 10 words. If you have a video, you might notice poor posture or a bad habit such as wiping your brow or scratching your nose.

By recognizing a weakness in practice, you can work to overcome that weakness prior to the interview. The more you practice and prepare, the better you will do in the interview.

One final note: You can never practice too much. Professional golfers will hit buckets of balls every day to continue to improve and perfect their skills. In fact, I have heard that many golf professionals practice even after finishing a tournament.

Work on perfecting your skills daily. This can be done even as you are driving your car. Talk out loud to yourself and practice your answers. You will be amazed at how this will sharpen your skills.

Try Practicing With a Mirror

One of the ways that I have practiced for my television interviews is to stand in front of a mirror and pretend that the mirror is the person interviewing me. By looking in the mirror, I can work on my smile, posture, attitude, and appearance. It is amazing how much I learned about myself in doing this exercise. Try practicing in front of a mirror...and watch how your skills will improve.

4. Review a Final Interview Checklist

Okay, now you are thoroughly prepared for the interview. You have researched the company, perfected your answers to possible questions, and you have practiced. You are almost there. But there are a few final things you need to do to be prepared for your job-hunting endeavors.

√   Get the Correct Spelling and Pronunciation

Before any interview, know how each interviewer spells his or her name, and how the name is pronounced. Correct spelling is imperative for thank you notes. Proper pronunciation is essential to having winning interviews. Do you like it when someone mispronounces your name? It's a sign of disrespect. Interviewers don't like it, either.

If you are not sure how a name is pronounced, ask the receptionist or administrative assistant prior to your interview. Also, make sure you know the gender of the person as well. Just the other day, I had an interview for a potential speaking engagement. The person interviewing me was named Morgan. I figured with a name like that, the person would be a woman. I was wrong! Other such names are Alex, Jaime, Joe, Pat, and Tyler.

√   Get Directions

If you get lost and arrive late, you will give a poor first impression. The Internet has many sites you can visit to get a map and directions on how to get to your interview. You can also call the company receptionist for directions. Make sure that you have the correct address.

Don't just go by what is in the phonebook. Call to be sure. A friend of mine once went to the wrong location. The company moved, but it wasn't reflected in the latest phonebook. Needless to say, he missed the interview and lost the job opportunity. Confirm the address!

If you live close by, drive by the location a day or two before your interview. That way you will know for sure how to get there. Sometimes online driving instructions can vary quite a bit from site to site. It is always best to be safe rather than sorry.

√   **Pick Out Your Interview Clothes in Advance**

By planning ahead, you can concentrate solely on the interview. Plus, you can avoid embarrassing mishaps. Years ago, I went to put on a suit the morning of an out-of-town interview and I discovered the zipper of my pants was broken. I had to get a safety pin from the front desk of the hotel to keep my fly shut.

Needless to say, I was so worried about my fly busting open, that I totally bombed the interview. Now I check my clothes at least a day or two before any important event.

You do not want to panic on the day of your interview because your favorite interview suit is at the cleaners, is dirty, or has a button missing. Hang your clothes on a doorknob at least a day or two before any interview so if something is wrong, you have enough time to rectify the situation.

√   **Plan to Arrive Early**

Arrange your schedule so you can show up for the interview at least 15 minutes early. That way you allow yourself some leeway for any traffic delays you might incur. If you arrive really early, find a local coffee shop and relax for a few minutes. You can never look bad by being a few minutes early.

Being late to an interview, however, will destroy your chances of success. If you plan on being late, then you might as well chew garlic before the interview, too. I don't care if you get struck by a train and neither will your interviewer! Being early gives you the chance to either get extra face time with interviewers or additional time to learn more about the company and its culture. Show up a little early and create that positive first impression.

**Secret #8: Prepare for Every Opportunity
—Checklist Summary—**

√   Any person you talk to throughout your job search may hold the keys to your next opportunity.

√   There are eight traits of ideal candidates.

√   Research your prospective companies and industries.

√   Create a list of possible interview questions.

√   Write down answers to those questions.

√   Practice, practice, practice.

√   Always go through a final interview checklist.

*Interviewers know within the first few seconds if they are interested in you.
Be prepared!*

Secret #9

Interview to Win

⦿ The five rules of successful interviewing.

Welcome to the *interview*, one of the most exciting aspects of the entire job search! This is the part of the job-hunting process that separates the winners from the losers. In this chapter, I am going to share with you the five rules of successful interviewing. Follow these rules and you will *interview to win!*

The Five Rules of Successful Interviewing

1. Visualize success.
2. Maintain a positive attitude.
3. Dress to win.
4. Master the three phases of a winning job interview.
5. Have fun.

1. Visualize Success

Back in Secret #1, we talked about something so important that it necessitates repeating. In order to be successful, you have to visualize success! Before each interview, close your eyes and visualize the outcome you want. If you are having a phone interview, imagine the interviewer saying to you, "You are just the type of candidate we are looking for. I am going to recommend you for a second interview."

If you are in a final in-person interview, picture the interviewer standing up from the desk with a big smile and gleaming eyes, shaking your hand and saying, "You are exactly the type of person I am looking for, I would like to make you an offer. Congratulations!"

Wow! Now that's powerful. Usually people envision the worst happening when they go on an interview. Then, they wonder why their expectations came true. You are a winner. Visualize success and you will achieve it!

Go for the Win

In sports you may have heard someone describe a losing team as having "played not to lose" rather than playing to win. In interviewing, it's natural to have this tendency because of the anxiety involved. However, if you approach the interview playing not to lose rather than interviewing to win, you *will* lose.

Don't be timid; be confident. Take some risks. No interview is life or death. Just remember everything happens for a reason. Don't put so much pressure on yourself. Have fun and go for victory.

Make Yourself Stand out From the Crowd

Imagine that you are talking to several strangers a day. Who will you remember? You will recall those who are unique and leave you with either a very positive or very negative impression. If you are stiff, boring, and seem in pain, you will be shown the door, not the job. However, if you are confident, exciting, and fun to be around, you will generate interest and enthusiasm. You will leave interviewers with a thirst for more.

Typically, interviewers will ask each candidate the same core questions. They will be looking for specific answers. If you do not answer the first couple of questions with what interviewers want to hear, the interview is over—you have lost!

Ask the Magical Question

Imagine playing darts. It is hard enough to hit a bull's-eye as it is. Now, imagine wearing a blindfold and trying to hit the bull's-eye. How difficult would that be? Hitting the target would be much tougher, right?

Yet, when it comes to interviewing, most people interview blindfolded. Some get lucky and hit a bull's eye. However, most don't and get rejected.

If there's one thing you should remember from this book it should be to *ask the one magical question*, in every interview, that can allow you to take off your blindfold and see your target.

The Magical Question
"If you had your ideal candidate for this position, what kind of qualities and characteristics would that person have?"

That's the magical question. Certainly, there are many ways you can phrase this question. You could say, *"Describe your ideal candidate,"* as well. When interviewers answer this question or a variation of it, they will articulate exactly the core strengths and competencies that they are looking for in their ideal candidates. Knowing this, you can tailor your answers throughout the rest of the interview. Focus on those strengths and competencies that demonstrate why you are indeed the right candidate for the position.

The key is for you to exemplify the traits and the qualities of the interviewer's ideal candidate. Why do you think politicians conduct so many polls? They do this to try to figure out what the voting public wants in candidates they will elect. By asking the interviewers, early in the interview, to describe their ideal candidate, you will know what is important and what to focus on. Armed with this information, you will interview to win!

2. Maintain a Positive Attitude

No matter what I say in this chapter, if you do not feel good about yourself going into the interview, all of your preparation will be for naught. If necessary, read Secret #1 again and remember that you are a *great* person! Whatever the outcome is, every interview offers an opportunity to learn. Each interview in which you participate gets you that much closer to the job you are supposed to have.

Believe in Yourself

If you don't believe in you, neither will your interviewer! A positive attitude is contagious and interviewers thrive on it. Show confidence and enthusiasm.

Imagine for a moment that you're interviewing real estate agents to sell your home. One agent comes in and fumbles through a predetermined presentation. He meekly gloats to you about how his company is #1 in your neighborhood. He doesn't ask you what is important to you in your decision. He just assumes, because his agency is #1, you should go with him.

Next, you interview a woman who walks in and says, "Wow, what a beautiful place. We'll have no problem selling this house. Look at the bathroom...the kitchen...this place is move-in condition. When would you like to list it?"

I don't know about you, but as an interviewer, I would much rather go with the woman who showed genuine excitement about the place...and was confident that it would be no problem to sell it. By far, she had a much more positive attitude and that is likely to help her succeed.

Interviewing Is Like Selling

The best way to sell something is to show confidence and excitement. Go in there and act as if the job is the best thing that could ever happen to you and that you are the best thing that could ever happen to the company that is interviewing you. Communicate the confidence that says that the best decision the interviewer could make is to hire you.

Make interviewers feel good about themselves, their companies, and the opportunities offered. You want interviewers to leave the interview pumped. When interviewers leave an interview jazzed up, it makes it very difficult for any other candidate to win their affection.

For example:

I just want to let you know how much I appreciate you taking your valuable time to meet with me. This position sounds so exciting and your company is the leader in the industry. I know I could make a great contribution to your ongoing success!

Be assertive about yourself. After all, if you don't speak highly of yourself, nobody will. Believe you are great and that any company would be *lucky* to have you as a part of their team.

When you are interviewing, don't put interviewers on a pedestal. If you do, you will be nervous and apprehensive. You have as much choice in this process as they do. No one is telling you what to do. You are your own person. After all, an interviewer may want to hire you on the spot but you might not like the company and choose not to accept their offer.

The most successful business relationships are those based on mutual trust, respect, and equality. When you view yourself as an equal, you will perform at your peak, both in the interview and on the job.

Develop a Personal Mantra

Be confident, have fun and, most of all, *be positive about the contribution you can make!* Repeat to yourself that you are the best candidate out there. Refer back to the ideal job mission statement you created. Believe in your destiny and you will achieve it. The worst that happens is you get bounced from an interview. If your mission is your destiny, then one rejection will not stop you from achieving it.

Having a positive attitude will give you every chance to succeed in the interview and to have a wonderfully fulfilling life! Happiness in life is based not on the events that happen to you, but on how you choose to interpret those events. Look to the positive in every situation and you will achieve success and happiness beyond your wildest dreams.

3. Dress to Win

When you knock on the door, the first thing interviewers see is your appearance. Whether you are dating, job interviewing, or meeting a stranger, first impressions are always important. Greater than 90 percent of all communication is nonverbal. You want to look good. It definitely has a major impact on your chances of getting a job.

Seldom will the way you dress actually get you a job. However, if you don't look good and dress professionally during the interview, you could easily lose one. Dress professionally.

Why is the way you dress so important? Think of flying. If you see the pilot wearing torn blue jeans and a stained white T-shirt, would you feel comfortable flying on that plane? Or would you rather fly with a pilot wearing a clean, freshly pressed blue uniform? Interviewers would rather fly with the pilot wearing the uniform.

Your attire says a lot about you and how you feel about yourself. If you are clean-cut and professional looking, you will make a far greater first impression than if you look as though you just walked out of a racetrack. Don't forget: People remember much more of what they see than what they hear. There's an old saying that says: "A *picture is worth a thousand words*." Need I say more? Dress professionally!

For Men

Wear a Professional and Well-Tailored Suit

The best colors to choose are dark blue, gray, black, or charcoal. The suit should be solid or feature a subtle pinstripe pattern. Loud pinstripes or bold plaids look great at banquets, but not at interviews. The suit fabric should be mostly, if not 100 percent, wool. A small touch of another material can help keep the suit's shape, but should be limited to less than 25 percent of the total suit's composition.

Sport a High Quality and Freshly-Pressed Shirt

The shirt should always be bright white and nicely starched. You can never go wrong with a white, long-sleeved shirt. If you want to wear a blue shirt, save it for when you play poker, not interviewing. Short-sleeved and colored shirts are less formal and not appropriate in the business setting. Save your short-sleeved shirt for the bowling alley.

Choose a Tasteful Tie and Conservative Shoes

The best styles for your tie are either traditional striped, geometric, or paisley. Red is perhaps the most conservative color to choose and yellow still makes for a great power color. Make sure the tie you choose is nicely pressed and free of any stains. You don't want the interviewer spending half the interview wondering if that spot on your tie is spaghetti sauce or soup.

For your shoes, you can never go wrong with a traditional, wing-tipped, or other conservative style of shoe. Make sure your shoes are shined and in good condition. Believe it or not, interviewers will look at whether or not you have shined shoes. Shined shoes present a professional image and demonstrate a good work ethic. If you wear shoes with holes in the sole, or shoes that are scuffed up, you'll convey a negative image.

Don't Overlook Your Socks

I have seen men walk into interviews with cleanly pressed suit and shined shoes, but mismatched socks. To avoid this problem, I suggest keeping on hand a couple of pairs of new, solid-colored socks that are still in the package. That way, you know the color and you know for sure that they match. If you are not sure what color to wear, black socks will go with almost any interview suit.

Make Sure You Are Well Groomed

Your hair should be stylish and short to medium in length. Unless you are interviewing for a creative position such as software development or musician, hair down to your shoulders is not a wise idea. If you have longer hair and do not wish to cut it, tie it back neatly to convey a professional image. Definitely make sure you are clean-shaven. If you have facial hair, keep it trimmed and shaped properly. Hands are also very important in conveying a positive and successful image. Your fingernails should be trimmed and clean or even manicured.

Minimize Any Jewelry

I recommend that you limit the jewelry on your hands to a wedding ring if you are married...and nothing if you are not. Watches are also acceptable, as well as modest tie tacks, tie clips and cuff links. Avoid wearing necklaces, lapel pins, chains, bracelets, and religious jewelry. And whatever you do...do not wear an earring or a nose ring. If you want to work in a coffee shop, maybe you can get away with that. Otherwise, it just isn't appropriate business attire.

For Women

Wear a Professional and Well-Tailored Suit

For more formal positions in industries such as banking, finance, and accounting, wear a skirt suit or a fashionable pant suit. For others, wearing pants with a blazer or sweater top is perfectly acceptable. In selecting the color, you need not limit yourself to solid gray, blue, or black, but do not wear wild patterns.

Try to stay away from long blazers, as often they just are not flattering. If you are wearing a suit with a skirt, keep the skirt at a conservative length. Short skirts do not convey a professional image and can detract from your positive message. The key is to be tastefully stylish yet lean towards the conservative.

Depending on the style of suit you are wearing, you may want to wear either a blouse or a simple shirt. Either way, selection is very important. Your blouse or shirt should be a solid color. If there is a print, it should be tasteful. The shirt or blouse should never be made of a transparent material. Items made of lace or satin should be avoided.

Match Your Outfit With Fashionable Shoes and Hose

Wear shoes that are in "like new" condition and complement your outfit. Heels should be totally in tact. When it comes to hosiery, wear a conservative color or a color that complements the suit. Conservative colors are nude, suntan, taupe, and black. If you wear bright-colored or white hose, it can be distracting to interviewers and take away from your overall professional image.

Sport Accessories That Are Tasteful, Not Distracting

In selecting a handbag or briefcase, choose one that complements your attire. Select one that is small or medium sized and made of leather. Large bags can be unsightly and create an appearance of disorganization. Ideally, choose either a purse or a briefcase, but not both. If you walk in with too much on your shoulders or in your hands, it can become awkward.

Hair, Makeup, and Hands Also Leave an Impression

Hair is a very important component to your overall presentation. Your hair should be manageable and preferably no longer than shoulder length. If your hair is long, you should wear it up or in a manner that is perceived to be stylish and professional. You don't want to look like you just walked out of a beach house or a nightclub.

Makeup should be subtle and tasteful. Don't use too much makeup. A bit of blush and lipstick can be worn to accentuate your features. Depending on your complexion, natural colors such as browns or tans may be best. For your lips, soft reds, corals, and pinks are the best colors. Use your best judgment. Too much makeup can be a detriment and a distraction.

Your hands should be well manicured. Fingernails should be painted either a conservative red, light pink, French style, or with a clear polish. As an interviewer, for some reason, nothing would distract me more than a woman who had fingernails that were either different lengths, strange colors, or improperly manicured.

In fact, when I interviewed musicians for my wedding reception, I rejected one band strictly because the lead singer's nailpolish was peeling off. I didn't want that kind of an image at my wedding. I wanted a band that was professional and cared about their appearance. Your interviewers will too.

Keep Jewelry to a Minimum

If you are engaged or married, feel free to wear your wedding and engagement rings. However, try to avoid wearing other rings. I have seen women in interviews wear a ring on every finger. This just does not convey a professional image. Plus, it is very difficult for either party to give a good handshake, when someone is wearing too many rings. In shaking a person's hand, a firm grip is essential. Too much jewelry can inhibit that.

Earrings can also impact your overall appearance. Too many earrings and extremely large earrings draw attention away from your presentation and message. Finally, do not wear religious jewelry. There is no need to bring religion into the interview. You want interviewers to focus on your skills and talent, not your faith.

Dress for success—not to make a fashion statement. Look professional, like an executive, not a nightclub patron. Dressing well is essential in creating a successful first impression.

For Both Men and Women

Politicians Provide Great Fashion Guidance

Whether you are a man or a woman, one of the best indicators of what to wear on an interview is take note of what the politicians of your gender are wearing in their current public appearances and who is in office at the time of your interview. In the United States, often when a Republican is President, business attire becomes more conservative versus when the Democrats hold power. When in doubt, always err towards conservative.

Freshen Your Breath

Believe it or not, breath contributes to your overall first impression. If your breath smells like garlic, onions, cigarettes, or even coffee, you might offend interviewers. Think about it: Do you feel comfortable when you are talking to a person with bad breath? Prior to the interview, brush your teeth, gargle with mouthwash, and use a long-lasting breath freshener.

Clean Your Car

What kind of car are you driving? Do you have a clean car? If not, clean it before the interview! Interviewers may want to walk you to your car. You want to leave them with a positive impression, not a negative one. Is your car presentable? Or does it have more dents than a beer can that fell off a five-story building? If your car is not presentable, rent one or take public transportation.

Insider Tip

When I interviewed candidates, some would say how organized and polished they were. To see if they were telling me the truth or not, I would walk them out to their car. If their car had leftover fries from lunch or other loose articles strewn throughout, I would reject the person strictly on that basis alone. Why? Their actions didn't match their words.

Press Your Suit and Use Professional Writing Instruments

What kind of condition are your interview clothes in? Did you just press your suit? If not, get it pressed! I can't think of a single article of business attire that looks better wrinkled than pressed. Wrinkles look cute on bulldogs, not on interview candidates.

What about your notepad? Don't walk into the interview with a grade school yellow notepad. Get a professional notepad. Also, use a nice pen. A.T. Cross Company manufactures attractive and relatively inexpensive pens that present a very professional image. Don't walk into the interview with a 10-cent disposable pen. You will leave a bad impression.

Leave Your Cell Phones and Pagers in the Car

If you must keep your cell phone or pager with you, turn it off before you go into the interview. Nothing is more annoying and disrupting than a cell phone or beeper ringing during the interview. It is distracting, ruins the flow, and if you (GASP!) take the call, you convey the impression that your call is more important than your interview.

You can always return your calls later. That's what caller ID and voice mail are for. If your interview is not as important as an impending phone call or page, then probably you are interviewing for the wrong job. Give your interviewer the appropriate respect and turn off your phone.

4. Master the Three Phases of a Winning Job Interview

To succeed in any interview, you must master each of the three phases of a winning job interview. Forget one phase and forget your chances of getting hired. Every moment of every interview can make or break your chances. You want to be as prepared and refined as possible, so you leave the interview with the job instead of the interviewer's foot on your behind.

The Three Phases of a Winning Job Interview

1. Introduction.
2. Qualification.
3. Summary/Close.

1. Introduction

The first step to winning any job interview is the your introduction. This is where that important first impression is made. It is during the introduction that interviewers see how you are dressed, how you shake their hand, and the presence you command when you enter a room.

You want to create a positive and lasting first impression. To do so, plan in advance how you are going to introduce yourself so you come across as confident, articulate, genuine and amiable. Write down a script and practice it over and over again. Smile, even as you practice.

Example:

Good morning, my name is _____ _____, currently of _____ company. I greatly appreciate you giving me the opportunity to meet with you today.

When Greeting Your Interviewers...Give a Good, Firm Handshake

The handshake is usually one of the first and most telling events in an interview. A firm, solid handshake demonstrates confidence and enthusiasm...and starts the interview in a positive fashion. However, a wimpy handshake is quite the opposite. A good handshake shows confidence and respect. A sweaty, weak and flimsy handshake says that you lack self-esteem and you don't think you're the right person for the job.

The key to the handshake is to be firm but not to squeeze. Be assertive and show the interviewer that you think you are the right person for the job.

Insider Tip

If your hands are clammy or sweaty, you can do something to help. Right before the interview, wash your hands in warm water and use lots of soap. Dry them off completely. The soap will dry out your hands and help eliminate the sweat.

After the handshake, the interviewer likely will ask you to sit down. At this time, if you see that the interviewer doesn't have a copy of your resume on his or her desk, it is a good idea is to take out an extra copy and hand it to the interviewer.

Example:

I have brought an extra copy of my resume for your convenience.

Also, if you have a business card, feel free to exchange it with the interviewer at this time.

By having a strong introduction, interviewers will remember you. The introduction step is usually the briefest step of the interview process. However, the introduction is one of the most important steps because first impressions are always the most vivid and lasting. The interviewer will likely be meeting with several people, so you want to stand out and be remembered positively.

As you are practicing and preparing for your introduction, think about people in your life that gave you the best initial impressions. What was their aura? How did they look? What kind of expression did they have on their faces? Try to practice and replicate those features that provided the most positive and lasting first impressions.

Try to Establish a Good Rapport Right From the Beginning

Developing good rapport is critical to any successful interview. Interviewers tend to like candidates who remind them of themselves. Think of the friends you have chosen to associate with throughout your life. Haven't most of those friends had qualities, characteristics, and interests similar to yours? In establishing a positive rapport with interviewers, you want them to, both consciously and subconsciously, feel comfortable with you (almost like a friend) and believe that you have many things in common.

This is done both verbally and nonverbally.

Verbal Communication Is Essential in Building a Solid Rapport

Interviewers each have their own unique styles of verbal communication. Tone of voice, pitch, rate, and volume can all vary from one person to another. Voice can show a person's emotions and personality. Some may come across as pleasant and friendly, while others may be very serious and cold. You do not want to mimic interviewers, but you do want to speak in a similar manner.

For instance, say the interviewer has a very friendly tone and is extremely cheerful. Do not try to be overwhelmingly businesslike and monotone. You will fail miserably. On the other hand, if the interviewer is intensely businesslike and shows little emotion, your dialogue should respect that style.

If you try to be overly cheerful to a person who is *not* as lighthearted in nature, you won't succeed. It is also very important to notice the pitch, rate, and volume of voice. If some interviewers speak in a low pitch, very slowly and softly, and you talk in a rapid, loud manner, you will overwhelm them.

Use words that are similar in conversation to those of the interviewer. If the interviewer uses emotional words such as feel, love, and beautiful, then incorporate some of those words into your conversation. Conversely, if the interviewer uses more factual-based words in conversation such as created, developed, and structured, then you want to use phrases that are similar.

People enjoy working with individuals who make them feel comfortable and who are like themselves. Use verbal communication to your advantage by talking in a fashion that matches your interviewers. If interviewers see some of their qualities in you, they will be much more receptive to what you have to say.

Nonverbal Communication Can Be Even More Important

Ninety percent, or more, of all face-to-face communication is nonverbal. Nonverbal communication includes appearance, facial expressions, posture, eye contact, gestures, and scent. You can interpret nonverbal gestures to understand the true feelings of interviewers and use nonverbal communication to build positive rapport and to make a point.

Facial expressions can tell a lot about how well you are performing. If the interviewer is smiling and nodding in agreement to your message, keep going, you are doing great. If you see a blank facial expression almost as if the interviewer is nodding off, then something is wrong. In this case, let the interviewer do more of the talking. Make your answers shorter and ask more questions.

Suppose the interviewer has a very serious face, as if it belonged on Mt. Rushmore. In this case, be serious. If your facial expression is all smiles and you look like Howdy Doody, you will agitate the interviewer. On the other hand, if the interviewer positively beams, then smile and be friendly.

Posture is also very important. If the interviewer is sitting in an *open position* and *slightly reclined*, this demonstrates a certain level of comfort or a general agreement with what you are saying. As such, you should also sit *openly* and *slightly reclined*. However, do not mimic. Instead, be discreet.

If the interviewer is sitting up *straight* and *forward*, do not sit in the chair like an oversized ball of putty. Position yourself like the interviewer. Otherwise, you will convey the attitude that you could care less how the interview turns out.

If the interviewer is sitting with *arms crossed* and *straight as an arrow*, then you are probably not doing too well. However, if the interviewer leans forward with the classic *hand-on-the-chin* pose then you really hit a hot button. Continue emphasizing whatever you said that interested the interviewer.

What Should You Do When Interviewers Have Their Arms Crossed?

Either you need to change what you are saying or you need to do something to get that person to relax. Typically, when interviewers stay with their arms crossed, they are either getting bored with what you are saying or for some reason, they are not believing you. Ask if you are focusing on the information that the interviewer wants to discuss. Try to get the interviewer to talk more and get more involved.

Insider Tip

A trick I learned years ago, when interviewers' arms are crossed, is that you also should sit with your arms crossed. Then, slowly drop one arm and then the other. Often, interviewers will follow you and drop their arms as well. If not, then you are in trouble and you need to understand where you are going wrong.

If the interviewer asks you a vague question where you could easily ramble on, try to pinpoint the question. Say something such as, "There is so much great information I could tell you, what would you like me to focus on first?"

When asked the famous "tell me about yourself" question or asked your job history, try getting the question more focused. Ask something such as, "Where would you like me to start?"

Eye contact is perhaps the most telling nonverbal clue. If an interviewer looks you straight in the eye, while listening to you, then you are communicating. If the interviewer is looking at the stuffed fish on the wall or the bubbles in the water cooler, then they are not hearing a word you are saying. Establish good eye contact with the interviewer. Eye contact shows that you mean what you say.

Gestures are also important and punctuate what you are saying. By smiling when you say something positive about yourself, or by being serious when you mention your work experience, you can emphasize your point. You can also lean forward or raise your hand to emphasize a particular strength or area of importance.

Depending on the interviewer, gesture can make a positive or negative impact. If the interviewer is reserved and does not talk with his or her hands, you should do so as well.

Scent can also impact your performance. Wear just enough cologne or perfume to create a light scent. Do not bathe in the bottle, it can be *offensive*. Some people have perfume allergies and you don't want interviewers to have an allergic reaction to you. Be subtle in your scent, or forgo it completely.

However, don't forget to wear antiperspirant or deodorant. If you smell like the inside of a gym locker, you will turn people off. If you sweat like an open faucet, wear light clothes. Also, wear a jacket or blazer that will cover up your stains.

Make That First Impression Count

Subtly employ and embrace the verbal and nonverbal communication styles of the interviewer. The more similar you appear to the conscious and subconscious mind of the interviewer, the greater the chance you will have of succeeding in the interview.

Not only is nonverbal communication significant in understanding the interviewer and building rapport, it is critical in emphasizing the message you're trying to get across. To enhance your nonverbal communication skills, look for nonverbal communication in your everyday life and practice it. Whether you are talking to a friend or meeting with a business associate, consciously look for nonverbal clues. The more you practice, the better you will be able to use nonverbal communication and gestures in your interview.

To Ensure a Winning Interview Generate Interest Quickly

Communicate what you can do for the company and person interviewing you. At the beginning of your interviews, it's what you can do for them...not what they can do for you. Express enthusiasm and excitement. Use a golden nugget of information that will stimulate the interviewer.

In the preparing for the interview, hopefully you identified key opportunities and contributions you could make to the success of the organization. Revisit these items and develop a couple of simple sentences that convey an interesting fact about you...that could intrigue the interviewer.

Example:

I am excited about this opportunity. In my current position I have successfully reduced expenses by more than 35 percent and increased productivity by more than 20 percent. This is a great opportunity to leverage my experience and become an immediate asset to your company.

Another great way to generate interest is to ask the interviewer a variation of the magical question we discussed in the last chapter.

Example:

If you had your ideal candidate for this position, what qualities and characteristics would be important to you?

The interviewer might mention characteristics such as motivated, team player, good communications skills and willingness to learn. Now you know what to emphasize. Focus on a couple of hot buttons.

Example:

That's great. Throughout my career, I have consistently demonstrated that I am a very motivated person and I have always prided myself on being a part of the team.

Immediately, you can generate interest. If you don't ask interviewers what is important, you may end up talking about attributes that they don't care about. So make sure you ask the magical question at some point early on in your interview.

2. Qualification

The next phase of the interview is where both you and the interviewers see if there is a mutual fit. Remember all of those questions you prepared for and answered earlier in this book? Now is the time you will put all that hard work to use.

In this phase, both you and the interviewers ask questions to qualify each other. If in the introduction you were not able to ask the question, "If you had your ideal candidate for this position, what qualities and characteristics would that person have?" then you must figure out a way at the beginning of this phase to ask it.

Ask Interviewers Qualifying Questions

- What is it about your company that you enjoy the most?
- What are the biggest challenges that you are facing today?
- What traits do your top performers have that are in common?
- What are the key attributes that make your company better than others in the industry?
- How do you reward top performers?
- If I exceed expectations, what is the typical timeframe to get reviewed?
- Do you have any additional questions?
- What is the next step in this interview process?
- When do you expect to make a decision on this position?
- How quickly could I start, if I was accepted for this position?

Ask positive and assumptive questions—ones that foster feedback and communication. These kinds of questions will impress the person interviewing you. By asking questions such as these, you display a confidence that says, "I know I am the right person for this job. Why look further?"

Don't be afraid to ask questions. You have the right to know the answers. Otherwise, how will you know if the position interests you and if it is the right job for you? Interviewers will sense your confidence and will be more than happy to answer your questions.

Ask Questions at the Appropriate Time

Don't just fire one question after another at interviewers, especially at the *beginning*. Usually interviewers will ask you at the *end* of this phase if you have any questions. That is the best time to ask them. Also, whatever you do, don't ask about sick days and vacation time during your interview. If you get an offer, then you can ask HR about that. It just isn't relevant to ask those types of questions early in the interviewing process. If you ask these kinds of questions, you'll come across as a lazy bum!

Insider Tip

Interviewers are schooled on making you do most of the talking. However, one of the best ways to succeed in an interview is to get the interviewer to do more of the talking instead. In sales, we have a saying, "We were given two ears and one mouth for a reason: We should listen twice as much as we talk." The same holds true for you.

The qualification phase is when interviewers justify or refute their first impressions. In most cases, interviewers try to justify their initial feelings. If they had a great feeling about you from the beginning, they will look for answers to their questions that confirm those feelings.

Again, throughout this phase as well as the entire interview, the more you can tailor your conscious and subconscious messages toward the interviewer's concept of an ideal candidate, the better your chances of success.

Review Your Strengths

Towards the end of the qualification phase, make sure you summarize your strongest points. Restate what interviewers say they are looking for in their ideal candidates. Make sure you know exactly the type of individual they want, otherwise, you could still lose in the final phase of the interview.

Be sure to ask at some point if there is any additional information that the interviewer would like to discuss. Ask, "Are there any other questions that you have for me at this time?" Then, position yourself for a powerful close.

3. Summary/Close

This is the best part of the interview. This phase is very similar to closing arguments in a court case. It is here that you make your final impression. Just like a lawyer wants to leave the jury with a final statement that is strong and persuasive, so do you. After all, the second most important impression after your first impression is your final one. So, make it good!

By this point in the interview, you should have a good idea whether or not you have a chance of getting the job. This is where you go for the close—a job offer! In going for the close, be confident and excited. Summarize your skills and relate how your expertise will benefit the interviewer and the company.

Example of a strong closing statement:

I want to thank you for giving me the opportunity to meet with you. This job sounds exciting and I know I can make an immediate impact. You mentioned that reducing costs and improving efficiencies are two of your most important objectives. Having reduced expenses by more than 15 percent in my last position and by increasing productivity by 20 percent, I am confident that I can jump in and immediately contribute to the ongoing success of your team. I am looking forward to the opportunity. Once again, I greatly appreciate your time and efforts on my behalf.

When interviewers want to hire you, they often will become as excited as you will. They'll show enthusiasm and give specific timeframes on when they will follow up. If they don't, you have a problem. It is *not* a positive sign when interviewers are inconclusive or vague at the end of an interview. Typically, when interviewers are evasive at the end, it means they have some sort of objection or reservation about you.

Try to pin them down. Ask, "What is the next step in the decision-making process?" If after asking that question, the interviewer is still elusive, you could be really bold and ask a pointed question that will definitely elicit a response such as, "Is there anything that would prevent you from wanting to hire me?"

When you ask a question that is bold and pointed like that, it gives you an opportunity to identify the objection or objections that the interviewer has about you. I only recommend asking a question like that if you think that for some reason, the interview is not ending on a good note...and there is something wrong that needs to be brought out.

Either way, during the close of the interview, maintain your composure, and remain positive, self-assured, and enthusiastic. As we have discussed before, if you do not exemplify these traits, you will be shown the door, not the job. Give interviewers a reason to want to hire you. Act like a winner, and interviewers will perceive you as one!

Insider Tip

Never ask an interviewer, "When will you get back to me?" Interviewers would rather gargle with razor blades than hear that question. It is much better to say, "What is the next step in the decision-making process?"

The close of the interview is also similar to the final seconds of a basketball game. Sometimes, if you have outscored your opponents throughout the interview, the close is just a formality. Other times, you may need to make that final shot to win the game. Before each interview, picture yourself making that game-winning shot and you will succeed! Practice that final shot over and over again!

5. Have Fun

The most important of all aspects of having a successful interview is to have *fun*! The interview is one of the most exciting aspects of job hunting. Enjoy it and have fun with the whole process. You may be thinking, "Interviewing gives me headaches and sweaty palms! How can it possibly be fun?" Interviewing is fun if you have the right approach and the right attitude.

Interviewing is nothing more than a game. There are winners and there are losers. In order for you to be the winner, you have to have better preparation, strategy, attitude, and performance, than your competition.

When I interviewed people in the past, I thoroughly enjoyed many of the interviews. Individuals who were confident in themselves, and knew how to have fun, were always the most enjoyable to interview. By coincidence, those were typically the candidates I hired.

As an interviewer, I wanted to come out of the interview pumped up! I wanted to be excited about who I was about to hire. Sometimes I was so enthusiastic, I couldn't wait to offer the person the job. When you generate that kind of enthusiasm, you win!

As in Sports...Talent Alone Doesn't Win

Don't worry if you lack "experience." Often, the sports teams that recruit and possess the best players still don't win. Regardless of the sport, every year there seems to be at least one team who, at the beginning of the season, no one thought would win. On paper, they looked like just an average team. Yet somehow, they reach the playoffs and sometimes win the championship.

The reason they make it that far is that they put no pressure on themselves to win, they just expect it. They approach the game to win and have fun. Being more relaxed and confident, the end result is they end up winning. Have you ever noticed that the people who have the most fun on their jobs tend to be the most successful people in their profession? Interviewing is the same. Have fun!

Treat Interviewing Like the Game That It Is

Why not see how many offers you can get? Why not try to anticipate questions before they are asked? I used to have fun by trying to guess how the people would look, just by thinking about their name. With the attitude that interviewing is like a game, you will be much more relaxed and confident.

Laugh at your learning experiences. The more fun you have, the better you will perform. After all, interviewing is a game for interviewers as well. They may have fun by seeing how you handle a tough question or how you stack up against the others. Some interviewers ask crazy questions...just to make candidates squirm.

One of my friends, a fellow sales manager at a company I worked for, asked the question, *"Why are manhole covers round?"*

In asking this question, he looked for how candidates handled a completely un-related and utterly useless question. He also looked to see how someone handled a situation where they did not know the answer. After all, one of the last things managers want is for an employee to lie or make up an answer. He bounced many candidates because they stumbled and tried to make up an answer. It's better that you admit you don't know the answer and ask if you can follow up with the answer at a later time.

If someone makes up an answer to this question in the interview, what would they do on the job in front of a customer? Managers never want their people saying something to the customer of which they are not sure. Instead, good employees will tell the customer they will research the answer and get back to them.

If you are ever asked a question where you do not know the answer, be honest and say you don't know. Say that you would be more than happy to research the answer and get back to them. Lying and making up answers to questions is the surest way to be rejected.

In fact, if you are nervous and not sure about a tough question, try to make light of the situation. Say something such as, "Wow...that's a great question...I have to admit you stumped me. Let me think about that one for a second." Or you could say, "Hmmm...that is one of the best questions an interviewer has ever asked me...how would you answer that question?"

When you add some levity to the situation, it helps to loosen you up and provides valuable stalling time for you to contemplate your answer.

Why Manhole Covers Are Round

The answer is that a circular-shaped lid, unlike a square or an oval, won't fall through the opening. There's no way to position a round cover to slip through a slightly smaller hole of the same shape. That's because a circle has a constant width (the same width all the way around).

However, an oval has a shape that is longer than it is wide. Thus, you can always find a way to slip an oval lid through a hole of the same shape. That's also true of a square or a six-sided, hexagonal cover. If you try to cut those shapes out of a piece of paper, you will see that you can slip the cut-out piece right through the opening created by it.

Insider Tip

As an interviewer, there was *one* question I always asked candidates to make the interview more fun.

"Why should I hire you instead of one of the other candidates I have interviewed?"

I couldn't wait to ask that question. It was amazing how differently people answered it. How will *you* answer that question...when it comes up in your next interview?

There Are Many Ways to Have Fun With Interviewing

You can win if you relax and do not put pressure on yourself. Look at every interview as an opportunity for you to sell yourself, an opportunity to learn, and an opportunity to have fun. Remember, if you get the hook around the neck, so what? You will have gained knowledge from the experience and you will be that much closer to your dream job.

Try Rewarding Yourself

To add fun to the process, a friend of mine would treat herself to something nice after each interview—regardless of how it went. That way she always looked forward to the interview. Maybe you want to reward yourself with a nice lunch or a relaxing massage. Whether you choose to reward yourself after each interview or to treat each interview like a game, you can have fun with the entire process.

You Have a Say Too

Yes, you have to sell yourself. However, don't be afraid to make the company sell itself to you. You have a lot of talent and positive qualities. Good employees are not easy to find. There are a lot of mediocre people out there. Don't sell yourself short. You have a tremendous amount to offer and you should be proud of yourself. If interviewers cannot express why you should work at their company, then maybe that company is not worth joining.

Each interview is an opportunity to shine, an opportunity to learn, and an opportunity to get your ideal job. Visualize success, believe in yourself and your ability to succeed, dress to win, master the three phases of a winning interview...and have fun. Do so and you will win!

Secret #9: Interview to Win
—Checklist Summary—

√   Visualize success.

√   Maintain a positive mental attitude.

√   Remember: you are equal.

√   Dress to win.

√   Master the three phases of a winning job interview.

√   Nonverbal communication is often more important than verbal.

√   Treat interviewing as a game and have fun!

Before each interview, close your eyes and visualize the outcome you want.

Secret #10

Follow Up and Close the Deal

- Summarize the interview.
- Make sure to say thank you.
- Three components of a winning thank you note.
- Sample thank you note.
- Give each offer careful consideration.
- Accept *good* offers with enthusiasm.
- Reject *bad* offers with dignity.
- Negotiate *debatable* offers with confidence.

Phew! The interview is over—or is it? Many people make the fatal mistake of assuming the interview process is over once they walk out the door. That couldn't be further from the truth. Just because your face-to-face time is over, doesn't mean you should sit idly by the phone waiting for it to ring. There are many things you should do both immediately after the interview and in the hours and days to come.

Summarize the Interview

Immediately after each interview, stop by a nearby coffee shop, library, or some other public place and sit down to write some notes that summarize the interview you just had. If you just completed a phone interview, then do so at your desk.

Make sure you have the correct spelling of the names of all the people you talked to. For in-person interviews, hopefully, you asked each person for a business card.

Write down key points you discussed with each person throughout each phase of the interview. This will help you prepare for future interviews with that company and also help you determine if you are interested in the position.

Often, I have been saved by the fact that I took notes after an interview. When talking with several companies, you'd be surprised at how hard it is to remember what has been said. Plus, in subsequent interviews, you may want to refer back to what was mentioned in an earlier interview.

Example:

In speaking with your head of sales, I learned that your company is very service-oriented. How do you maintain this image?

By writing down notes immediately after the interview, the information you just received will remain fresh in your mind. This information will also be helpful when you compare one position to another. One company may have better working conditions while another may have a position that is more stimulating. By having good notes, you can accurately determine which job is best for you.

Rate Your Performance

Also, when summarizing the interview, rate your performance during each phase of the interview. Summarize the areas where you think you did well. Also note the areas where you need to improve. This will help you learn from each interviewing experience. Later, you can practice on those areas that need improvement.

When you take the time to summarize each interview, suddenly, there is no such thing as a bad interview. You can learn from the experience. *The only way you can fail on an interview is if you don't take the time to learn from it.*

Make Sure You Say Thank You

Within a few hours of your interview, you should type a thank you note to each person with whom you spoke. If you have good handwriting, a handwritten note on good stationery can be an excellent touch as well.

Even send the receptionist or secretary a thank you. You might be surprised to discover how much power a receptionist or secretary can have in an organization. They can either help or destroy your chances of getting your ideal job. Once you have typed up your letters, either e-mail them or send them via priority overnight service.

Why go to this time and expense? Well, if you *really* want the job, then you need to do what it takes to get it. I can guarantee you that if an interviewer is on the fence and not quite sure which person to choose, a simple *thank you* can make all the difference. If you send an e-mail or overnight package, that person is going to say, "Wow! That's the kind of person I want to hire!"

I remember a time when I was really torn between two candidates I interviewed for a district manager position on the West Coast. Both people did a great job interviewing. Both were polished and had excellent experience. I actually tried to convince the company to allow me to hire both of them. Unfortunately, upper management said no.

The first applicant I interviewed e-mailed me *immediately* upon her return to California, that *same* day. In the e-mail, she told me how excited she was about the opportunity and how successful she would be in the position. The second candidate I interviewed took more than two days to thank me. Well, as you might imagine, I ended up hiring the first person due to the simple fact that she thanked me in a more timely and enthusiastic fashion.

When writing a thank you note, there are three components you should include to make the message as powerful as possible. When you include these items as a part of your message, you will leave a positive and lasting impression.

The Three Components of a Winning Thank You Note

1. Thank the interviewers for the opportunity.
2. Summarize why you are the best candidate.
3. Go for the close.

1. Thank Interviewers for the Opportunity

As simple as it sounds, start out your thank you notes by thanking the interviewers for their time and consideration. Then, tell them how excited you are about the opportunity. Your interviewers' time is valuable. They appreciate it when you show some gratitude.

2. Summarize Why You Are the Best Candidate

Provide a brief summary of the qualities that the interviewer identified as important in an ideal candidate. Then, show why you are the best person for the job. After interviewing several candidates, the minds of hiring managers can get as cluttered as a house after a birthday party. Reminding them why you are the best person for the job may just be the thing that puts you over the top.

3. Go for the Close

End your thank you notes by once again thanking them and saying that you are looking forward to the opportunity to be a part of their winning team. Your thank you notes should be short, to the point, and convincing. You don't want to say too much— you might "buy back the sale." However, you want to say enough to remind them why you are the best candidate for the position and that you want the job!

Sample Thank You Note

Dear Jamie:

Thank you for taking the time to meet with me today to discuss the technical support managerial position at High Tech Industries. I am excited about this opportunity. During our discussion, you mentioned that your main goals are to reduce employee turnover, improve customer satisfaction, and reduce the number of abandoned calls coming into technical support.

Having reduced employee turnover by more than 20 percent, and significantly improving the overall customer experience for my previous employer, I am confident that I can help you achieve your goals and make an immediate contribution to your organization.

I am looking forward to having the opportunity to be a part of your winning team. If there is any further information I can provide, please feel free to contact me at 555-555-6400 or tbermont@10stepjobsearch.com. I look forward to hearing from you soon. Once again, thank you so much for your consideration.

Sincerely,

Todd Bermont

Do the Small Things That Make a Big Difference

In interviewing, as well as in life, it is sometimes the smallest things that can make the biggest difference. By doing the little things like saying thank you via e-mail, you can make a difference. What's the worst that could happen? You waste a few minutes of your time. At least you will be at peace with yourself knowing you did everything you could to get the job.

One of the most frustrating things is failing at something because you didn't give it your best shot. So what if it takes a couple of extra hours or you spend a couple of additional dollars? In the grand scheme of things, what's the big deal?

If you had a great interview, you properly follow up, and if you pay attention to the small things that make a big difference, you will get the job! Realistically, when interviewers like you, they will get back to you quickly, usually, within a couple of days. Unless otherwise specified, it should never take more than a week to hear back from an interviewer.

If you don't hear back from the interviewer in a timely fashion don't hesitate to call. Time, energy, expense, and emotions are invested into each of your interviews. You have a right to know where you stand. If more than a week goes by to where you don't hear from the interviewer, then by all means, call the interviewer.

If you get voice mail, then leave a professional voice mail such as:

Good afternoon Jerry, this is Todd Bermont. I wanted to call to thank you for taking the time to interview with me last week for the accounting position. It's an exciting opportunity and one that I know I can succeed at. I just wanted to follow up with you to say that I greatly enjoyed our conversation and to see where things stood. I look forward to hearing from you soon. I can be reached at 555-555-6400. Once again, thank you for your time and have a great day.

Then, give it a few days. If you still don't hear back, then keep calling until you reach the interviewer. Most likely, if you don't hear back in a timely fashion, it means you didn't get the job. But keep calling anyway. The only way you will truly learn from the experience is to understand why they didn't want to hire you.

If you didn't get the job, then ask them why. Ask a question such as, "Jerry, I thought I was an ideal person for the job. I was wondering if you could tell me where I fell short, so I can learn from the experience."

The interviewer may bring out an objection you can handle. If that is the case, you might be able to turn around the situation. But, if not, at least you will know why you got rejected. Often, it is something you can't control. Either way, it is good to know why.

By reading this book, you should have many more good interviews than bad. I know that you can interview to win! You *will* succeed and get *many* job offers! Keep the faith!

Give Each Offer Careful Consideration

So, if all goes well, you will get the job offer. Now what? For sure, the greatest prize of all in your job search is to get a job offer. But just because you have an offer doesn't mean your job search is over. You have to analyze the offer and decide if it is the right job for you. Then, you have to follow the appropriate steps to ensure a happy ending.

Contain Your Emotions

Regardless of the quality of the offer, contain your emotions. It is easy to get caught up in the heat of the moment. By remaining calm, you will make the right career decision. Choosing a job is one of the most important things you can do in life. Don't rush to a decision.

Ask Yourself Some Important Questions

Before making a decision, ask yourself a few questions about the opportunity. Following I have listed 10 questions that I have used in the past to evaluate job offers that I received:

1. Is this a position I *really* want?
2. Are they offering me enough money and benefits?
3. Is this a short-term position or one with a good career path?
4. Will my personality match well with this company?
5. In three years, will I still want to work for this company?
6. Do I want to work for this type of boss?
7. Is the position in alignment with my purpose, mission statement, and values?
8. Is this a job I can be passionate about?
9. Is this a job I can succeed at, yet still have a balance in my life?
10. Can I truly picture myself in this position?

Make a Decision and Follow Up

Once you have studied the offer, it's time for that moment of truth. To call the interviewer and either accept the offer, reject it, or try to negotiate it. For the remainder of this chapter, I will give you some guidelines to use to help you, regardless of your decision. Just to get to this point is fantastic. Whatever your decision may be, you should be very proud of yourself to have made it here. I know that I am proud of you for investing your valuable time and money in this book, and I am confident that you will have many opportunities to evaluate job offers in the very near future. Let's take a look at what you should do when these offers start flowing in.

Accept Good Offers With Enthusiasm

Call interviewers in a timely fashion. There is no reason to wait too long. Reply in a timeframe that is long enough to show that you are not desperate, but short enough to demonstrate your excitement for the job. I recommend thanking the person for the offer and saying that you will get back within a day or two with a final decision.

You want to convey an image that you are in demand. However, it is perfectly acceptable, if you are happy with the offer, to accept it immediately. Only you will be able to judge the situation and do what is right. Either way, thank them so much for the offer and show your excitement.

Limit Your Conversation

You do not want to "buy back the sale." Often, interviewers make the mistake of talking too much and actually losing or "buying back" the job offer. Don't make this mistake.

When you do decide to accept, do so in an excited tone. Accept the position and restate your enthusiasm. Then, ask what the next step should be, and when and where you should report to work. Most importantly, thank interviewers for offering you a job and tell them that they made a great decision!

Example of accepting an offer:

Good Morning Mr. _____ this is _____. I want to thank you so much for the job offer and I am calling you to accept. (Be enthusiastic!) You made a great decision, and I know you will be thrilled with my efforts. What is the next step in the process? (Pause!) Again, thank you so much for giving me this opportunity. Have a great day!

When You Show Up for Your First Day

The absolute final step in the job-hunting process is your first day of work. Give it your best. Just like your first impression in the interview, when you start a new job, you only get one opportunity to give a first impression. Make it count.

Be on your best behavior. Wear your nicest clothes. Nothing is official, until you sign all the paperwork. Like the interview, show up early and be as enthusiastic as can be. Your goal for your first day should be that your new boss is thrilled to have made the decision to hire you.

Ideally, everyday thereafter, you too want to give it your all. That is the best way to have a career full of joy and happiness. I know for me, I always feel better at the end of the day when I know I gave my fullest efforts. When you give 110 percent...you'll feel joy and satisfaction as well.

Reject Bad Offers With Dignity

Make Sure You Are Making the Right Decision

The job hunt can be a very emotional journey. Various emotions can cause you to make rash decisions. Before you decide to formally reject an offer, make sure the position fails to match your criteria of an ideal job. Review the 10 elements of job satisfaction on page 53.

The key is to take your emotions out of the decision and look at the situation objectively. If after doing so you are not comfortable with the job, then reject it. If you are not sure, ask some of your friends and family for advice. And don't hesitate to ask your interviewer any questions you are not sure of as well.

Respond Quickly and Courteously

If you want to reject the offer, give interviewers a chance to look elsewhere. Try your best to respond in a timely fashion. You never want to "burn any bridges." A phone call or a letter is appropriate. I personally prefer a phone call, but that is up to you.

Either way, thank the interviewers for their time. Flatter them a bit. Say it was a tough decision, but it was not the ideal fit at this time.

Try to Keep Your Options Open

Mention that you are very impressed with the company and that you would like to keep your options open...if an opportunity that is a better fit opens up in the future. You never know when in the future you might want to work for the company. Try to be as complimentary as possible towards the person and the company and part on gracious terms.

Example of how to reject an offer:

Good afternoon Ms. _____ this is _____. I want to thank you so much for the job offer. Unfortunately, at this time I have to decline. I am extremely impressed with both you and your company. This is a very difficult decision. The offer just isn't the right fit at this time. I greatly appreciate the time you spent with me and I'd like to keep the dialogue open for the future. Again, thank you so much for your time.

Negotiate Debatable Offers With Confidence

What if you really like your potential employer and boss, yet you are disappointed in the offer they gave you? What should you do? This is really a touchy subject. First, review the questions from earlier in this chapter. Then, go over the exercise you did on determining your ideal job.

See how closely this offer matches the criteria of your ideal job. Look at all of the accompanying perks. If you still feel the offer is short of your expectations, then be honest with yourself and try to negotiate for more. This is a difficult topic, because in any negotiation, you can lose.

In this case of negotiating an offer, you can lose the job altogether. However, if you are not going to be happy working for what they proposed, then you have no other alternative than to negotiate. The last thing you want to do is to accept a job with which you are not happy.

Following, I will share with you seven steps to a successful job-offer negotiation. If you follow these, you have a solid chance of scoring more favorable terms and conditions.

7 Steps to a Successful Negotiation

1. Research the market.
2. Exhibit confidence.
3. Create demand.
4. Demonstrate excitement.
5. Find a win-win.
6. Expand the playing field.
7. Once again...go for the close.

1. Research the Market

Before entering into any job negotiation, research the market to see how your job offer compares with others. Look at the title of the position you are being offered. For instance, a director will typically get paid more than a manager will. See what comparable titles earn in your targeted industry. In doing research, you will have an idea of how your offer compares with others and you will have an indication of how much negotiating room you have.

2. Exhibit Confidence

When negotiating with interviewers, you need to maintain your confidence. Any weakness here will cause interviewers to not budge on the offer. They may even yank the offer off the table altogether. If you come across as confident, and willing to lose the job if necessary, you are more likely to get a better offer. After all, out of all the people they interviewed, these companies chose you! That means they want you! Be confident!

However, being confident does not mean being demanding or cocky. People don't like to be told what they have to do. Have balance in your approach. Be firm, not demanding!

Example of how to show confidence:

I know I will be a tremendous asset to your company and I appreciate your offer, however, I must tell you that I was expecting a salary of about $10,000 more. The position is awesome and your company is fantastic. But, unfortunately, I can't accept the job under these terms. I would very much like to work for you and your company. Is there any way we can meet somewhere in between?

3. Create Demand

In any negotiation, when one party is in demand—or has more control of a situation—typically, the other party realizes they need to be flexible. Remember our dating analogy from earlier in the book? Right or wrong, many people feel that if their significant other is also seeing other people, they need to be more generous and considerate towards that person. In other words, couples are sometimes more flexible with each other when they are not exclusive.

Negotiating for a job is much the same. You want to show an image that other companies are looking to hire you and that your skills are in demand. Convey the message that there are additional offers or opportunities out there.

Example of how to create demand:

I have been looking at several companies. I must say, I am the most excited about your position...However, the numbers you offered are a bit less than my expectations.

4. Demonstrate Excitement

It is critical to show excitement for the job at hand. If you do not appear enthusiastic about the job, then they will not sweeten your offer. On the other hand, if you are excited and confident and they are just a few dollars short, then you will have a better chance of getting a sweetened offer.

5. Find a Win-Win

For any negotiation to be successful, the end result has to be a win-win situation. That means both sides have to feel like they are better off as a result of the negotiation. Many companies will purposely leave a little room for negotiation. The key here is to show how the company will benefit by giving you more money.

You also need to demonstrate that you are willing to give as well.

Example of a win-win:

As I mentioned earlier, the offer is about $10,000 short of my expectations. I know with my tremendous enthusiasm, experience, and proven track record, I will more than make up for that difference. However, to show my willingness to come to work for you, if we can meet somewhere in the middle, I can enthusiastically accept your position.

The key here is to start with a figure that is higher than for what you are willing to settle so that you can meet in the middle. For instance, if the offer was $5,000 less than you had hoped, then say it was $10,000 less and ask to meet in the middle. If the offer was $10,000 less, then say it was $15,000–$20,000 less than your expectations.

The same technique can be used on vacation time and other aspects of the offer. If the company wants you bad enough, they will be willing to negotiate. Just realize your limits and don't push for too much.

6. Expand the Playing Field

Another aspect of negotiating is to expand the scope of the negotiation. For instance, let's say the company offered you $10,000 less than your expectation. Would you accept the offer if they doubled the number of stock options or if they granted you an extra week of vacation? Sometimes, companies may have more flexibility in one area than another. So be creative. Don't limit your negotiations to just salary.

If salary remains a key sticking point, but you really want the job, then try negotiating for a review (for a raise) after three or six months, instead of the standard one year. Some companies are willing to accept this idea because it lowers their risk. However, if you agree to this, get it in writing.

Many a manager has either moved on or conveniently forgotten items such as this. By having the outcomes of your negotiations in writing, there is no room for interpretation.

7. Once Again...Go for the Close

After you have put out on the table what you want, whether it is a higher salary or more benefits, finish your negotiations by once again going for the close. Summarize your excitement for the position and exhibit confidence that you can become an immediate asset to the company.

Example of going for the close:

I can't tell you how excited I am about this position. I know I can make an immediate contribution to your team. I am looking forward to hearing back from you on this request. My goal is that, in the days and months after you hire me, you are not only satisfied in my efforts, but you are absolutely delighted. Once again, thank you for your time and consideration.

There are many ways to come to a resolution that makes both sides happy. Figure out what you are willing to accept, and go for it. Just be aware that the company always reserves the right to refuse negotiation and may tell you to take it or leave it.

If their final offer is still unacceptable, then reject it. After all, you want to be happy. Just do so with compassion and dignity. Let's face it, compensation is an important factor in job satisfaction. Compensation cannot be ignored if you want a position you can enjoy and have longevity with. If a company is not willing to negotiate, then it is not a very flexible organization and probably not one you want to work for anyway.

Only you will be able to decide what is right. Negotiation can bring you a better offer but it can also cause you to lose your offer. Weigh all of the risks and potential rewards before you enter into any negotiating process. Then approach the negotiation with confidence. Visualize the outcome you want...and go for it!

For more tips and techniques on how to negotiate your job offers, once again, go to your favorite search engine on the Web. Type in search phrases such as "negotiating job offers," "salary negotiation," and "free job search negotiation tips." You'll find many sites than can give you some additional great advice.

Secret #10: Follow-up and Close the Deal
—Checklist Summary—

√   After each interview, summarize what you discussed and learned.

√   Rate your performance.

√   Identify areas of improvement.

√   Send a "thank you" note as quickly as possible.

√   If you get rejected, ask why.

√   Respond to offers in a timely fashion.

√   Accept *good* offers with enthusiasm.

√   Reject *bad* offers with dignity.

√   Negotiate debatable offers with confidence.

Visualize the outcome you want and go for it!

Some Final Thoughts

- Secret #11: Take immediate action!
- You are great!
- You will get the job you *really* want!

Congratulations. You now have the foundation you need to be successful in your job search. You have learned everything from developing a positive attitude to selling yourself in the interview to following up to closing the deal and getting the offer.

Hopefully, this has been a fun and rewarding experience for you. I know I have enjoyed sharing my knowledge and time with you. These secrets, tips, and techniques will undoubtedly help you achieve success.

Before we can conclude, there is one secret that I have to mention. Unfortunately, without this secret, you cannot succeed in your job hunt. On the other hand, if you embrace this secret, you'll be well on your way to getting the job you want at a salary you desire!

Secret #11: Take Immediate Action

You must take the knowledge you have gained from this book and take immediate action. I can't tell you how many people I have seen who just sat on their duffs waiting for a job to drop in their lap. Then they wonder why they can't find a job.

I know the concept of taking action is not easy. Change is always scary. But without action, you cannot succeed. Sometimes it is easier to start by taking baby steps. What I have found helpful is to put together a daily to-do list. I include items such as "research 10 companies" and "make five phone calls." When you write out a step-by-step list of what you have to do, it makes things much easier.

Jump in...the Water's Fine

I am sure you have been in a swimming pool or hot tub before. Have you ever stepped in and felt the pool was too cold or the tub too hot? I know I have. Every time

I went into a pool or tub one foot at a time, it was always difficult. I discovered that it was much easier to just jump in. The first couple of seconds are always tough, but the body adjusts quickly. Beginning your job search is the same as jumping into a pool.

If you start too slowly, or not at all, you will never fully get into it and you will prolong your misery. But, if you jump into the job hunt with both feet, you will realize it is not so bad. Just jump in and you'll do fine.

Like a Locomotive...It Takes Time to Pick Up Speed

But...once you build the momentum, you can't help but succeed. The faster you start, the more momentum you will pick up. The more momentum you will pick up, the greater your chances will be of getting the job you have always wanted.

Now It's Up to You

Hopefully by now, you have completed the exercises in this book and you are ready to begin your job search. If not, complete the exercises as soon as possible and start implementing the secrets. Having read this book, you now have the foundation necessary to succeed.

If you are *employed*, you can either stay in a job you are not happy with...*or* you can take action and live out your dreams.

If you are *unemployed*, you can either stay unemployed...*or* you can go out there...start selling yourself...and bust your hump.

If you are a *student*, you can either remain a permanent student and not deal with reality, *or*, you can get excited, jump in, and get your dream job.

I can't make the ultimate decision for you. Only you can!

You Are Great!

I know you are a fantastic person with awesome credentials. You are the type of person that any company would be fortunate to hire. It is my sincere hope and desire that you go out there and get the job you *really* want!

My purpose in writing this book is simple. I want to help as many people as possible improve their lives, by *getting* the jobs they want, fast and easily. If I have helped motivate you to go *find* the job you want, then I have only partially achieved my objectives. My ultimate goal is for you to go out there and actually *get* that job of your dreams!

Go out There and Do It!

Jump in and, most importantly, have fun! Life is too short to get stressed over the job search. If you follow what is discussed in this book, you will succeed. Relax, take action, and be proud of who you are. I am proud of you for having the courage and taking the time to read this book.

Are you smiling and having fun yet? If not, you should be. By following the advice given in this book, you will succeed!

Get psyched!

You Will Get the Job You Really Want!

You are among the select few who can conquer any challenge presented to you in an interview. Just the fact that you took the time to read this book and improve your skills demonstrates that you are a winner!

By investing the time you have just invested in yourself, you will get that job you *really* want! Also, hang onto this book for future reference. Keep the book with you in your car.

The job search is nothing more than a game. Be prepared and confident. If you want to stay in touch or provide any feedback, please feel free to visit my Website on the Internet at *www.10stepjobsearch.com.*

Believe That You Are #1 and Have Fun!

At this time, I would like to thank you again for investing your hard-earned time and money in this book. I wish you wonderful success in your job hunting as well as in your personal life. It has been a tremendous honor to be able to share these moments with you. Once again, thank you! Now go out there and get that job of your dreams! Best wishes to you!

Are You Interested In...?

- A personal career coach.
- Customized assistance with your job hunt.
- Having Todd speak at your next event.
- A guest for your TV or radio program.
- Contribution on job-hunting or sales articles.

If so, for more information visit *www.10stepjobsearch.com,* or call (888) 894-6400! Once again, thank you for investing your valuable time and money in this book!

Frequently Asked Questions

Since coming out with my first book, I have had the privilege of coaching several clients, speaking in front of many groups and appearing as a guest on numerous radio and television programs—including CNN and FOX. As a result, I have had the opportunity to talk with thousands of job seekers just like you.

Interestingly, there have been 10 common questions about the job-search process. I thought I would share these with you to give you that final edge you need to get that job you *really* want!

1. When are the best times to interview?

Most companies will interview more than one person for a given position. Like a horse race or automobile race, your "post" or "pole" position for the interview can often influence your chances of success.

How does timing affect your opportunity? If you are the fifth person to interview, and the third person made an incredible impression, you'll have a difficult hurdle to overcome. The precedent will have been set and the interviewer may have already made up his or her mind.

You should always try to be the first person to interview. By being first, you can set the expectation level. Everyone will have to measure up to you. Also, as with first impressions, the interviewer will remember the most about the person who interviewed first. If you have an outstanding interview, it will be tough for anyone after you to succeed.

Tuesdays and Thursdays Are the Optimal Days to Interview

Mondays are bad because they often are spent getting organized and planning for the week. Wednesdays are sometimes unpleasant because people like to take a mid-week break, and it is a typical day for internal meetings. Fridays are poor because everyone is more focused on the weekend than on the tasks at hand.

Mid-Morning and Mid-afternoon Are the Best Times to Interview

- Best time to interview 9:30 a.m.–10:30 a.m.
- Worst time to interview 1:00 p.m.–2:30 p.m.

If possible, you should schedule your interview in the morning, about 9:30 a.m. People are usually more alert in the morning and have not had enough time to have a bad day. It is usually after 10:30 a.m. when problems and disruptions start. You should not interview before 9:30 a.m. because people take a good hour to get through the morning mail and paperwork...and to get their bearings. By 9:30 a.m., however, the coffee has kicked in and interviewers will be ready for you.

Avoid Interviewing Near Lunch

After 11:00 a.m., interviewers will start to get hungry and will be thinking more about lunch than your skills for the job. It is much better to interview earlier in the morning.

The absolute worst time to interview is right after lunch. Typically, after eating, neither you nor the interviewer will be alert, and the interview will not go well.

When I interviewed candidates, I hated that first interview after lunch. Inevitably, I would become sleepy. This always caused me considerable distraction. The person I was interviewing had to be extremely good to make a big impression on me.

After eating, most people need a good hour to fully digest their meal and wake up. If you must interview in the afternoon, try to schedule it between 2:30 p.m. and 3:30 p.m. After 3:30 p.m., interviewers will be thinking more about going home than about your job credentials. For me, the last interview of the day was always the pits. At that point, my voice was dead and I was tired of asking the same questions over and over again. I have yet to participate in a good interview at the end of the day.

2. What if I can't be the first person to interview?

If you are not the first person to be interviewed, the key is to raise the bar so that you stand out from your competition. You can do this by changing the rules of the game. By expanding the role of the position and what you can add to it, you can become the *new* first impression in the minds of interviewers.

When you raise the bar and redefine what qualities and experiences are necessary for the position, you totally change the playing field. You can now become the *new* first impression.

3. What are the small things that make a big difference?

In everyday life, it is often the little things that can make or break a situation. Interviewing is no different. The tips that I am going to give you in this section should not be taken lightly.

Avoid Eating, Drinking and, Smoking During Interviews

When interviewing, do not drink, eat, or chew gum. Not only is this unprofessional, but it could annoy interviewers. I have actually interviewed people that chewed gum like a cow gnawing on grass. All I could think of was watching their mouths go up and down, up and down. What did they say? Who knows? Who cares? All I wanted to do was get them out of my office.

There may be times when interviewers might offer you a soft drink, coffee, or water. What should you do? I recommend that you politely turn down the offer. I say this for two reasons. First, having a beverage gives you one more thing to worry about. You start thinking more about the drink than the interview. Second, a beverage gives you a great target to knock over. If you are like me, and use hand gestures when you speak, you could spill a hot cup of coffee into the interviewer's lap—not a good idea!

Finally, you shouldn't smoke during an interview unless both you and the interviewer are smokers. Smoking can inhibit your concentration and also irritate interviewers. The only time it is okay to smoke on an interview is if both of you are smokers, and the interviewer wants to take a smoke and offers you a cigarette. Otherwise, smoking just is not a good idea...regardless of whether you both smoke or not.

Listen, Listen, and Listen

As humans, you were created with two ears and one mouth for a reason. You should listen twice as much as you talk. Quite often, people hear but do not listen. Pay attention and keep good eye contact. If you are well prepared, your mind will not need to wander while the other person is talking. By listening carefully, you will be able to respond more intelligently to statements and questions.

Never Interrupt the Interviewer

Often, you will be so excited about something that was said that you want to respond...before interviewers have a chance to finish with what they have to say. If you do this, interviewers will get upset and eventually tune you out. Wait for interviewers to finish their thoughts before talking. I know it can be tough. But remain silent until your interviewers are finished with what they want to say.

More Interviewing "Don'ts"

a. **Don't share proprietary information about your existing employer.**

b. **Don't ramble on.** An interviewer's time is valuable. Don't waste it. Make sure that before you say something, you answer in your mind, "*So what?*" If you were the interviewer, would you care about what you are going to say? If the answer to "*So what?*" is positive, then go ahead. If not, don't say it.

c. **Don't ever disparage your current company.** Be positive when stating why you are leaving. Give your current boss and employer high praises. Then, shift the focus to the fact that you are ready for the next challenge. Nobody wants to hire a complainer or a chronic problem.

d. **Don't tell interviewers what you are currently earning.** If you mention how much you are currently making, you have just capped your potential offer. By not mentioning current compensation, you place yourself in a much better bargaining position.

e. **Don't show up late to the interview.** That will immediately leave a bad taste in the interviewer's mouth. You most likely will be rejected just because of that.

More Interviewing "Do's"

a. **Sit down**...only when offered.

b. **Cross your legs**...only if the interviewer does.

c. **Eat lightly before the interview and at least an hour in advance.** You can celebrate with a good meal *after* the interview.

d. **Brush your teeth and use mouthwash before the interview.** Bring breath mints with you. Keep your breath fresh!

e. **Ask to take notes**...if you wish.

f. **After each interview, grade yourself.** Ask yourself what you did well on and where you could have improved. Write down notes on these areas so you can improve on your interviewing techniques.

g. **Smile and have fun!**

4. What can and can't interviewers ask?

When it comes to interviewing, hopefully you will not have to deal with any legal issues. But no book on job hunting would be complete without giving you an overview of your rights.

I would like to preface what I am about to share with you by saying that I am not a lawyer and much of what I will say can be left up to interpretation. This is for information purposes only and shall not be construed as formal legal advice. To find out exactly what your rights are, you should refer to a lawyer or your local or federal governmental agency.

With that disclaimer made, I want to give you an idea of the topics and questions that are off limits to interviewers. In an interview, it is important for interviewers to keep the questions to relevant work-related history. Very personal topics (that is, age, religion, etc.) have no relevance in an interview. In fact, many of the following topics are illegal to discuss in the interview setting.

Inappropriate Interview Topics to Avoid

Marital status.	National origin and/or citizenship.
Number of children.	Sexual preference.
Age.	Medical history.
Religion.	Physiological or psychological disorders.
Political affiliation.	Economic status.

Interviewers are not allowed to ask a man questions they would not ask a woman, or vice versa. In addition, interviewers cannot ask any question of a minority that they would not ask of a non-minority.

Unfortunately, there are interviewers who have unlawfully used their position for personal gain. You should know what your rights are, especially when it comes to harassment.

For More Information, Try the EEOC

If you want further information on what your rights are, you can contact the Equal Employment Opportunity Commission (EEOC). The EEOC is a U.S. government commission that promotes and enforces equal opportunity in the workplace. The EEOC has a Website that is very helpful and goes into tremendous detail about your rights as an individual in the labor force. You can reach this Website by going to *www.eeoc.gov*. If you live outside the United States, then check with an equivalent agency in your local geography.

Keep the Interview Focused on "Position-Relevant" Information

If you are asked questions that you feel are not appropriate, or are in a situation where harassment is present, my best advice is to politely state that you would like to keep the interview focused on relevant topics and not discuss personal aspects. If the situation gets worse, your best bet is to end the interview. Most likely, if people like this are managing and working at the company, you don't want to work there. Depending on the severity of the situation, you may want to obtain the advice of legal counsel.

You have a right to an open and fair interview, where you are judged on your merits, not on your race, gender, beliefs, and other non-relevant personal information.

5. What is the best way to approach a "panel" or group interview?

Sometimes companies will have two or more people interview you at the same time. I'll never forget one interview I had, during my senior year of college, with a major appliance manufacturer. They had me sit at the head of a boardroom table. No less than *eight* people sat around the table, firing questions at me like I was a punching bag. At first, I wasn't sure what to do. So, I tried to treat each person as if they were the final decision-maker. It worked! I got the job offer.

As it turns out, the best strategy to use is to treat each and every person with equal importance. When you are answering a question, be sure to look at each individual. Just like a teacher tries to make eye contact with every pupil, do the same thing in a group interview.

At the end of the interview, ask the group *"What is the next step in the process for me to become a part of your team?"* At that point, they should tell you the person that you should follow up with. Then after the interview, send each and every person a thank you note. If they all took the time to participate, most likely, they all have input in the decision.

6. How should I prepare for a phone interview?

The best way to prepare for a phone interview is to put forth the same kind of effort and energy that you would for a face-to-face interview. In fact, I even recommend wearing business professional attire. Believe it or not, people can sense how you are dressed, even over the phone. Plus, when you are dressed professionally, you will be much more likely to perform at the top of your game.

Follow each of the interview phases we discussed earlier in this book and know your objective before you pick up the phone. Just like you would end a face-to-face interview…at the end of the phone interview…go for the close! In this case, the close will most likely be a follow-up interview.

7. Any suggestions on interviewing during a meal?

Interviewing over a meal can be very challenging. It's hard to balance eating and interviewing at the same time. Typically, if an interviewer wants to interview you over a meal, that person wants to foster a more casual environment than that of a stiff office.

When interviewing during a meal, order something that is easy to eat and relatively inexpensive. Stay away from dishes such as pasta and nachos. Always wait for the interviewer to start eating before you do. Don't talk with your mouth full and don't finish the entire course. Unless the interviewer insists, stay away from dessert. You don't want to become tired during your interview by getting a "sugar crash."

Try to be a little more casual than you would be in an office environment. Also, try to make your answers a little more concise. If it is a crowded restaurant, it will be difficult to hear. Keep your message as short and to the point as possible. At the end of the interview, thank the interviewer and once again go for the close.

8. What should I do when asked about compensation?

At all costs, try to avoid giving a specific dollar expectation during the interview. If you provide a figure that is too low or too high, you will lose. And if your figure is in the ballpark, you have just capped what your offer can be.

The best way to approach this topic is to say something such as, "I fully expect to be a top performer for your organization. As a result, I expect to get compensated accordingly." Or you could say something such as, "Based on my track record, I expect to be compensated at a similar level to other top performers in your company."

But, whatever you do, try not to give any salary specifics. If they keep trying to nail you down on a specific figure, say to them, "I am really excited about the opportunity. What I can tell you is to just give me your best shot and I will do the same."

9. What is the most common job-hunting mistake?

The most common mistake people make is to just jump into the job hunt without first deciding what they *really* want to do for a living. Consequently, their focus and messaging is confused and they have a very difficult time finding a job. After all, if you don't know what you want to do, how is anyone else supposed to know?

You will be competing against people who are absolutely passionate about what they want. You need to be able to match that passion in order to succeed. No one can tell you what you want to do for a living. Only you can decide that. Take your time and go for a job you can be passionate about.

10. What is the best way to handle an objection?

First, be honest. If the concern is true, acknowledge it. Then, put yourself in their shoes. Say to them, "If I were in your shoes I'd be concerned about that too, however, let me show you why I am the best person for the job...."

Then, turn the negative to a positive. "Granted, I don't have a lot of experience, but you would have to hire two people to give you the same kind of energy and enthusiasm that I will bring to the table." Finally, ask, "Did that answer your question or concern?" If not, try again. If so, move on.

Two of the most common objections people encounter in interviews are the classics *"you have too little experience"* and *"you have too much experience."* Following, I will show you some key selling points and benefits you can focus on to overcome those two most common objections. Regardless of the objection or the concern, there is always a way to turn a negative into a positive.

"Being a Recent Graduate, You Have No experience"

- Will work twice as hard because of my youth and energy.
- Learned the latest techniques in school.
- I can introduce fresh ideas.
- Driven to succeed because I have to prove myself.
- Too young to have learned bad habits.
- You can pay me 1/3 less...yet, get greater productivity and results.
- Being young, it is easier for me to fit in to your corporate culture.

"You Have Too Much Experience"

- Why invest time and money training someone...I can jump right in.
- Being experienced, I'll be twice as productive.
- I can make an immediate contribution to your team.
- I have a proven track record of success.
- I know what it takes to succeed.
- You'll gain immediate and measurable results.
- With me, you'll get an immediate return on your investment.
- Why take a risk on someone with less experience?

Frequently Asked Questions
—Checklist Summary—

√   When possible, try to be the first person to interview.

√   The best times to interview are 9:30 a.m. on Tuesdays and Thursdays.

√   Don't forget the small things that make a big difference.

√   Never interrupt interviewers; let them finish their thoughts.

√   Know your legal rights before you go into the interview.

√   When interviewing with a group, treat each person like a decision-maker.

√   Dress and prepare for phone interviews...like you would in-person.

√   Avoid talking about salary during your interviews.

√   Know what you want...and you will get it.

√   To overcome objections, turn negatives into positives.

In interviews you should listen twice as much as you talk.

Recommended Books and Audio Programs

Motivational Books

Brown, Les. *Live Your Dreams*. New York: Avon, 1996.

Grabhorn, Lynn. *Excuse Me, Your Life Is Waiting: The Astonishing Power of Feelings*. Charlottesville, Pa: Hampton Roads Publiching Company, 2003.

Robbins, Anthony. *Awaken the Giant Within: How to Take Immediate Control of Your Mental, Emotional, Physical & Financial Destiny*. New York: Simon & Schuster, 1992.

Tracy, Brian. *Goals: How to Get Everything You Want—Faster Than You Ever Thought Possible*. San Francisco, Calif: Berrett-Koehler Publishing, 2003.

Additional Career Books

Dawson, Roger. *Secrets of Power Negotiating*. Franklin Lakes, N.J.: Career Press, 2000.

Covey, Stephen R. *Seven Habits Of Highly Effective People*. New York: Simon & Schuster, 1990.

Index

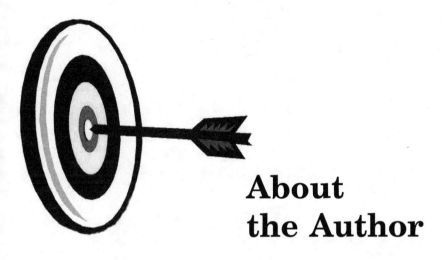

About
the Author

Todd Bermont is president and founder of 10 Step Corporation, a firm specializing in sales training, sales consulting, keynote speaking, and career coaching.

Todd Bermont graduated with honors from the University of Illinois. He has been a frequent guest lecturer at the University of Chicago and has taught job-hunting online through many colleges and universities across the country including the University of Wisconsin.

Todd Bermont has been awarded the "Certificate of Merit" by *Writers Digest* magazine and "Businessman of the Year" by the Business Advisory Council. Todd Bermont has also received numerous other sales and management awards throughout his career and has appeared several times on radio and television, and in newspapers across the country.

Having been a hiring manager as well as an expert in sales, Todd Bermont brings a unique perspective to job hunting. Even today, as an author and speaker, Bermont uses the tips and techniques shared in this book. He is truly one author that "walks the walk."

Prior to founding 10 Step Corporation, Bermont worked in executive management and corporate sales at some of the world's leading corporations, including Royal Dutch Shell, NCR, IBM, and American Power Conversion.

Todd Bermont has worked in more than 20 countries, with more than half of the Fortune 500. As part of his goal to give back to the community, Bermont has also volunteered some of his time teaching job-hunting skills to inner-city high school students and to underprivileged individuals. Throughout his career, Bermont has helped thousands of people, across the globe, succeed.

Today, Todd Bermont is an internationally renowned author, professional speaker, sales trainer, executive career coach, and consultant. You can find out more about Todd Bermont by visiting *www.10StepJobSearch.com*.